Terence Stamp is best known as an actor and autobiographer. He lives in London. This is his first novel.

Stamp Album (Autobiography)
Coming Attractions (Autobiography)
Double Feature (Autobiography)

The Night

TERENCE STAMP

PHŒNIX

A PHOENIX PAPERBACK

First published in Great Britain by Phoenix House in 1993
This paperback edition published in 1993 by Phoenix,
a division of Orion Books Ltd,
Orion House, 5 Upper St Martin's Lane, London WC2H 9EA

Copyright © Terence Stamp, 1993

The right of Terence Stamp to be identified as the author of this
work has been asserted by him in accordance with the
Copyright, Designs and Patents Act 1988.

A CIP catalogue record for this book is available from the British Library.

ISBN: 1 85799 008 0

The two lines quoted on page 158 from 'I Get Around' (Brian Wilson) are
reproduced by permission of Warner Chappell Music Ltd.

Printed and bound in Great Britain by
The Guernsey Press Co. Ltd, Guernsey, Channel Islands.

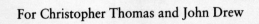
For Christopher Thomas and John Drew

CONSCIOUSNESS returned as the fire started. There was a moment without thought, and then he remembered how it was.

How cunningly he had been led to this moment, how willingly he had followed the path. As the ache cleared, he could work out dim shapes and knew where he was. They had piled leaves against the door, no doubt pushing them in until the last moment – closing the two halves, fastening them together and finally shooting the bolt – when the fire caught. The window behind him was open and, if he craned his neck, he could follow the pain from his wrists, link by link, through the open frame to the point where he was manacled – probably to the spokes of the larger back wheel. His dog was howling with fright. The sound was close. Tied to the same wheel no doubt. Just like our great elder, he thought, to keep with tradition: all possessions to be burned with him.

The dead leaves were taking now, their scorching fumes filling the air with the smell he had loved as a boy, a smell which reminded him of all the good things of life on the road.

To end this way. He examined the voice within him, whose whisperings assured him that everything was all right, that rescue was at hand – and saw the folly of it. What was this insane optimism? It had been with him as long as he could remember. But now he must cut himself loose. Tonight he was surely to die. He had to admit it to himself, had to prepare for his last great adventure. But there was no one to pray to – no one to listen. He called to his dog – poor, dumb creature. It yelped at the sound of his voice, as trusting of him as he was of . . . who?

How would it be to die? To die in the fire?

From the birth of his race, fire had been the tradition: 'It is only a moment of discomfort,' his father had told him, 'then you are somewhere else.'

His feet were closest to the line of flame. He could see his brown lace-up boots, not new, but not old – they would take the heat first. And how would his feet burn? The same as hedgehogs cooked in mud, probably.

He found himself staring at the basket beside him, filled with quince and medlars, the last fruit they had picked together. He had known even then. Been watching. Seen him gazing at the slimness of her back, loving the head that turned profile as she reached up, aching to caress the small imperfection in front of her ear – the butterfly birthmark that moved as the seasons changed. Yes, he had been watching. Seen him take her. Seen her give herself. And now – the price.

His eyes started to smart. The leaves crackled into flame. His eyes – would they melt? He supposed they must, they were water: but what of the radiance? Did it melt, too? He had always wanted eyes like hers – maybe it was part of his love for her. Did he love her more than himself? He tried to remember her eyes the first day he had seen her, the day she had joined their camp. Blue, as blue as the stone in his grandmother's ring. There had been days when they had been grey, too, when he had followed her to the river and watched her washing linen. And green. He mustn't forget the green, when she sat under the willow. The first time she had smiled at him. She had entered through his eyes, seen who he really was.

A patch of light fell near his foot and he was filled with an urge to see the moon one last time.

He leaned forward, his arms shackled behind him stretching until his joints cracked, the auburn hair on his wrist shaking with

2

strain. There she was in her fullness, grey streams of cloud scudding across the black sea she floated in and . . . a terrible scream echoed across the ravine. His name. She was calling his name. He filled his lungs with the smoky air, choking as he cried to her: 'Rawnie. Rawnie, my love. You will never be alone. I will always be with you. Now. This night. For ever.'

He could feel his grasp on life easing away, taken by the smoke he had not allowed for. So this was how it was.

Her cries were becoming fainter; they took on a mournful unworldly note, like a train whistling in the darkness. A train? How strange that this word he had never heard should come into his head. Her cries to him were drowned as a great gust of wind passed over him. He saw her face as lovely as he had ever seen it, and with the vision came a haunting refrain.

THE DAY

On the morning of the night, Zeno awoke early, yet his waking was so unusual it felt indelicate to move. He had been having a dream, a vivid dream; but, then, lots of his dreams were vivid. Then he had seen the face of a loved one he knew was dead, and asked himself if he was dreaming. In that instant two things happened: he understood that part of him was awake and witnessing the dream – although his body was still asleep, safely alongside his wife; whilst in the dream itself, his body began a headlong tumble into a dark chasm.

If this is a dream, he assured himself, I should be able to fly.

No sooner had he reached this conclusion than his panic stopped, the air rushing past him became velvety smooth, and he found himself suspended, weightless.

I should be able to fly, he repeated. In answer to his wish, his body began to move upward, and he assumed the flying posture of his earliest comic book hero, Captain Marvel.

It was dark and smoky, but he rose above it, moving effortlessly towards the horizon where the sun was about to rise. He lay without movement, flying over a Turner landscape. He had no way of knowing how long the condition lasted, and it was only when the mattress moved – his wife getting out of bed – that the dream canvas faded and the sounds of Victoria Road reached his ears.

The experience left him fragile. Analysing the sensation, he found it similar to one of his first memories. His breathing was soft and finer than usual, and he had less sense of the perimeters of his body. He lay motionless, afraid of rupturing the sensation, the passage of time monitored only by the sedate chimes of the long case clock in the ground-floor hall. His sense of smell was heightened: he could recognise the flavours of the teas being brewed in the kitchen and, when the refrigerator door was opened, the aroma of celery was strong, as though freshly pulled from earth alongside him.

He heard his family leave, felt the early rays of the sun come through the east-facing window without stirring, and even the pneumatic drill in a road near by did not breach his silence.

When Zeno was young he saw things that weren't there; at least, others couldn't see them. But they were real to him, and he would chat to them in the same way he chatted to other kids. This became an embarrassment to his parents, mainly his mother, who would take young Zeno everywhere with her. When she stopped for a chat with a neighbour, he would carry on a conversation with one of his 'chums'. Finally, she had to ask him to talk to these friends in the privacy of their own home.

The problem solved itself by the time he reached puberty, when the companions faded from his life. He did not pay much attention to the going of them, being preoccupied with more pressing matters. It was only when he matured that he realised the extent of the gift he had lost – yet his outlook remained different. For while he could no longer see into the unseen world, he knew it was there – rather in the way a person suddenly forced to wear spectacles knows that it is his vision that is impaired, not what he is looking at.

This particular morning, getting out of bed, he remembered an image from his dream, and wished he still had one of his 'chums' to discuss it with. It was to return to him more than once that day – a procession of figures carrying circular trays. He recalled one figure in particular, a ginger-haired youngster whose tray radiated light. In this moment he felt lonely, a loneliness no amount of company could fill. It was as if something or someone he had known and cared for had been taken during sleep, and some form of psychic surgery administered to leach the memory-bearing atoms from his mind. Sometimes an iota was revived and he experienced this hollowness of absence.

He folded the linen sheet to the bottom of the bed and plumped up the pillows. It had been unusually hot during the weeks leading up to Midsummer's Eve and the English had, with their typical contrariness, begun to regard the sun as an enemy.

Friday, he said to himself. A day of prayers answered and dreams realised.

It was his habit to remind himself of the symbolism of the day when he woke every morning. There was much of this kind of clutter in his life, left over from the Sixties and Seventies. He paused in his chore to regard the unusual angle of the bed, remembering the day his wife had helped him move it to match the changing fluctuations of the Earth's electromagnetic field.

'When the circadian rhythms are harmonised, the proper amounts of hormones are released while we're asleep,' he had told her. Of course, he had long since moved through his bio-rhythmic fixation, but he didn't have the heart to revise their sleeping arrangements again since he had overheard her repeating to a friend, 'It suits the Caucasian rhythms of our bodies.'

He had married young, in the grip of biological tyranny. As a teenager, he had come across an erotic illustration by the artist Vargas and vowed that if he ever met a girl who looked like that he would marry her. He had. And he had.

Prudence wasn't much of a talker, but she was a great kisser. And her passion and unexpected innovation had reduced him to mindless vapourings. He was married by the time he realised that this rapt lover – who listened so intently – did not understand very much of what was being said. When their daughter was born, he took steps to insure that she remained an only child: it was not so much that he didn't want to have more children – he just wasn't sure he had the stamina to persevere with married life.

Zeno looked again at the large bed he had positioned for the summer equinox, and the mural he had painted on the wall behind it – a nude of his new wife. Was it so long ago? He remembered the erotic studies he had done of her when they had returned from their honeymoon; how he had pinned them around the walls. He found the memory stirring, and thought of the first time he had undressed her, every moment anticipating a flaw – and finding none.

'Kings kiss the dust whereof the fair spring from . . .' he quoted to no one in particular. 'I must make this marriage work,' he said firmly. It was a sentence he repeated regularly. Something he had picked up from a book which advocated frequent vocalisation as a way of making wishes become facts. Not that Zeno's heart was in the statement, for by now it was only a habit, something he said automatically. Are all marriages this way? he mused.

Who's asking this anyway? he wondered abstractedly. There were lots of such unanswered fragments behind his tall brow; phrases he didn't understand, yet had committed to memory in the hope that the meanings would unfold by themselves. He had led most of his life this way – 'education by the senses' was what he called it.

It was a topic which never came up on the many talk-shows in which he had taken part during his long and intermittent career. In fact, he didn't regard it as a career at all. He had been lucky enough to be in the right place at the right time: he had landed a minor role in a television series which had lasted a season, and in which he had sung a song. The song had become the surprise hit of the summer, climbing up the charts and displacing the inevitable American single from the top spot.

Zeno found himself a celebrity, even winding up on the road with Billy Fury. His voice outside the echo chamber was hardly equipped for the rigorous tour of the coastal cinemas in which he gyrated, but he persevered. His sullen look pleased the entrepreneur, and his hangdog expression brought instant gratification to the teenage groupies of the time.

Zeno was smarter than most of his hip-swivelling contemporaries, and remained level-headed in spite of the groundswell of adoration. While others partied late and slept soundly – their new surnames and pancake make-up intact – until late afternoon, he rose early. Investing his money in odds and ends he felt would suit the home he shared with his mother, he explored the many antique shops sprinkled around the provincial town in which he woke. It didn't take too long for him to recognise the discrepancy between provincial and London prices, and soon the charabanc conveying the bevy of pop swans was also transporting Zeno's finds.

The personal manager who had rechristened him (he had been magically transformed from Jenkins to Studd) and the other acolytes – Biberfeldt, Solly and Crump had become Ripp, Havoc and Stiff – introduced Zeno to the gay underground of West End dealers, and he soon became a freelance supplier of antiques to the trade who just couldn't find the time to scavenge the provinces themselves. It was a role that suited him, combining as it did his natural interest in unfamiliar places with an uncanny knack of finding pieces almost at will, sometimes from only a pencil sketch or a long look at an illustration.

'You sure you've no family in the trade, dear?' one slightly miffed queen had asked when Zeno had materialised a striking piece of Boulle marquetry after a one-nighter in Hastings. Zeno had grinned lopsidedly. It was a mannerism he had been told passed for an answer – and he was surprised that most times it did. He didn't have family 'in the trade', but his lighterman dad – now passed away, God bless him – would have been amused to hear it. Zeno himself wondered at his luck and the ease with which he had adapted to life on the road.

On the advice of one of his new-found dealer chums, he began investing the bulk of his rock-and-roll loot in small terraced houses in Fulham, so when his star set, unlike his other stellar chums who turned to minicabbing, Zeno Studd was able to continue living in some style. After his marriage, he was even able to purchase the grand Kensington house in which he awoke on the morning of the night.

Zen stretched out on the banquette in the kitchen. It was a comfortable spot, in close proximity to the red Aga stove. During the summer months Zen had it to herself. Unlike her mother and father, Zen liked extremes, so both very hot and very cold were to her liking.

The other reason she was so fond of this seat was that, when she lounged full-length along its needle-pointed surface, it made her invisible to anyone entering the kitchen. This morning she lay there in cotton pyjamas brought back specially for her from India. She rarely wore them in bed, yet loved to swan around in them watching videos in the evening, or in the morning before getting dressed proper – a habit she had picked up from Zeno, giving credence to his theory that a child was a mirror in which parents could view themselves.

Zen appeared to be in that unengaged state common to children when the mind is conscious but empty. But this morning this was not the case. She had noticed that the kitchen tap was dripping in perfect time with her pet starling's cheeps from the window-sill. When the grandfather clock's chimes joined the duet, Zen made it a quartet by tapping the downbeat on the underside of the breakfast table.

Zen loved the house in which she had been born – loved its familiar sounds and melodies, the rhythms of which she alone heard. She had retained the openness and warmth noticeable in children of acid-taking parents – the fragile innocence not frag-menting when teething and the formation of her little mind began. In their way, both parents acknowledged the sweetness of their child's nature, with Zeno perhaps aware of it earlier than most fathers.

Zen didn't see any difference between herself and the other kids at school, the majority of whom came from single-parent homes. She remained content in the knowledge that both her mum and dad would be there for her every morning, and always one of them to put her to bed at night. Although she knew of the disturbing currents that sometimes passed between them, she kept the sense of well-being that made her childhood a kingdom.

Zen's little concerto ended, and she sat up as the wooden stairs creaked. It wasn't the expected weight of her dad's bare feet they were announcing, but the slippered sounds of her mother.

Prudence could not remember in all her years of marriage when she had woken before Zeno. It was something he often pointed out to their friends. 'Prudence is not a morning person,' he would say, touching her arm or tousling her hair to let her know it wasn't a criticism.

She watched him as he slept next to her, lying flat on his back with his head resting on a Japanese pillow, as still as a sarcophagus. For a moment she thought he was dead. She was very frightened of death, and held her breath until she saw the rise and fall of his chest. His hair was grey now, yet he still wore it long, in the same way as when they had first met. Ivanhoe, she thought the first time she saw him. Because his sleeping late was so unusual, she decided he must need the rest. She climbed out of bed without waking him.

Zen, their newly nine-year-old daughter, was downstairs in the kitchen. She had made tea, apparently expecting her father because the concoction in the glass teapot was red and herbal, just as he liked it.

'Where's Dad?' she asked.

'He's . . . resting this morning.'

'But is he all right?'

'Yes, he's fine. Tired from all those questions you ask him, I expect.'

She smiled, hoping to end the inquisition before it started. Zen considered the statement and returned to stirring honey into her drink. Prudence reached into the giant box of teabags above the stove. Pushing the kettle to the middle of the hot plate, she turned and stared at the back of her daughter's head; her hair was scruffed into what look like a bulldog clip with teeth. She felt a rush of emotion and told herself not to be silly.

Sometimes she found it hard to believe that she had given birth to this little creature. Seeing the perfection of her made her feel grateful in a way she could never have put into words. As she watched her daughter scribbling intensely in her dream diary, she thought about the day she had announced to Zeno that she was pregnant.

Her announcement had triggered a previously unseen energy within her husband. He began by withdrawing both caffeine and wheat from her diet; he even gave them up himself by way of encouragement. He searched for and found little-known herbs and plant oils, which became part of her everyday life. They were measured into her bath – which he drew for her himself – and dropped on to the four corners of her pillow at bedtime. He also rubbed them into her handkerchief, to be sniffed during the day. These special potions would vary, and he prepared the combinations with the tender loving care of an ancient alchemist.

She absentmindedly put some breadcrumbs on the counter near the open window, the starling's feeding table. Her husband had arrived with the damaged fledgeling one morning so that their daughter could have a pet. With one foot in its world and the other in theirs.

Prudence never understood much of what Zeno talked about, but she always listened intently, and this seemed to satisfy him – at least for a while. Then a change had occurred in their relationship, which she felt long before anything actually happened that she could pinpoint. He did not stop talking to her, but he began explaining to her rather than just talking. Spontaneity was something she missed – especially when she noticed it being lavished on others (it was about this time that

Prudence consulted her mother, who advised her to stop taking the pill).

In an attempt to explain the function of the oils – they took on an element of magic after their daughter was born – he told her how, in ancient times, herbs and other naturally occurring substances were used by women – the herbalists, nurses, midwives and GPs of the day – as they spent their lives planting and gathering. The alchemy of herbs was understood and used throughout the ages simply because there was nothing else – empirical knowledge (which she looked up in the dictionary) being acquired by practice so that a real herbal lore was passed from generation to generation.

'It was only after the development of experimental chemistry – the forerunner of the patriarchal medical profession – that these ladies were burned as witches; the word "witch" being Old English for "wise",' he had said with the smile she knew frequently accompanied interesting titbits. Modern scientists were now confirming with specialised equipment what these ancients had always known. The rose, for example – with its five thousand components – combined with Indian sandalwood, would be perfect for her pillow; it would help her sleep and influence the limbic part of her brain so their child would be born with intelligence and beauty.

'Clary sage will give our child courage, and lavender in your inhalant will prevent you from getting anxious.' For Prudence, the relief from anxiety came with knowing that Zeno wanted to have the baby.

The double brass whistle on the kettle began its shrill moan, and Prudence was preparing to make her tea, when Zen said, 'Oh, let it blow, Mum, I love that noise – it reminds me of the trains in the films.'

'It goes right through me,' she retorted, thinking how much Zen took after Zeno. One of the quaint theories Zeno held was that the sound of a steam whistle developed the pineal gland; he claimed he had successfully beaten his dependence on marijuana by listening to the sound of the kettle boiling every morning. She would often return to the house to find the kettle boiling like mad, and Zeno going about his business, seemingly oblivious.

'Would you like me to come shopping with you, Mum?' Zen asked, changing the subject.

'If you like,' said Prudence, getting down to making the tea. 'I'll go and put some clothes on.'

'Mum, put your Alaia on.'

'For shopping? It shows everything I've got.'

'It suits you, though. And I like it when people look at you.'

She meant she liked it when people look at them; Zen had yet to have her first period, but she did have a friend who had started, and she and her classmates had talked of little else but that and boys last term.

During such conversations, Prudence thought there might be some truth to her husband's theory that she had been Zen's child in a previous life. She went to put on her jeans.

Zeno brushed his teeth, trying to see how many of the sixteen herbs in his Ayurvedic toothpaste he could recognise, and then went to the attic room for his workout. He did his short exercise routine and then chose a spot on the carpet where the sun shone on his face. He sat crosslegged, the sun's early rays warming his pituitary gland – or 'recharging his battery', as he called it. In spite of this, his concentration wandered, and he found himself inhaling the golden rays and mentally projecting them on to the image of the youth in his dream. Which was curious because, although Zeno's ambivalence had been much speculated-upon during his early years, he had never been sexually drawn to males.

Zeno didn't do his affirmations at all. This was partly because he knew he wasn't concentrating very well; but mainly because he knew Zen was not in her hiding place. Her bedroom adjoined his quiet room and most mornings, as soon as she heard him enter to do his yoga exercises, she would give him a moment to sit and close his eyes, and then creep in and join him. She believed her hiding place – under the day bed with the carpet over it – to be completely secure, and Zeno was only too pleased to let her go on believing it. He often recited things he wanted her to hear. He had promised himself that if he ever had children he would teach them how to breathe properly. And although Prudence had doubts about the success of his plan, he felt Zen had already been learning for some time.

Zeno had been married for years before he realised the extent to which fear played a role in his wife's life. The abandon which she expressed sexually was in no way reflected in her daily life; she feared almost everything new. It was some time before she would venture out of the Victoria Road house without her mother or sister with her; and even now she preferred to go shopping with Zen in tow. Zeno found this frustrating socially, but he trod warily around the long toenails of his wife's phobia, for he had experienced great fears himself, fears that had kept him a virtual prisoner in Britain. Not only did he have a fear of flying, but he also had a severe aversion to heights. This was to change in part some years after his daughter was born when, to his wife's astonishment, he announced his intention of going to India.

He was gone for a month. His mother-in-law – something of a wag – said the flight out must have been so terrifying that he was too frightened to come back. When he did come home, his fear of heights had not actually subsided (which Prudence was secretly pleased about), but something had changed. And although she thought about it a lot at the beginning, this change gradually became another of those things about her husband that she pushed to one side of her mind. She simply continued loving him in the little ways that she understood: making the dishes of his ever-changing diet tasty, always hanging his shirts on the line in the garden (even though he had provided her with a German tumble-dryer) whenever there was a little sun in the sky.

15

'Went to see a man about a dog,' was all he offered her by way of explanation after his Eastern odyssey.

The room in the attic that Zeno had allocated himself upon his return from India had been put together haphazardly – something he fully intended to remedy someday, but never got around to. In fact, he grew to like the chaos. No one was invited to the room, and its disorder came to represent a part of himself that he had rarely acknowledged. Over the years, the various effects, souvenirs, and odds and ends that had touched him found their way to the top floor, and a random order had established itself. In a Victorian chest with a brass name-plate he kept the outfits he had worn for his nights on the road, some too fragile to be worn regularly. One old silk shirt which he had not used in a very long time suited his mood. Putting it on, he recalled the day that lilac shirt had caught his eye. He and Kenny Wisdom had been strolling past Hung On You.

Kenny had been his first real friend after fame had swept him up and away; Kenny the teenage cat-burglar, an erstwhile member of Brooklyn's Aces Wild, and a reformed teenage junkie who became the founder of the Diggers. When Kenny began supplying free food to the poor of San Francisco, he became acknowledged as the Robin Hood of his time. It was the heroin – or 'Joan of Arc' as he called it – that did for him in the end. One temptation too many: overdosed on the subway to Brooklyn. A Sunday, when the Methadone Center was closed.

Kenny, whose ancestors came from the 'old country', stayed with the Studds when he crossed the Atlantic. His Hell's Angels leathers caused a stir amongst Zeno's lofty neighbours, but the disapproving glances were a small price for the pleasure of Kenny's company, which Zeno enjoyed greatly.

As he dressed, Zeno looked out at the one blot on his day – the Victorian chimney-stack which rose over a hundred and fifty feet into the air, the property of St Mary Abbot's Hospital in the Marloes Road. It was visible from every front window in the

Studd house. This chimney, stoutly constructed from Victorian bricks, was not in itself an eyesore – but its top was. Instead of being finished with the expected nineteenth-century flourish, it narrowed into a wimpy inner rim.

Zeno grinned as he remembered the afternoon he and Kenny had smoked a joint and devised a plan to transform that eyesore into a National Monument.

Kenny had noticed that the chimney was having its annual facelift and that at least half of its height was sheathed in scaffold. He examined it through Zeno's telescope and discovered a series of iron rungs built into the brick that began where the scaffolding ended. They formed an escalade to the top.

The next day, Zeno was woken by Mr Wisdom who had already scaled the smokestack and brought back measurements to start work on the transformation. A model of the proposed construction was put together by tea-time. By the weekend, the construction proper began. Zeno, however, had been unable to overcome his fear of heights, and Kenny, who could easily have completed the job alone, protested that he could not, and would not, undertake the installation without Zeno accompanying him.

'It's no fun climbing a mountain alone,' he said.

Kenny Wisdom was his father's son, a man's man who could macho most guys into doing anything he wanted. But not this time.

Zeno always kicked himself for not taking on the job. The neat jigsaw of plywood components remained stacked in Zeno's cellar.

He selected several cookies from his daughter's biscuit tin for a walking breakfast. But as he was replacing the lid, he had the uneasy feeling that someone was watching him through it, as if it were a two-way mirror. He hastily replaced the tin on the shelf, pocketed the cookies, grabbed a few nuts, and made his way on to the street, where the tarmac was already hot.

*

In spite of the fact that Prudence had not worn the black dress, she drew many glances from other shoppers, both male and female. Not being a morning person she was unaware of all the looks. However, not too much escaped her daughter, who was.

Prudence had wanted to hit the latest fave rave coffee shop first for a kick-start cappuccino before tackling the week's shopping. Zen's plan, on the other hand, was to complete her shopping before the check-out queues became long and boring, and hit the coffee shop when the task was completed.

Zen won, and it was a masterpiece of timing; they completed their shopping while the bread was still warm and before the hippies arrived for their chunks of organic pizza.

Zen stocked up on ingredients for the wheatless gingersnaps she baked herself. Prudence was constantly confused by her husband's rapid changes in nutrition, but to Zen, with the open mind of a child, her father's search for perfect health only meant more fun in the kitchen. The sugarless snap, baked without wheat, was one of their more successful inventions, and once the basic recipe had been arrived at, Zen took over the baking, and even improvised. Like most good cooks, potential or otherwise, she was secretive about her concoctions; yet Prudence, who organised the house-keeping, always allowed for large amounts of vanilla essence, oat bran, concentrated apple juice, powdered ginger and cinnamon. Zen shaped the biscuits by hand – too sticky for any other method – and laid them individually on the baking trays. When the undersides were cooked dark, she placed them one at a time into her favourite cake tin, the one with the picture on the lid of Little Lady Bountiful giving food to the gypsy children.

Like most children given free rein in the kitchen, she enjoyed the chance to cook. But what pleased her most was the idea that her father carried her cookies in his pocket across alien territory where only pizzas, croissants, sandwiches, buns, rolls and doughnuts, which flooded the system with acid, were sold. And Zen loved to see her father smile – even if it did make his face look like rubber.

When the girls – which is how Zeno thought of them – reached the snack bar, it was buzzing. Zen spotted two empty seats, and steered her mother towards them.

'You wait there and I'll get us a drink.'

Zen took off for the counter, soon to return with a cappuccino and a glass of hot water into which she dropped a sachet of Orange Sunrise from her travelling stash. After Prudence had skimmed the powdered chocolate from the top of her cappuccino and spooned several mouthfuls, Zen considered her mum sufficiently awake to chat.

All summer the topic had been her impending period. Zen considered it to be imminent, and Prudence didn't argue. The other topic was when Zen's first brassière could be purchased.

Prudence found it hard to think about what went on at Zen's school. She had somehow suppressed the fact that she herself had been seduced – or 'done' as it was termed then – at the age of fourteen. She was a natural, and loved it straight away. From that first time, she had dreamed only of a man and a place of her own where she could do it whenever she wanted, and not be confined to the park after dark or the deep doorway of the sweet factory. She did not know why she sought to delay her daughter's maturation as long as possible; it was simply an instinct that she followed blindly. She was relieved when Zen changed the subject and asked how Prudence had been wooed by Zeno.

'When did you know, Mum – when did you know you loved him?'

'Well, all the girls wanted him. We'd never met anyone famous. Nobody round our way had seen anything like him. He had this real long hair. Everyone's got it today, but then it was, well, it was like a girl's – it was sort of shocking. I caught hell when I first brought him home. Me mum . . .'

'Granny Em?'

'Mm-mm, Granny Em. She took one look at him and burst into tears.'

19

'What did you do?'

'I didn't do anything, but Zeno immediately said to me mum, "Cheer up, love, it might have been worse, I could have been a Rolling Stone." She liked him after that, probably because he made her laugh.'

'But you, Mum, when did you know?'

'We met at the Lyceum. I used to go for the Friday dance. They had a live band on Fridays.'

'You went on your own?'

'No. I usually went with my friend, Eileen. We were dancing together, Eileen and me, and he was dancing on his own, and he came and danced near us. Well, we were giggling – he looked so weird. His hair was up in a ponytail and he had a funny suit – some kind of powder-blue job. He saw we were laughing at him and he said, "You think I'm a right Mary Ann, don't you?" '

'What's that?' Zen wanted to know.

'Oh, it's a man who behaves like an old woman.'

'Like Daddy's friend Ciro who wears the eyeliner?'

'Kind of. Well, anyway, he asked us to dance.'

'Both of you?'

'Yes. Well, he didn't ask us, really, he just kept dancing near us. Everybody was looking at us. I wanted to sit down. I didn't know what to do with myself, but Eileen was loving the attention, so we kept dancing. He was good though, you know – he made up his own steps. Anyway, he took us for tea.'

'Where to, Mum?'

'To an old coffee stall in Covent Garden; it's not there anymore. He talked mostly to Eileen, because she knew about music – jazz and that – but he kept looking at me. He had this way of holding his cup near his face, every now and then looking at me through the steam. I felt like he was looking right into me.' She paused, looking at Zen. 'You have his eyes, sausage. At any rate, he walked us to the tube and said perhaps he'd see us there next week. Eileen's boxer friend was around the next weekend, so I went on my own.'

'You didn't!'

'I did.'

'Mum!'

'Well, I couldn't stop thinking about him; there was something about him, and I knew if I didn't go I probably wouldn't see him again. So I went. He was waiting outside, but we didn't go in; he took me to a jazz club instead.'

'Did he kiss you goodnight?'

'No.'

Prudence didn't continue. She looked out across the crowded café, and Zen knew her mother was transported back to the night her prince had come. She gave her a moment and then brought her back to earth.

'So, Mum, what did he do?'

Prudence was touching her wide, unmade-up mouth, and her daughter knew that her mother was thinking about that first kiss. But when she spoke, it was to tell her something else, something she had never spoken of before; believing in her superstitious way that the charm of a secret is broken once it is spoken of, even to a loved one.

'When he saw me outside the Lyceum I was a bit flustered – travelling on my own and all that – which I think he understood. I didn't tell him, but he took my hand and we walked to this jazz club in Soho and on the way he told me he knew I would come because he'd had a dream about me the night before we had met.'

'Did he tell you the dream?'

'Yes, but it was the night before the dance at the Lyceum.'

'Before he'd even seen you?'

'That's what he said. He told me that when he was a boy, they had these trolley-buses that he went everywhere on, and in this dream he was coming home with a gang of his mates when a family got on a trolley; a mother and three daughters, all dishy, who sat at the front of the bus. He and his mates were pretty sharp, but because he had the gift of the gab, he was chosen to go

21

and chat them up. He sat behind them and, being a smart cookie . . .'

'Which he is.'

'. . . began flattering the mum. The woman was swallowing his line about him and his friends coming to call for tea, when the daughter next to her pointed to him and said to her mum, "Just him, not the others. Only him." '

'And?'

'The girl, the daughter, was me. Well, looked like me.'

'That's awesome.'

'She wasn't exactly like me, but similar enough that he recognised me at the dance, the red hair and everything. What was the word he used? Idolised?'

'Idealised?'

'Mm-mm, that's it – an idealised version of me.'

'How . . . how . . . romantic.'

'Yes. If it's true.'

Prudence returned to her introspection, and this time Zen didn't intrude. Her mother was lost in the fond memories of those early years – before the distance she had always felt in Zeno finally surfaced. He had stopped performing or writing songs, and he spent hours – sometimes days – alone, poring over books, books she couldn't understand: where did he find them?

This avid reading had started while she was still breast-feeding Zen. And then new procedures entered into their life: the Billings ovulation method – where had he come across that? Those embarrassing evening classes he had taken her to, drawing her attention to the mysterious mucus patterns that had changed their lives, made their spontaneous passion a thing of the past, their daughter an only child. She doubted if she could ever have more children, even if she lied to him. She had left it too long. Even though he still shaved and bathed before coming to bed with her, she man she had married was becoming more of a stranger every day.

'If it's true,' she repeated to herself, 'if anything he told me was true. Me mum warned me against marrying above myself.' Tears came to her eyes. Then she remembered that Zen was with her, and she tried to blink them away.

'Mum, I'm sorry. Don't be sad – let's talk about something else.'

She thinks it's her fault, thought Prudence; isn't it strange that whenever a marriage goes wrong, the kids blame themselves?

The whistle blew and the train was about to pull out when the door opened and a young woman struggled in. Nick, slouched in his corner seat, perked up. He wasn't one of those people who felt his privacy invaded when someone entered his carriage – he welcomed a travelling companion. He regarded the newcomer as acutely as an anthropologist presented with a new species. In her flurry, she was unaware of his presence. He appreciated this, as it gave him an edge. Her face was away from him as she placed her basket – a Third World affair with a stripe and leather straps – alongside a pair of plastic bags in the overhead rack. He noted that, viewed from the rear – not the most flattering angle to view a woman's legs – hers showed unusual promise. He was even more intrigued when she turned and proved to be attractive. Not that it would have made a great deal of difference to Nick – he wasn't that sort of guy. In fact, in a bygone era, he could easily have been one of those warrior chieftains who bedded all the women of his clan, not just the pretty ones.

She was wearing a great deal of jewelry – so much so that virtually all her movements were accompanied by jangling and tinkling. He was not especially put off by this, as it was his custom not to divide sounds into harmonious or inharmonious, but rather to extend the field of his listening until he arrived at a comprehensive conclusion.

He had always felt that you could tell a lot about a person from their jewelry and how they wore it. Thus, he first noticed the most obvious items – the wedding and engagement rings. He glanced down at the ring on his own forefinger, painstakingly copied from the portrait of a pope in a Venetian palazzo. If his carriage companion had been interested – which at present she was not – she might have been intrigued by the oblong of black amber held in place by the plain gold hoop. Intrigued by the theory that, worn on this finger, it denoted a desire for power over others.

His attention returned to the girl, who was rummaging through her handbag, probably for her ticket; he wondered if she realised that she was in a first-class carriage. She held her legs together, providing a stable place for the bag, and he casually glanced at the fine shafts of hair above her knees, noting that the colour corresponded with her strawberry-blonde hair, which was cut into a fashionable page-boy.

Nick also believed that humans retained traces of the lower kingdoms in their physiognomy, and this signified a similarity with the nature of that creature. It was one of the insights that had given him unexpected success in his chosen pastime.

Continuing his analysis, he divided her form into two parts, body and head; the one for action, the other for thought. From his present observations, he deduced that the former most resembled a horse or foal, and that her frequent stretching conveyed a desire for action. Contemplating the head, he could almost deduce her feelings, which he read as waves that passed across her face, as deftly as a sea captain reading the mood of the ocean. The momentary puckering of the lips suggested pleasure, perhaps at the idea of being on the loose, on her way to the big city. The upward twist of her eyebrows indicated that she was not without ego, yet a certain expression about the eyes told him she was not above a dash of submissiveness. Of his many talents, Nick most appreciated his ability to read the language of the eyes, for it was his opinion that in the speed and direction of the glance lay the mystery of the expression.

The ticket inspector drew aside the door and Nick, nearest the corridor, produced his ticket. He was half expecting the girl to be directed to the other section of the train, when she produced what appeared to be a special pass.

'On the railway?' asked the inspector. He resembled the tubby half of Abbott and Costello.

'That's right,' she replied.

'Where do you work out of then?' he went on, chatty for a change.

'Barking.'

'Going back to work, eh?'

'That's right. Been to see me sister in Brighton.' Her voice had a foggy London accent. The inspector returned her pass.

'Be lucky,' he said as he closed the door.

Nick recalculated: not a girl from the shires up for the day, but a Londoner going home. Barking. Let's see . . . that's out Essex way. The train comes in to Victoria; is she in a hurry to get directly on to the Underground and home, or is it a window-shop in the West End? He noticed that she was still stretching from time to time.

He drew his chiming pocket watch from his waistcoat and flipped it open, watching her face as he wound the hands to the hour. She looked up as it chimed, saw him staring at her, blinked and crossed her legs. Nick saw the skin of her thigh pucker.

'Wot's your game, then?' she asked, levelling his glance.

Nick opened his eyes a fraction, letting her feel his power, and said, 'I bet I could show you how to make your eyes up so they'd be the envy of every woman in Barking.'

Fleur didn't stir until Mister Owl's needle punctured her foot. It said much for the acupuncturist's skill that she didn't actually wake until he had half a dozen needles in place (her own needles, kept in her personal case: a recent precaution since the advent of AIDS). She felt the extra energy moving through her body, and opened her eyes. Her tongue was coated, and she remembered that she had deliberately forgone supper in order to ensure that her tummy was flat for the party.

25

At her best, Fleur didn't sparkle until after midday. As a teenager, she had been asked to leave more than one finishing school for simply refusing to get out of bed. Waking this morning with a tingling coursing through her meridians brought to mind the bearded Dutchman who had all too briefly warmed her life. He would probe her gently before sun-up so that she would wake on the threshold of orgasm. A pity there weren't more like him. What was his name?

Mister Owl removed the long needles and began massaging her foot. He's making a meal of it today, she thought, her mind segueing from the memorable Dutchman; perhaps the maid's been talking. Then she recalled why she had booked the squat Oriental so early. She had two appointments, both in the Harley Street area: the dentist for her bi-monthly clean-up, and a colonic irrigation. She was due at the dentist at 10.30. Fleur's vanity had won out, and she was bent on overcoming her fear of the occasion, albeit with a little Chinese help. Mister Owl had progressed up her calf and was now pummelling away at her knee.

What is the man doing? she thought, reaching for her robe and sliding from under the sheet.

'Thank you, Doctor,' she said tetchily. 'See Vanella on the way out. Still thirty pounds, is it?'

He mumbled an unintelligible reply. Amazing how these people don't bother to learn English, she thought; she knew for a fact that he had arrived from Hong Kong over ten years ago. As she proceeded to the bathroom she found her progress impeded by two short golden arms around her midriff, and turning her head, found Mister Owl's face buried in her shoulder.

'I huv you,' she thought he said.

For a moment she felt like she was being subjected to some extreme form of shiatsu, but when he continued to grapple with the cord of her robe, repeating, 'I huv you, I huv you,' she realised his intentions weren't solely therapeutic.

'Pull yourself together,' she said sternly. 'And go and collect your money from the maid or I shan't pay you at all.'

The thought of forfeiting a fee struck fear into the heart of Mister Owl. He immediately released her, hastily pulled his black judo shoes on over his white socks, and departed to see Vanella. The Madagasque maid handed him three clean ten-pound notes – like the Queen, Fleur withdrew only new notes from the bank – and went to linger in the doorway smiling. Glancing once more at Fleur, he turned and left.

'Your bath is ready, Madam – would you like coffee now?'

'I'll take it while I bathe, thank you, Vanella.'

She dropped the silk skin where she stood and proceeded naked to the adjoining bathroom, where she sprinkled extra lilac oil into the water to help regain her composure. Stepping into the bath she called: 'Have you been gossiping with Mister Owl, Vanella?'

Vanella was in the bedroom. She had not yet started stripping the bed – Fleur liked clean sheets every day; linen in summer, cotton in winter – but was holding Fleur's discarded robe against herself, admiring her reflection in her mistress's floor-to-ceiling wall of peach mirror.

'Only on the phone, Madam. He likes to talk dirty on the phone.'

'Well, don't,' said Fleur from the bath, evidently an important feature in her life judging from its position in the middle of the room; the wall-to-wall carpet ran up its sides as if to prevent it getting a chill. Years ago Fleur had tried to decide between comfort and taste and, born with her ascendant in the sign of procrastination, came down somewhere in the middle.

'He was rubbing himself against me as if I was a bitch in heat,' said Fleur absently.

Vanella, who was as delicious as her name, smiled and kept her own counsel.

'Will you be wanting me any more today, Madam?' the maid asked, filling a Hadden Hall cup with coffee from a small stainless-steel flask. She had found herself a tousle-headed Scotsman who had introduced a little bondage into her young life,

27

fashioning her a velvet blindfold and binding her with a silk skipping rope. Vanella had been looking forward to her day off all week.

'Has the curry been put on?' enquired Madam.

'Yes'm. All fixed and bubbling smoothly since six this morning,' Vanella said as she entered the bathroom and balanced the flowered cup on the end of the tub.

'In that case you can take the rest of the day off. Oh, and Vanella – if you come back early, use your own door, please.' The maid, who had her modest quarters in the basement, popped her head back around the door, and with a delightful enamelled grin said, 'Yes'm. Have a wonderful salty time, Madam.' And she was gone before Fleur could think of anything else she needed doing.

'I'd kill for a smile like that,' she said to herself. 'I wonder who's going to be looking down at that face tonight?'

As she rough-gloved her back, she had second thoughts about letting her maid go, yet she reassured herself that it was never a good policy to have anyone as young and tasty as Vanella around when entertaining a new man. At least not until he was familiar with Fleur's special feature.

She finished her coffee, which had been made just right – Blue Mountain on Fridays, ground fine for that extra zing when you sniffed it. She had taken Ian Fleming's word on it when as a young girl she'd met him in Jamaica. Stepping out of the bath, she spent a moment admiring her breasts, breasts that the two great conveniences of the twentieth century – the pill and cosmetic surgery – had improved. Mirrors played a big part in Fleur's life. A camp decorator (who wasn't so camp in bed) had told her that marble, mirrors and fur created an air of luxury in a home – 'horny luxury' were the words he used – and Fleur had taken him at his word. Fleur was not a great one for original thought, but, like her walls, she reflected a great deal; a sympathetic screen on which to project almost anything. As one taxi driver, with a Leslie Howard forehead, once exclaimed after an enervating night: 'You're not a great fuck, darlin', but you're great *to* fuck.'

It was a peculiarity of Fleur's make-up that, whilst most of her life was spent satisfying her peculiar sense of refinement, the men she found most acceptable were invariably a little on the cheap side. The kind that really turned her on can best be described as the sort that wear short socks and reveal a hairy ankle whenever their trousers are hitched up. This penchant manifested itself early in her life. And it was due to her mother – who understood that trait – being sympathetic and concealing the incidents from her father, that she inherited the fortune she did when she reached thirty, by which time Fleur had at least learned to discriminate between actual gangsters and gents who looked enough like gangsters to get her off. She never entertained the idea of getting a beating, but the threat caused her considerable excitement. In her own way it was as near as she came to realising that pain and pleasure were intimate strangers.

Seeking therapy from a renowned mystic therapist when such things were fashionable, she confessed during an early session that her first orgasmic sensation had been induced during a spanking administered by her father, when she had peed herself in fright, the wetting being accompanied by a thrilling feeling. The distinguished psychologist had smiled and commented that the punishment was providential, as not every girl found herself released into womanhood that simply – or that early.

Fleur didn't have too many female intimates, but one, a blonde model with luminous skin, could only find satisfaction with negro men. Fleur felt sorry for her because her field of endeavour was so restricted – never for a moment considering that her own predilections restricted her in much the same way.

She thought about what she would wear for her ordeal in Harley Street, and promised herself a Sobranie with her cappuccino in Fortnum's – or num nums, as she had called it as a child – as a reward when it was over. Before sliding open the mirrored doors of her summer hanging space, she sat on a low padded satin chair, spread her legs, and regarded the neat blonde triangle covering her pubic bone (its shape waxed geometric by an expert in Putney), the triangle that housed the 'magic wherewithal', as the bearded Dutchman, who spoke such quaint English, had termed it; the magic wherewithal being a clitoris so distended that it protruded like an erection when it was stimulated.

Fleur closed her legs and concentrated on some new games for her party.

The Rose had always been an addictive personality. Even before medical college focused his obsessive nature on study and left his contemporaries in the dust. His decision to become a surgeon seemed natural, and nobody doubted his eventual success. He rose like a spark, securing rooms in Cavendish Street, an apartment with a view of the Thames, and a black Bentley – brain-surgeon black, as he called it – with single headlights. 'The last elegant car that Bentley made,' he was fond of saying.

He was abstemious by habit (the strongest drink he'd ever taken was black coffee) and the idea of sex, the great appeaser of the big ego, was something that seldom entered his noble head. All this changed one country weekend in a grand house when the hostess doused an indifferent trifle with sherry. The Rose did have a sweet tooth, and he ate two portions. He was found an hour later on all fours, still in the dining room, an empty bottle of Dow's near by. He later confessed to a colleague that when the trifle hit his palate, he had let forth a 'Wow!' of recognition, the kind of recognition which is known to any hereditary alcoholic who recalls sampling their first drink.

At first this addition to his lifestyle didn't affect his work; it was two years before he experienced his first hangover. But what a hangover it was. Driving to work that morning, he remembered acknowledging the seemingly lethal headache and deciding that he would have to find a way of getting used to it, because this was how it was going to be from now on. He was soon greeting each day with a sandwich, as he called it: a dash of lemonade with a Fuller's E.S.B. and a Carlsberg Special Brew – both concoctions available only in countries where there is no legal requirement to display ingredients on the container. Publicans all over London were impressed by the constitution of the well-spoken gent who could sink a 'shandy' of this type at eleven o'clock in the morning. It was only when an older colleague noticed his shaking hands that he was warned of the error of his ways and pointed in the right direction. Shandy liveners and vodkatinis became a thing of the past; now, Dexedrine pepped him up before surgery, and Demerol and Percodan smoothed him out at night. And Daliudid – the pill that Elvis reputedly loved so – became his weekend treat.

The Rose understood early that life was energy, to be willed as directed. The paradox of his addiction was that his chosen path was fast undermining the force of will that directed it. His system would snap. It was simply a question of when. After a year, the Dems and Percs were jettisoned, and self-administered IV Valium was dripping into his arm before bed. The same nerve ganglia which showed increased sensitivity during intoxication were becoming increasingly lifeless without it. So, lacking the energy or determination to do otherwise, he simply stopped worrying, and concentrated all his remaining energies on planning the next fix.

He took to mixing cocktails in his chambers and taking them with him to surgery. One afternoon, he became so fragmented that he took a break during a three-hour operation to inject himself in the anteroom adjoining the theatre. In his haste he grabbed the wrong ampoule and was found minutes later in a state of complete paralysis. The Rose had not lost consciousness – he knew precisely what he had done. Shortly afterwards, the head of the hospital took him aside.

'It would be a pity if this kind of behaviour continued. I suggest you take a break – a long one. Perhaps a period of convalescence. I believe there are rehab centres that are both good and discreet.'

He was called the Rose – in his early years as a surgeon he had placed a red rose on the life-support machine of a patient in intensive care. The patient had survived. Since then he had always worn a rose in his buttonhole though he never admitted or denied his belief in the healing power of flowers.

He set off for his month in the rehabilitation clinic with half a dozen bottles of chilled Ladoucette. The chauffeur – hired to drive him and return with the car – drove leisurely, as instructed, and the Rose sat in the back with the cooler, sipping the wine as a palliative against the withdrawals he was experiencing.

The guards at the lodge of the clinic put an end to this, and the driver returned to London with the remaining three bottles. 'A month,' mused the tipsy neurosurgeon as he walked like a captive between the porters. A month indeed.

The male inmates of the clinic were boarded in groups of six. Their routines were continuous, and supervised either by a member of staff or each other. The first couple of weeks were a nightmare for the Rose. He sulked in silence. Finally, one of his circle got on his case.

'I don't know why you're not joining in – anyone would think butter wouldn't melt in your mouth.' The Rose didn't respond.

'Come on, junkie, share your shit with us.'

'I'm not a junkie, I'm an impaired practitioner,' the Rose snapped.

Everyone in the circle laughed, except a serious-faced individual who may very well have signed the Hippocratic oath himself at one time. In the silence that followed he smiled at the Rose and said, 'Just because you don't buy your junk, Doc, doesn't make you any different. You shoot up the same as the rest of us.'

That afternoon the result of his brain scan arrived, and he viewed it with the MD in residence. His brain had begun to be affected by the abuse. However, his metabolism, in its wisdom, had allowed the least-used part to be sacrificed first: the Rose saw that the section of his brain which had absorbed the most damage was responsible for abstract thought.

'It has only been affected recently,' said the doctor, sensing his patient's distress. 'It might not be irreversible. I'm sure I don't need to explain the theory of Vis Medicatrix to you.'

The Rose didn't respond. But that was the moment when he knew he wouldn't be able to indulge again.

He committed himself to his routines, doing his share of the cleaning and tidying of the group quarters, and enjoying it. He had never done day-to-day tasks, and manual labour was a mystery to him (unless eight-hour stretches in the operating theatre could be termed manual), yet he found the purely physical jobs refreshing. In his journal he talked of 'getting myself back into my body' and by the third week he was 'less morose and sleeping astonishingly well'.

He was allowed visitors, provided they submitted to a body search and agreed to leave all alcohol and banned substances in their cars – but the Rose didn't want any reminders of his past life anyway. His intellectual stimulation came from the weekly sessions with the psychoanalyst, which generally opened with:

'And what shall we talk about this week?'

'Why don't we talk about you, Doctor Plante?'

'Perhaps when I know you better. Cup of herbal tea, while it's hot?'

'No chance of a proper cuppa?'

'Anything that is a mood-altering substance increases your risk of slipping. Try to get used to life without caffeine, sugar, tobacco. All craving has the same root. You are an addict, but you're not stupid.'

The Rose considered. 'Herbal is fine, thank you.'

During their first session, the Rose saw the potential of debate with the 'doctor of the mind', but felt too fragmented to put forth any line of serious discussion. However, by the third week, he was confident enough to steer their discussion to the subject of right and wrong. Dr Plante took up the challenge: 'My feeling, reinforced by some years in the field, is that the most reliable way to view good, or right, is that which comforts the mind, and bad as that which causes discomfort.'

'So you completely disregard moral law?'

'If you mean moral law outwardly, yes. After all, each mind has its own opinion of what is good or bad, which is usually a jumble of what one has learned from one's parents, or read, or one's belief in a certain dogma, birth of a particular colour or nation . . .'

'And inwardly – how would you describe inner moral law?'

'Conscience.' Plante paused. 'Cultivation of conscience, if you like.'

The Rose pondered a moment, and then said, 'In other words, a man should consult his own conscience, his own spirit, to make the distinction between right and wrong?'

'I think so, yes. Outwardly it appears that it is discomfort that produces wrongdoing, but my belief is that it's the other way around.'

'That wrongdoing produces discomfort – psychological discomfort?'

The psychoanalyst drank some of his tea and looked into his cup as though expecting an answer from the herbs. Then he said slowly, 'Look, the pain of the mind, in my experience, is often far greater than the pain of the body – do you agree?'

'Yes,' said the Rose, thinking back over the last three weeks. 'The psychological emotional discomfort can often be extreme, and the remedies are . . .'

'. . . are no escape.' Plante smiled. 'Because they kill you. Unless you're lucky enough to wind up here. So abiding to moral law outwardly is an artificial standard. You can conform to it all your life, feeling emotionally out of sync . . .'

'And find yourself dying of cancer.'

The doctor pointed his pen in the Rose's direction. 'Are you agreeing with me?' he asked.

'No. I was finishing your sentence. I'm familiar with the holistic theory that a life lived at odds with one's nature results in the manifestation of an additional "personality" – the cancerous growth.'

'You disagree then?'

'Privately no, I think it's uplifting – the idea that man should be able to consult his own feelings to discover what is good or bad, right or wrong for him. Because that's what you're saying, is it not? That this artificial standard being passed from parent to child and taught in classrooms is itself burying the human spirit? So would I therefore conclude that if the world at large were, say, taught at an early age . . .'

'They could develop a better sense of what it was that truly gave them comfort . . .'

'Or discomfort.' The Rose finished his Cinnamon Dawn, which was lukewarm.

'Of course, it can't be imposed.'

'Which would be a contradiction in terms.'

'So there you have it. It can only be initiated by the individual willingly, as and when he or she sees the sense of it.'

'The world only being the individual in the collective sense.'

'Which brings us to you,' said Dr Plante. The Rose managed a smile.

'I thought it might,' he said.

'What do you think made you bury your spirit so deeply?'

'The drugs, you mean?'

'Yes.'

'The drink – I was trying to bury the hangover.' Plante looked at the Rose and smirked.

'Oh, Mister – you who are so intelligent.'

'I was making a joke.' The Rose grinned. It had been a winner on the wards.

'I know. But this may be our last session.'

'Please forgive me my transgression. I'll promise to be . . . to behave properly.' Plante nodded his head like a cardinal and said, 'To sum up, you are cross-addicted. You cleaned out from the drink by shooting up the stuff, and vice versa. A bit like a thief dressing up as a policeman and trying to let himself out of jail.'

'I wasn't allowed any alcohol as a child.'

'Your parents kept a tight rein on you?'

'My father had travelled – he was a great one for the evils of sex and drink, always warning me against them. His mother liked to drink, you see, and his dad had been a bit of a lad, I think. A sailor. The old Spirochaeta pallida finally got him.' He caught the doctor's blank look. 'Syphillis. He died from syphillis.'

'I see. You're celibate?'

'No.'

'Not celibate – you don't practise celibacy?'

The surgeon seemed to find the doctor's even glance disconcerting. After a moment he replied: 'Continence. More like continence. Celibacy breaks itself, doesn't it? Anyway, energy is energy, you can use it how you choose. Sex is a direction.'

'That's true. The reason you are in relatively good shape is probably due to your abstinence.'

'Relatively, yes. It's about the only area I've abstained in.'

'You're alive,' Plante said assuringly. The Rose nodded.

'And you have wet dreams?'

'I do?'

'Well. You said celibacy breaks itself. I assumed that's what you meant.' The Rose nodded. It wasn't exactly assent.

'Do you have wet dreams, then?'

'Doesn't everyone?'

'We're not discussing everyone.'

'No, of course we're not. Yes, I do have wet dreams.'

'Frequently?'

'I don't exactly keep a wet-dream journal, you know.'

36

'I understand.' Neither of the men spoke for some time, and then Plante said, 'When you have these dreams, are they accompanied by an erotic image?'

'I suppose so. Frankly, I don't remember.'

'Why not?'

'They stopped some time ago. When drugs became my . . . girl. Do you think my addiction is hereditary?'

'It may be genetic. Why d'you ask?'

'I wonder why I didn't start drinking earlier.'

'You may have been traumatised as a boy. Only started when life became too painful.' Plante looked at his watch. 'Well, I think that's fine for today. Thank you for dropping by.'

'Thank you. It was my pleasure.' The Rose rubbed his hands. Strong hands, capable of working many tension-filled hours at a stretch. He felt the hardened tendon in his left hand, and Plante caught the gesture.

'Dupuytren's contraction?'

'Yes.'

'Is it operable?'

'It is, but it's risky – for a surgeon.'

'I've heard it's caused by a massive shock to the central nervous system.'

The Rose considered this, and said, 'Both Reagan and Thatcher have it.'

'Which would figure,' said Plante with a smile.

'I suppose it would.'

'It might recover with sobriety.' A discreet tap on the door signalled that the next patient had arrived. The men shook hands.

There was a Russian bath at the rehabilitation centre, which the Rose found a great help in the morning when he was low. The steam cheered him up, and he imagined it was purifying his spirit. He hadn't known it was there until one of his group asked him along.

It is a fact that a lot of long-term addicts approaching mundane things newly sober find them terrifying, and one of the strengths of the centre was not allowing patients to isolate themselves too much. This was a problem for the surgeon who, for most of his life, had had most things his own way.

In his group was a man named Dave, whom the Rose took an almost instant dislike to. Dave was known as DD, short for Denial Dave, because in spite of the fact that he had been consuming in excess of a bottle of gin per day for the last ten years, he would not admit to being completely powerless in the face of alcohol. The Rose's aversion to DD at the first group-therapy session no doubt stemmed from the fact that Dave reflected his own denial – but this initial impression changed when Dave took him along to the bath and showed him the ropes with all the tenderness of a Jewish mother. And although when they said their goodbyes Dave was still vigorously denying he was an alcoholic, the Rose rarely entered a steam bath without a thought for DD, and wondered if he'd ever 'got it'.

Once he had gained confidence and started coming to the bath on his own, he discovered it wasn't dissimilar to the one he'd been to as a boy with his dad, which was in the neighbourhood where his grandmother lived. When they visited the old lady, his father sometimes took him to the baths. He soon learned how to control the steam at the rehab, and took to dropping by the baths in the evening before turning in.

On the next to last evening before his scheduled departure, he was savouring a moment alone in the steam before bed when he sensed a presence near him more by the extra heat created than anything else. Nothing felt amiss, and he didn't bother to open his eyes. He may have dropped off for a moment, because he suddenly felt very hot, and came to to find a vapour swirling around him like a fog. A vague outline moved and sat on the marble bench adjacent to him. The skin of the figure was dark against the white-on-white of the room. He felt his own skin prickle without reason.

'Hello,' said the voice, its breath propelling a path towards him through the steam. 'Thought I had the room to myself. Nice isn't it – steam before dream?'

There was something exotic about the speech, more in the lilt than the dialect, but the Rose, who was a listener by nature, recognised it immediately as Indian.

'Yes. Relaxing.' He kept his reply short, caught midway between his old habit of remaining detached, and his new-found openness. By the time he'd realised he was isolating – as they called it at the clinic – and relented, the stranger spoke again, and he was glad of the second chance to interact.

The man stood up and moved in a circle around the room, allowing the vapour to flow over his body, chatting all the while. The Rose saw he was young, probably in his twenties, and there was a certain feline grace about him – the way his legs moved and the manner in which his feet made contact with the tiled floor.

During one of his circuits of the room, he stopped directly in front of the Rose. About three feet separated them and, without pausing in his monologue, he drew his right foot up and placed it against his left thigh, behind his scrotum, which was considerable. He straightened his left leg, rested his left arm on his hip, and raised his other arm above his head. Unlike the Rose, who had his loincloth wrapped sedately around his waist, the youth wore his around his neck like a college scarf. He was perspiring heavily, and the aroma he gave off was both rich and strange. The hand draped over his hip wore a silver bracelet – a Sikh wedding band – and the Rose was looking at this and pondering its significance when the youth, using his free hand, whipped the loincloth from his neck and, with a sharp flick of his wrist, snapped it in front of the Rose's face. The crack echoed around the room.

'Are you staring at me?' he demanded.

Regaining his composure the Rose said, 'No. I was . . . appreciating you.'

'That's all right, then.' The youth looked at the Rose and smiled. 'Are you gay?'

'Why do you ask?'

'Just like that – are you?'

'I've never thought about it. Probably nothing. Like Jesus.'

'I wouldn't say that. I'd say you were gay.'

'What makes you so sure?'

'Because you're so sad.'

'I don't feel sad.'

'Maybe not, but your eyes give you away. They're sad.'

The Rose couldn't think what to say, so he didn't reply. The youth, swaying his torso on his stretched leg, continued speaking. The Rose thought he resembled a young tree, and wondered how long he could balance this way. It added to the tension in the room. The tree spoke. 'My eyes are sad too. We all have them.'

'Do you?'

'People say.'

'People say so many things.'

'Do so many things, too.' He paused. 'Are you married?'

'No. Why do you ask?'

'Oh, it's my lot in life. Every man I open up to seems to go off and get married.'

'Open up?'

'You know what I mean.' The youth paused again, looked the Rose squarely in the eye and asked, 'Do I interest you?'

Again the surgeon was at a loss for words; neither a yes nor a no seemed appropriate. So he said 'ah cha,' which on the continent of India is always accompanied by a waggle of the head, midway between a nod and a shake, and meaning the same.

The youth laughed and, still balancing on his one leg, leaned his face a little closer. He spoke again, his voice low and sultry. 'This, how I am standing, is a yoga posture – it is called vrksasana. It is only relatively difficult to balance, but with eyes closed it becomes more difficult because one has to listen to balance. I am going to close my eyes now and count to ten. If you are here when I open them, I am going to take you where you've never been.' He closed his eyes.

The Rose left the clinic a changed man. He wore the same conservative three-piece suit he had arrived in and, although he was by no means completely fit, his body had begun to lose its recent flaccidity. In addition, his bowels were functioning properly – junkies hate to own up to the chronic constipation they all suffer from – and during the last week of rehabilitation he was having a movement after each meal, which the doctor in attendance said was natural, albeit not normal.

His new friend, Kerim – it means 'generous' – had given him some advice: 'You are not old, but you already dress old. You are a powerful chap and you should wear powerful clothes, powerful colours. I will tell you which ones,' he'd said.

The Rose didn't telephone his driver. He needed time to think, and returned to the capital by rail. The trip took four hours. He ordered the tawdry British Rail lunch, and was astonished when all three waiters attempted to ply him with alcohol. It wasn't difficult to refuse, but he felt the need to stay alert.

The train journey was as strange for him as his first visit to London Zoo. He observed his fellow passengers sinking drinks, as he had done until recently. As a spectator he was aware for the first time how he must have behaved. By the time the train arrived at Euston, he'd made several decisions.

His career as a neurosurgeon was over. The contraction hardening the tendon of his hand would not get worse if he stayed straight, but it was unlikely to improve. Traditional medicine had no knowledge of its cause, but the holistic view that it was started by a serious shock to the central nervous system was feasible, the nervous system being the body's principal battery. It was operable, with a sixty–forty success rate, but he wasn't prepared to chance the odds. And although the damaged

41

hemisphere of his right brain had recovered, the Rose did not feel good about returning to neurosurgery.

He went back to college and studied the art of plastic surgery. He practised his new art in off-the-rack clothes. They cost as much as or more than the best of his Savile Row suits – although most of them fell to bits after one season. In an effort to attract younger men he traded in his Bentley and bought a leather jacket to go with his new motorbike. He kept his pair of rooms in Cavendish Street, although he could easily have moved to a grander practice, considering the fees he commanded now that he was in the cosmetic business. He thought of it as making people more attractive, making them how they wanted to be.

He had turned forty, and had celebrated his first sober birth-day, when he agreed to give Fleur's eyes a tuck, and dispense with 'those nasty little droops on my chin'. When the job was successfully completed, he was added to her party list and, although he did not attend her weekends in the shires, he frequently dined at the house on Stanley Crescent.

On the morning of the night, Phyllis awoke, still in the arms of Somnos. At least that was how she entered the event in her Opera House diary. In the moment between sleep and waking she stirred, and the contours of her dream slipped away, leaving her with only the memory of a woman's face. She kept her eyes closed, holding the impressions of feelings, alive but disem-bodied, and trying to recapture more fragments, or even drift back into that state that makes beggars the equals of kings. She didn't succeed.

Her cat knew she was awake. He came into the bedroom, black and glossy, mewed hello, and settled on the pillow for his morning cuddle. He had an unusually engaging voice; a trait, along with his eyes, that must have been inherited from a Burmese ancestor.

Her flatmate's bed was empty, the sheets without warmth.

Early turn, she remembered. Phyllis showered, drank a cup of coffee, gave the cat a snack, checked that his backdoor flap wasn't bolted, and set off for the Underground.

Phyllis had been born in America. From birth, the auburn curls and high colour of the red-headed child had assured that she was showered with affection from almost every quarter. It was her destiny to fill the role of a beloved. In spite of this, she grew up with an innate modesty. In fact, there was a seriousness about her that was often interpreted as indifference – even coldness – by some. This wasn't strictly true, although by the time she attended junior high school it was clear she was wary about any show of emotion. She developed no visible passions, save an addiction to the classic black-and-white musicals shown on TV, and a crush she developed on her music teacher, a Miss Vincent from Glasgow in Britain. She was late becoming a woman; she didn't own a bra until well into her freshman year at Bard. There she was a competent student without excelling in any particular field. The only constant in her life was music – but even this became a private matter after Miss Vincent moved on at the end of Phyllis's first semester.

At that point, something in Phyllis closed down. For reasons known only to her, she sang, like some girls masturbate, in the dark, and frequently at night. In the edition of the college magazine that marked her graduation, Phyllis had listed her three wishes for the future as: to have her own bathroom; to wear only satin underwear; and to visit Greece. She left college without a best friend, and with no idea of how she intended to make a living. She didn't go home, but instead made her way to New York, where she checked into a modest hotel and postponed her decision about a career by presenting herself to a model agent who specialised in hands and feet.

She was soon earning enough money not only to stay in the big city, but to put a little by as well. Phyllis had always harboured a longing to travel, evident as soon as she could walk. Her parents had been forced to keep her under constant surveillance because, left alone, she would wander indefinitely until someone recognised her and brought her home.

Finding herself with enough cash for a passage to Europe and an international meal-ticket (her hands and feet apparently equally in demand in Paris, Milan and London), she packed her few belongings – including the softening cream and cotton gloves to wear at night – and set sail, crossing the Atlantic for the first time in style on the *QE2*, albeit in a modest cabin near the waterline.

The decision to fulfil her wanderlust was prompted by two things; she doubted that the normal relationsips her fellow models repeatedly tried would ever be hers, and wanted to 'find herself'. As far away from her parents as possible.

Her other reason was less defined. Miss Vincent had once or twice spoken of her own teacher, and Phyllis had remembered the name: a Miss Sage, who taught voice in London.

She had stopped modelling after a trip to Rome and a visit to a fortune teller, *una strega*, an old lady with a chatty mynah bird, who lived in a garret with a balcony that looked out across the russet rooftops. She had originally gone to see the old woman with friends for a lark, but stayed to talk privately. The old woman told Phyllis that only if she followed her heart's desire would she be showered with inner and outer gold.

Later, in a moment of insight, she realised that she had perhaps overdone the solitude. Soon after returning to London she halted her wanderings, found a flatmate, and together they rented a small house in the suburbs. Phyllis had taken a job in an office close by the Green Park tube. It was a large airy space on the sixth floor, with a view over the park, staffed almost exclusively by women. The work she did wasn't very taxing – her choice of employment being more geographical than financial – and she spent a lot of time thinking about other things; twice a week anyone strolling down

Half Moon Street would have seen a still figure sitting on a stoop, an apple in her lap and a thermos flask by her side, her head tilted like the HMV dog, as though listening – which indeed she was.

One of the first things Phyllis had done upon returning from the modelling trip to Italy was to look through the telephone directory and see if Miss Sage – her voice teacher's teacher – was listed. There was an 'I. Sage' listed and, on impulse, Phyllis dialled the number, half expecting to discover it was the wrong Miss Sage or, worse, that she had passed away. Phyllis knew that the renowned teacher had not been young when she'd taught Miss Vincent.

At last the telephone was answered, and the voice that came through the receiver was unmistakable. Too overpowered to speak, she replaced the receiver. It was a Tuesday. Phyllis located the address and was several houses away when she heard the sound of a piano and knew that a lesson was in progress. She stood on the doorstep near the window and, listening with all the attention she could muster, heard most of the tuition being given.

Phyllis soon knew the routine of the Sage household well. A neat Spanish maid named Solacia came each day and stayed from midday until four, frequently bringing shopping with her. Early in September a coalman from Chessington delivered smokeless fuel. The man from Fortnum and Mason with the white fluffy dog in his van brought bottled water – Evian and Badoit – once a month, and on Tuesdays and Fridays at twelve o'clock a pupil arrived for a lesson: on Tuesdays a black tenor with a large vocal range rat-tat-tatted the knocker, and on Fridays a soprano with a celestial voice (and legs to match) rang the bell.

Subconsciously, Phyllis may have been intimidated by the superb voices at work inside, for she never thought to present herself for a lesson. She lost interest in modelling, took the job in Stratton Street, arranged to take her lunch break early, and fell into the habit of eating her lunch on the doorstep of the Sage residence, listening in on Tuesdays and Fridays. She didn't start putting into practice what she overheard, and may never have, had not the soprano left her lesson early one day wearing a pair of soft-heeled shoes instead of the customary stilletos which tip-tapped across the parquet hall floor.

This time, with the soft-soled shoes and no warning, Phyllis was startled, and jumped to her feet, reaching the middle of the road before realising that the flask and its beaker were still sitting on the doorstep. Turning, she intended to retrieve them when she saw the soprano facing her. Phyllis froze, but the singer was so intent on stretching her tongue up to her nose and down to her chin in clockwise and anticlockwise rotations that she didn't notice either the thermos or the flummoxed figure tempting fate in the middle of the road. Phyllis found herself imitating the palatal gymnastics on her way back to work, and realised that they were exercises to strengthen the tongue. As soon as she felt she was doing them correctly she practised religiously alone in the bathroom at home. She was soon doing other exercises that she overheard from the inner sanctum of the Sage residence.

Six weeks before Christmas both pupils disappeared and Phyllis, not realising that professional singers often take work in the provinces over the holiday (the soprano principal boy in *Cinderella*, the tenor the genie in *Aladdin*), began having serious withdrawal symptoms. She was prompted to send Miss Sage a Christmas card, stating that she had been a pupil of Miss Vincent and asking if she might call and say hello.

A few days later she received a reply on embossed Smythson's notepaper; Imogen Sage would be at home for tea on Saturday or Sunday.

Phyllis decided on Saturday, as it was her monthly turn for the half-day at the office. She dressed that morning with a care that had been recently absent from her working life, choosing her fitted blue coat with tobacco-brown frogging and embroidered barrel buttons, and her brown cossack hat. Phyllis never wore make-up, but she took a toothbrush to work, brushing her teeth – even scrubbing her tongue – in the cloakroom before she left the office.

She whiled away an hour wandering around the park before buying a bunch of odorous rusty chrysanthemums from the flower man outside Green Park station, wondering what on earth she would say to Miss Sage as she slowly paced the route to number twenty-five that had become so much a part of her life.

The chimes sounded a long way off today as she pressed the bell. She heard birdlike steps sounding across the wooden floor, and the door opened.

Sky-blue eyes looked up from beneath a velvet alice band. The hair tucked under it was white and framed the face. Phyllis felt a lump come to her throat.

'Come on in, dear, you must be frozen,' tinkled the voice she knew so well.

Phyllis was having trouble seeing clearly, and Miss Sage – or Imo, as she preferred to be called – led her to an armchair beside an open fire, peat-burning ('a treat from Ireland for Christmas, you see'). A cat, black save for its eyes, sprawled in front of it. He eased himself up on to his back legs, stretched, and came to investigate Phyllis.

'You must be a soprano: his favourites are sopranos. Aren't they, Winston?' Imo said with a smile.

Imo Sage was very old, and as fragile as the Worcester china that was displayed in glass-fronted cabinets around the room. Her eyes had a limpid quality which Phyllis had seen in the expression of Catholic priests she had known as a child.

They sat in the Victorian carpet armchairs across from each other and chatted like sisters who had been separated and were catching up on old times, the elder pouring the tea. Miss Sage talked first, her melodic voice giving Phyllis a sense of well-being that she had rarely experienced.

Listening to the teacher, Phyllis began to understand the theory she had heard at college of the left brain perceiving speech, whilst the right perceived song. She knew that certain sounds caused this cerebral duality to be lost, both halves listening simultaneously.

Miss Sage's voice, pitched as it was between the two, seemed to do that.

Miss Sage was telling her of her one love who had died when she was young.

'God moves in mysterious ways,' she quoted. 'Perhaps I wouldn't have devoted myself to music if he'd lived – wouldn't have seen all the beauty that I have.' Her eyes moved to the middle distance. Perhaps the old teacher saw things like a prospector – always working in dirt, yet only seeing gold.

'I have met them all – McCormack, Rosa Ponselle – she came to see me when she was singing Norma at the Garden. Oh, and Lanza – my dear, what a character! I went to see him at the Dorchester. As we were leaving the Oliver Messel suite he hit a high C. He held it all the way down in the lift, and when we arrived on the ground floor he strolled over to the piano in the lounge and, still singing, played the high C. He turned to me and grinned. He was in perfect pitch. And McCormack – how proud he was when he was made a papal count.' She smiled and turned her head, looking so pointedly at the stairs that Phyllis turned around expecting to be joined. Winston chose that moment to jump on to her lap.

'There, you must be a soprano. Sopranos are your sweethearts, aren't they Winston?' Winston's only reply was a yelp in a minor key. He was apparently not in a talkative mood today.

'Given some of them help, too,' Miss Sage was saying. 'Most of them only need reassurance – such babies they are, opera singers. Mind you, they have to be a little crazy to do what they do, if you think about it.' Phyllis smiled. She had. 'Yes,' Miss Sage continued. 'They all came to see Imo, at one time or another – so close to the Garden, you see. And we were a soft touch, always ready to drop everything and jump in a cab to go down the Strand.'

'We?'

'Doctor Punt and me. He was the throat specialist. Me with my exercises, he with his spray. We always got them through, somehow or other.' She gave another modest smile.

'Oh, it's so nice to have a visitor. More tea?' She poured from the old silver teapot, which reflected the firelight, and Phyllis inhaled the tarry aroma from the steam.

'Now don't let me do all the talking, or I'll scare you away. Tell me about you.'

And so Phyllis, warm and secure in the company she had longed for, unwrapped her secret. And Miss Sage listened as only one trained in the art of listening can.

She heard how something had always been missing from Phyllis's life, a piece which somehow kept the puzzle incomplete; even the woman she shared her body with didn't fill this gap. Relief came when she sang, but it was temporary, and the need for this relief was held in check by her intense fear of performing. She spoke of having no defined ambition, of not being fuelled by potential fame or fortune. Her desire was resolution.

As her heart told its story, she became aware of an exquisite fragrance on the very edge of her senses. It appeared to be without source, and like nothing she had ever smelled before. It had the richness of a deep rose and the freshness of new-mown hay.

A cosy silence followed.

Miss Sage switched on some lamps and drew the curtains. Sitting in her carpet chair, Phyllis heard kitchen tinkerings through the open Victorian doors, and Imo returned with fresh tea, crumpets and a toasting fork. Phyllis took the iron fork and knelt in front of the fire, browning the spongy griddle cakes a safe distance from the heat, and passing them to her hostess for buttering. Miss Sage had a taste for tangy things, and the butter from Mont Saint Michel was salty to Phyllis's palate. She crunched while she toasted, her hair lit by the flames, and Miss Sage, regarding the intent figure, was only aware of the halo around her head.

'You see, my dear,' began Miss Sage to the halo, 'the voice is a unique thing. Darwin thought the throat area was the last remaining characteristic that humans have kept from their time as birds. Singing is our most natural expression. Which is why we feel good when we sing. But my own feeling is that the voice is a precious instrument, because it makes visible something which is invisible, namely the breath, and proves that something exists of which we are conscious, but the source of which no one knows.

'When we sing – keeping in mind that we are the only creatures that have this in common with birds – we are rejoicing, as they are, at one with our state of being. Every movement we make – stretching, yawning, sneezing – are devices used by the breath to spread its influence throughout the body. When we sing, especially if we are blessed with a developed voice, we not only magnetise our own body, but we can vitalise the minds and bodies of all who listen.

'This is why a great singer is in such demand. Their love and sympathy go out to others via their voice. People feel it – it is healing for them. No doubt they may also feel something from the phonograph or the wireless, but it is not nearly the same as being in the presence of a great vocal personality. The boundaries of a person's influence are as wide as the reaching point of their voice, and an audience senses this, if only at a subconscious level.' Without pausing, Miss Sage stood up and kindly but firmly took hold of Phyllis's arm, and led her to the piano, a baby grand, which sat impressively near the front window.

Phyllis, mesmerised by the teacher's presence, allowed herself to be placed alongside Miss Sage as she sat on the stool and rifled through her song sheets, all the while tapping notes with her right hand to find her new pupil's range.

'So you are a coloratura,' she said, delighted, and suddenly Phyllis had sung clear through 'Nel Cor Piu Mi Sento' with a finely decorated repeat section, and Miss Sage was saying, 'How good you are, my dear, and I do believe you are blessed with perfect pitch. Whoever taught you?'

To which Phyllis replied, 'I'm afraid you did.'

*

People poured out of the train at Mansion House, but others poured back in. Phyllis was feeling the urge for a cigarette. It hadn't been so bad this morning – the calm state she had woken in had helped – but all this thinking about her friend was making her edgy, and she couldn't stop the flow of memories.

One of the promises she had made to Miss Sage was to try to stop smoking, and even the suggestion frightened her. Something else had frightened her even more – for the teacher had exercised a sweet touch of emotional blackmail by telling Phyllis that, until a pupil performed in public, she didn't feel she'd earned her fee (no matter that she would never take a penny from Phyllis – 'You know what I mean,' she had said). Phyllis always arrived with something – flowers, tea, liver for Winston – yet Miss Sage bore witness to something Miss Vincent had told her: that the best teachers are never the expensive ones; that a great teacher invariably has a bigger need to pass on what they know than the student does to receive it.

In the crowded Underground, the electric overspill from one of London's immigrant music-manic populations was fraying her nerves. Why didn't they make Walkmans illegal if they weren't silent? To Phyllis, sound was just as polluting as smoke. She retreated back into her daydream. And to her mind came the day of Miss Sage's birthday.

The long winter had ended. Green Park was kindled with crocuses, and Phyllis had bought a posy of snowdrops to give to her teacher. Imo Sage was a Pisces, and Phyllis remembered her birthday whenever she saw the first snowdrops. The Friday commuters, anxious to be home after their week's labour, were pushing and shoving their way into the mouth of the Under-ground in an un-English way. As she jostled through them, protecting her fragile bouquet, a low spring sun shone on her face.

Imo had loved her flowers, and Phyllis, who had been preparing Bellini's 'Qui La Voce', had given a nervy rendering. But instead of running through it again, Miss Sage had risen from the stool,

51

leaving Phyllis standing in the bow of the piano while she went to the kitchen. She returned a moment later with tea and biscuits.

'I'm a little weary today, dear. Let's have a natter.' She beckoned her to the chair by the fire. 'That was charming, and well supported. That rendering would have filled the Opera House.'

'Oh,' said Phyllis bashfully. 'I've been working on it at home. It seems to make it easier in Italian.'

'It is, dear. The open vowels, you see. Does your room-mate help you?'

'No,' said Phyllis, a tad too quickly.

'Doesn't she like to listen to you sing?'

'I practise when she's out, which is often. She works evenings, you see,' she added lamely.

'So, it is still our little secret: I'm the only one who has the pleasure of hearing your lovely voice?'

'Yes,' confessed Phyllis with a downward turn of her lips.

'I see.'

There was a pause while Miss Sage poured them tea, followed by a crunch, as Phyllis bit into a wafer-thin biscuit, flavoured with lime peel and tart. Obviously homemade. Phyllis had never thought to make anything for Imo; she wasn't a very capable cook. Phyllis put a hand to her mouth and Miss Sage beamed a smile across at her.

'Good, aren't they? Made with love, like your voice.'

Phyllis flushed and her pale neck reddened, 'Oh, Imo.'

'I'm not flattering you undeservedly, dear. I tell you for selfish reasons. There's nothing like a star pupil to brighten an old lady's day – if that old lady is a teacher, which this one is. It is a catastrophe for a teacher to die without a distinguished pupil to carry on the line.' Phyllis, sensing what was coming, stopped drinking her tea and began to speak. But Imo raised a pale hand. 'I know I have other pupils. Damien is a virtuoso, and Phoebe is – will be – superb, but they only come to me for toning up. You, on the other hand – you were placed on my doorstep. Imo has been your only teacher. You are blessed with perfect pitch.' The old teacher looked Phyllis squarely in the eye. 'I've said it before and I will say it again: your career will not end early, because when you don't want to sing anymore, you can pass on what I've taught you and what you've learned yourself. Perhaps some little primrose will come and sit on your step and give you the joy you've given me.' She stopped and regarded her star pupil with a bright eye. 'Now, give me your word that you will perform publicly. If you do not let others appreciate your gift, I will not have done my job. And that will slow me down from wherever it is I'm going next.'

Phyllis couldn't trust herself to speak.

'We could fix you up in no time. There are lots of folks who would fight to have a lovely girl with a voice like yours sing to them . . .' Phyllis's jaw dropped in horror. 'But I'd like you to arrange it yourself when you're good and ready . . . but not too long, eh?' Her eyes twinkled across the tea-tray.

'Not planning on leaving, are we?' asked Phyllis after a hefty swallow of Darjeeling.

'You never know. It's best to live every day as though it's your last . . .'

'But Imo . . .' But Imo was looking into the near distance towards the stairs.

'Your true self is that part of you which knows itself to exist, which is conscious of itself. When you take breath as its vehicle instead of this body . . .' she paused. 'Now, when I'm not here, you continue to practise. You have your tape and you won't need another teacher. And . . . and someone will come to help you. If you don't like them at first, that's all right, they will understand that.' The eyes, a little mauvy today, settled back into focus. 'How are we doing with the habit?'

'You mean the smoking?'

'Yes, the smoking.'

'Not good. Better, but not good.'

'I see.'

'It's hard. When I'm with you it's easy, I don't think about it, but when . . .'

'I know, I know, nicotine makes a strong impression upon the mind. It's like an illness you suffer from for a long time – it becomes part of you. Even after you're cured, the impression stays. It has become a part of you. You don't feel right without it.'

'I can't seem to stop.'

Miss Sage lifted her hand. Blue veins showed through the translucent skin. 'Don't say "can't", dear, it only deepens the impression. Deny your weakness. It won't be telling a lie. It's not a reality, it is only a shadow, and a truthful confession of something unreal is worse than a lie. Never say "I can't do it, I can't sing in public." Decide for yourself what you wish to do, wish to be. If you fail to act how you want to be, think of it as a stumbling before you get the pitch of it. You will become how you want to be sooner or later.'

Phyllis had leaned back in the chair, her head resting against the antimacassar, and was listening so intently that it took a moment to realise Miss Sage was expecting a comment from her. In a voice that sounded distant – even to herself – Phyllis said, 'It all seems so straightforward, so clear, when I listen to you.'

Miss Sage shifted in her chair and changed tack. 'The breathing exercises won't give complete results if the channels aren't clear. The external organs of the body have to be clean to function correctly, but the inner ones, or centres, are the instruments of the mind, and the cleaner the channels of the breath, the more active they become. When your inner centres are working as they should, your skin will not only feel the vibrations of music, but the vibrations of another's breath. Then music will, as it were, touch every particle of you. Above all be patient. The hand of providence may be very close, and if one loses one's patience, the opportunity can be missed.'

A sheet of music fell from the stand with the clatter that paper sometimes makes. Winston shot out into the room from his hiding place under the stairs.

'Now, now, sir,' said Imo, offering the cat a spot on her lap. 'It's only a spirit passing, nothing to fret about.' Phyllis was holding her breath, trying to keep the air, and the words, cushioned inside her as long as she could.

Imo Sage passed away the next day as the clocks in St James's were chiming eleven. Her housekeeper, Solacia, swore that the house was lit full of angels, and she continued to come every day to feed Winston and keep him company. Then Miss Sage's will was read, and Phyllis inherited Winston, along with the piano and Miss Sage's collection of sheet music.

From the moment that her teacher passed away, Phyllis drifted into a torpor. There was no question of her rousing as she slipped into a lesser existence, as unknowing as one who falls asleep; and as the dream appears real to the dreamer, so did Phyllis's life seem whole to her.

She continued with her practices in the privacy of her home, listening to the scraps of Imo instructing her between scales on her practice tape. Occasionally – for he had her garden now, and the run of everyone else's – Winston would turn up when he heard the voice, and Phyllis would find him staring at her. This would make her feel guilty in a vague sort of way, yet not enough to shake her from her stupor. She continued to smoke, albeit periodically going through the motions of quitting – changing to a weaker brand, not indulging until mid-morning coffee. Her voice however, continued to grow. As did her sense of smell, albeit unnoticed.

The ascending escalator at Green Park was crowded, as usual, but both escalators were in service. This was such a novel event that Phyllis's eyes kept glancing towards the one descending, and the few punters getting a free ride. A figure backed on to the top of the near-deserted moving staircase and proceeded to travel down backwards. He immediately caught her attention – as an American she never ceased to be amazed by the number of eccentrics this little island produced – with his velvet jacket and what appeared from the back to be a white lace ruff around his neck. She was curious to view this oddball's face, but as they were about to draw level the melody of an old ballad came into her head, the title of which eluded her, and by the time she finally placed it as 'I'll Walk Beside You', her escalator had arrived and the whimsical passenger had disappeared.

As the exit came into view, and other sufferers started reaching for cigarettes, she also felt the pull of the familiar urge, but to her surprise she assured herself, I can wait. I will wait . . . until coffee at least. Perhaps I won't smoke today at all.

Miranda married late in life, by the standards of her friends – she had met the man when she was thirty-two and taken the vows a year later. None of her circle, including her family, could understand why it had taken so long, for she had an enviable combination of intelligence and looks. The problem (although Miranda herself didn't see it like that) was that almost from the beginning of her physical adventures, she had been able to separate the climactic sensation from attachment to its provider. This gave her an emotional autonomy, and although many men regarded her as a bitch ('She uses her pussy as a gadget,' one disgruntled Lothario had hissed), Miranda felt that it put her on an equal footing with men. And as her sensual appetite was well beyond restraint, the idea of matrimony didn't feature too high on her list of immediate personal needs. In fact, her husband was the first person she met who intrigued her beyond the first coupling – new flesh providing most of the erotic in her life.

Miranda had been enrolled in a boarding school in Sussex when she was fourteen, and had succumbed to seduction almost immediately by one of the prefects. Unlike most young ladies with crushes on their seniors, Miranda didn't grow out of it when she left school – she simply widened her scope to include boys. Partners of both genders felt threatened by this ambivalence, and by the time she was out of her teens she had become duly diplomatic. This was to end when she met her future partner.

As a youngster she'd been athletic, which prepared her for her second passion, dancing. Having enjoyed the benefits of discipline early, it was to become a welcome tool in her considerable kit. As soon as her academic schooling was over, rather than go to Florence or Geneva for 'finishing', she opted for a theatrical school that emphasised ballet, and improved not only her voice and poise, but also her physique. It was the high regard she had for her body that saved her from a life completely without moderation.

Another of her unusual characteristics was the ability to train alone, and although she enjoyed a formal class now and then, generally favouring the Pilates system, she didn't allow this luxury to become an excuse for not training alone on the other days of the week. One of the changes that marriage brought to her life was a live-in training partner. Her husband's knowledge of anatomy and its muscular structure was extensive, and he furthered the work she began.

Working under his guidance, she achieved the vital quarter-inch on each calf (so that they, along with her ankles and knees, touched when she stood with her legs together), and also, once she'd seen it, a washboard stomach similar to her husband's. Urged on by him, she entered the 'Most Beautiful Body in Europe' competition; he had supervised her training, even carrying with him a pair of scales to calculate her food intake whenever they dined out. When she won hands down, she was glad she had taken her husband's advice and entered under an assumed name.

Her husband never allowed too much mundanity to enter their lives. Even a supper at the Savoy Grill could be transformed by having her dress up as a hooker for the evening. Miranda didn't feel diminished by any of the escapades he put her up to; in fact, quite the opposite: a whole new and different world had opened up to her after their union. He sharpened himself against her and she formed herself upon his edge, or so he believed.

Those people who had known them individually before they were married – and were not shocked by the subsequent antics – considered their coming together as delightful. One wag, who had been briefly included in their shenanigans, likened them to the combination of fresh pepper and salt added to fruit salad.

On the morning of Fleur's Midsummer's Eve party, Miranda awoke with the same excitement she felt on the first mornings of her freedom away from home. She switched on the upstairs radio, expecting to find the mishmash of music and minor celebrities that accompanied her initial workout. Instead, she found the station her other half had been tuned to; a ball-by-ball account of the Lord's Test match. As she reset the wavelength, she was already thinking of him.

In fact, she woke with a tender sensation that reminded her of the first time she had been held; the wide-shouldered prefect with the dirty laugh. But this memory soon turned to the more feral feelings she had experienced with her husband. She found herself missing him even though she knew he would be returning before evening. In his dressing room, she held his suits near her to catch his odour, looking for missing buttons, socks in need of darning – tasks which didn't usually preoccupy her. Later, as she sweated in the sauna, she pondered her current appetites. The strong need she felt for her spouse at this moment would have seemed inconceivable to her a few years ago; yet she knew there would be other moments when the flash of a smile or the lowering of an eyelid would have her aching to touch thighs as smooth as her own, and she would be taken with the ease and swiftness of a harlot on the troll.

She had learned at a young age that no one can go against their nature. When the mind was held in abeyance – in sleep, for example – was there one sex or another?

Miranda cooled herself with cold water from the high-pressure shower, wrapped herself in a bath towel, and wandered around his dressing area, presenting herself in front of his 'Upper Boats' team

58

photograph, framed and set on the military shaving stand. The youth in the front row had the same large eyes – at once both penetrating and impenetrable – that she had noticed the first time she had seen him. Where was it? Yes, at the home of that artist and his scrawny wife, close by the V&A. She'd been aware of his stare before she saw him, had felt the skin on her back goose-pimple under his charged look, but had dismissed him as altogether too small. Sizeable hands though, she'd thought. The eyes had lingered. Still, rather sombre; at ease, yet alert.

She had witnessed the same patient expression the night a yahoo on the piss had tried to touch her up – the calm eyes that watched and waited as he ducked and weaved, slipping punches, waiting the moment to uncoil a throat-closing left cross. He had taken her arm and steered her across Shaftesbury Avenue as though nothing had happened. She knew there was a demon inside him, yet she had never seen it unleashed. Miranda felt sure he must have cut quite a rug at Eton with those eyes that saw everything and judged only when it suited him.

She smiled to herself at the boyish image in front of her, and replayed in her mind the evening they met. It wasn't until she spotted the hostess knotting and unknotting her bony legs in an effort to attract his glance that she had decided to give him a serious once-over. He must have noticed, for he approached her in the hall as she was trying to retrieve her coat. She was slightly taller than him. He had said, 'Hello.' And as she turned to face him, 'How'd you like to fuck a midget?'

She couldn't help but laugh. He had taken her arm, whisked her out of the house, hailed a taxi in the Cromwell Road, and seen her all the way to her apartment in W12. If questioned closely, she would have admitted that, if it hadn't been for the fact that she'd already decided she fancied him for more than a flingette, he could have parked his hand-benched shoes under her bed that same night.

She continued to fancy him, in spite of all the 'larking around',

59

as he called it – or perhaps because of it. And although, since they married, he had never disappointed her, she always felt there was that little something held in reserve that might be revealed at any time. More than a little.

'Spotting' him as he worked out, she noticed that during the exertion of his final sets of exercises, tears of gleet would issue from his member. She would lubricate her middle finger with them and slide the tip between the semi-stiff head and its loose foreskin, delicately circling the almost raw conflux of nerve endings. Sometimes, waking in the night, she would observe the sleeping head on the pillow beside her, often on such occasions covering his flaccid penis until it grew in her mouth like a crazed mushroom.

She supposed she had met her erotic match, yet often wondered whether another man could stir her the way he did – binding her emotionally as well – and pondered a phrase heard from her eldest sister; that there comes a day when a woman only feels comfortable undressing in front of her husband.

She wondered what was keeping him, and hoped that he would come home soon.

Routes did not present a problem for Zeno. Left to his own devices, the journey itself became the objective; the destination was simply the excuse for, or focus of, the journey. He had viewed the day from his window and assessed it worthy of an inbreath – which meant he wouldn't engage it with any exertion, he would simply observe it and let it come to him; 'loafing', his wife would have called it.

The trip he loosely planned for himself was a stroll across Kensington Park Gardens to the Porchester Terrace Gate, where he would cross the Bayswater Road down into the Queensway station, catch the Central Line (changing to the Northern Line at Tottenham Court Road), and zip up to Hampstead, where he knew a delightful tea-shop that had resisted all attempts at modernisation – a word associated with 'ugly' in Zeno's mind – and was still in the 'home style' of its Hungarian owners' dream. They also sold the only proper poppy-seed slice in London, which, although it was made with both wheat and sugar, he occasionally indulged in when his daughter wasn't about.

The destination with its poppy-seed treat was in no way fixed in his mind, and he knew he might digress at any step, but his route did hold certain other points of interest, the first being a tree which Zeno felt was special. Today he found himself sitting and resting his back against its ancient trunk, appreciating a particularly blue sky, pondering the passing of his youth, and shelling his four almonds (eaten every day to prevent cancer), one of which contained two entwined so perfectly as to fit the space made for one.

Both his parents were resting in peace, but before his mother had died, Zeno had finally persuaded her to tell him how he came to have his unusual name. As long as he could remember – which was quite a long time – his name had made him feel special. 'Jenkins, Zeno,' his form master would holler when calling the register, ensuring all his charges were wide awake. And as he was squeezed between 'Isaacs, Molly' and 'Jones, Stanley', it always presented a thrilling start to the day. It was not just unusual in a school filled with Toms, Georges and Alberts, it was unique.

The fact that neither his mother nor his father would divulge the whys and wherefores of their choice of name convinced him that, deep in the annals of the Jenkins or Johnson clan, lay an ancestor – another Zeno – whose name he bore. As a youngster he'd quizzed all four of his grandparents, gazing up into their faces with the sincerest of blue eyes. However, the four elders of little Zeno could not (or would not) recall another Zeno. And in his boy's mind, this denial gave dark credence to a 'black sheep' ancestor: a smuggler, perhaps – a pirate or a horse thief. Yes, probably a horse thief, so disgraced as not to be spoken of.

As Zeno grew, so did his belief in the legend he had created. And in the way that every past is eager to enhance its own tune, so did Zeno boast of this ancestor whose namesake he was. Once set upon the path of exaggeration, however, he found it impossible to retreat; his fancies grew, as did his resolve to unearth the secret.

At primary school, his illustrious relation was 'Zeno the Transylvanian Horsetrader', with one leg shorter than the other. Crippled taming a wild horse, he became the wheelwright of his troupe and, because of the great strength of his arms, the fashioner of all the leather tack – which was a lot, as the band was horse-drawn.

The Firemaker was another of his titles: able to raise a fire anywhere, even in the rain. This fiction continued well into secondary school, when necromancy became the fad of the day and 'Old Blacky' – as he had become – was magically transformed into a great soothsayer.

One afternoon when his grandma met him after school, she was perplexed to find herself surrounded by a gang of children who couldn't take their eyes off her shawl and gold hoop ear-rings, unaware that two days earlier she had inherited 'Old Blacky's' powers of secret crystal gazing and the reading of tea-leaves. Zeno was caught unawares but once he found out that she hadn't actually spoken to any of his classmates, he explained the next day that she spoke only Rom – Romany for 'the uninformed'.

It was at the height of his fame – he was eighteen, and his record had just entered the *Billboard* charts with a bullet – that the mystery was finally resolved. Posing, as is often the case, a far greater mystery.

Zeno's mum, Enid, lived to enjoy her son's fame, and her fiftieth birthday was celebrated, at Zeno's instigation, by a luncheon at the Orangery in Holland Park. Enid had a sweet tooth, and on the advice of the wine waiter Zeno ordered for her a split of Château Yquem. His mother, ignorant of its potency, yet approving of its taste, downed the half-bottle as though it were a shandy. The plan was to stroll in the gardens amongst the irises that smelled like prunes, and then put her on a number-nine bus home. She made it as far as the mulberry tree, where she had to sit down. The robust sauterne had loosened her tongue and she confessed the much-speculated-upon secret without so much as a prod.

During the pregnancy – which had come late (they had been trying for twelve years) – she was convinced a daughter was expected. This was in part because Mrs Askew at number eighty-four who read the cards (and doubled as the back-street abortionist) told her so, and because of her own longing for the daughter/friend that would keep her company during the lonely hours of the days and nights that her husband had to work.

She had knitted masses of pink four-ply baby clothes, and chosen a name – Zena. Dumbfounded at giving birth to a boy – an eight-pounder, to boot – she found herself at a loss for words and a name for her newborn son. She wouldn't even listen to her husband's choices: Alfred, like his father, Ron, like him. Her best friend on the block was Mrs Bianchi, who owned the corner ice-cream shop. During rationing, this ingenious Italian had sold ice-cubes on sticks, flavoured with sarsaparilla, and slices of turnips soaked in tinned pineapple juice. It was to her that Enid went for advice.

'Zis is nothing. You like "Zena". So it's a boy – it's a Zeno. It'sa beautiful, like your son,' who at that moment was beaming happily from behind a flush of pink in his pram.

Mrs Askew, the card reader, was shocked by the decision, and may have exaggerated the long-term effects of such a name for the boy (this in an attempt to win acceptance for her choice – Gideon – before the christening). Mrs Bianchi prevailed, and Zena became Zeno without even a second name to fall back upon.

Eighteen years later, the shock effect on Zeno was equally profound – even with a record, accompanied by a bullet, in the US charts. The bullet may just as well have been shot into his stomach. Dismay quietly consumed the rest of his day, and a lengthy melancholia may have set in, had not fate – in the shape of a Yale graduate doing a thesis on the English pop scene – found its way on to the grey-green charabanc; destination: Bournemouth, the very next day. His neat haircut and Jack Kennedy suit with softly moulded shoulders set him so apart from the muster of peacocks and shaven-headed roadies that Zeno was struck by him immediately. He had no sooner sat alongside the young man than his eye was caught by the title of the book resting on his lap: *The Confessions of Zeno*, by Italo Svevo.

When Rick – for that was the scholar's name – and Zeno traded introductions, he appeared as delighted by the coincidence (synchronicity, he termed it) as Zeno. A discussion followed that took them through the night, and both were surprised to find the coach pulling to a halt, the sun highlighting Bournemouth's manicured lawns.

By the time the tour finished, Rick had begun his career in rock and roll, and he went on to promote some of the most memorable Sixties happenings in the US. Meanwhile, Master Studd was off searching in an altogether different direction.

Zeno passed the ornamental lake and was heading into the shadowy section of the park, which was generally deserted, when he saw three figures: a middle-aged-spread jogger with jaws clamped on a glowing Churchillian cigar, the earphones of his antennaed Walkman giving him the appearance of a mutated insect; and a man teaching a boy to shoot a bow and arrow.

Zeno slowed his pace to study the lesson. The resemblance between the two was striking, even though the father was in his sixties. Another case of a man who had become a parent late in life. And why archery? Perhaps this latter-day merry man had inhabited Sherwood Forest in a previous life. The boy aimed his arrow at the straw-backed target, shot – and missed. The arrow in its short flight brought to mind the second part of his quest; the part that had opened like Ali Baba's cave on the charabanc to Bournemouth.

It was Rick's theory that Zeno of Svevo had been named after Zeno of Elea, a pre-Socratic Greek born around 485 BC. Not much was known of his life, except the floruit he left, a small collection of philosophical puzzles of astonishing ingenuity. These puzzles were known to students since Zeno's day as the paradoxes of motion.

It was by way of these that Zeno of Wapping transferred his identification with an imaginary gypsy ancestor to an even greater outsider. For he came to believe that in the solving of these conundrums he would prove himself a worthy inheritor of his name. He applied himself daily to the many unsettling limbs of Zeno's arguments that he learned had defeated more accomplished thinkers than himself. Bertrand Russell was said to have taken with him to his grave the disappointment of failing to solve Zeno's puzzles. And Aristotle didn't appear to have seen the implication of his fellow Greek's artful gem.

For months Zeno had addressed these paradoxes of motion, facing them in his mind from different angles, as a mountaineer studies a seemingly unscalable rock face. As time passed and he found he was no nearer a solution, he narrowed his field to the third conundrum in the series, which stated: 'The arrow in motion is at rest.' To which the ancient Greek had commented, 'For what is in motion moves neither in the place it is in, nor in one in which it is not.'

The boy yelled as he put an arrow in the bullseye, but by then Zeno had moved on.

On this Midsummer's Eve excursion, Zeno felt no nearer to solving the puzzle, yet there had been moments when a solution had felt close. Once, on an overnighter from Glasgow to Leeds, while the other young men were busy kissing and cuddling with groupies at the back of the coach, Zeno had been dozing across two seats near the front. He'd woken to find his mind curiously clear and receptive. He discreetly asked himself, Why was the arrow in flight at rest? and waited. The front of his mind remained tranquil, but from its depths came a sensation of movement as though a trapped bubble of air was slowly surfacing from the darkness. The sensation increased, spreading throughout his body, and he knew without thinking that if his brain tried to reach for it consciously, the very action would halt the movement. It was moving closer, ever closer to his comprehension when Slim Stiff – Iron Dick, to some – shouted from across the way: 'Oi, Zeno – what's the collective noun for actors, four letters?'

Zeno had not looked at a crossword since.

As he strolled, he wondered what had become of his rocker compatriots. Like himself, they had swallowed fame without chewing. And when it ended, had they reverted to their original names and moved back to the suburbs? Or had they tried to live up to their limelight personas – not realising that their fame was an abstraction, filling the shallowness left in its wake with booze or hallucinogenics?

As he made his way down into the subway, he thought again of the archery lesson he had witnessed, and a phrase – 'where your heart is, there will your treasure be' – came into his head and almost at the same time it occurred to him that desire itself could cover the heart. It was the law of gravity in the abstract. But surely everything had its opposite. What was the opposite of gravity? Levitation? The abstract of levitation – evolvement? Could that be right? Again he felt on the verge of something. The conundrum had not yet yielded its secret, but the one-pointedness his mind had practised seeking it was bearing fruit.

He was standing alone in the old lift, and the downward jerk as it began its descent below Bayswater Road brought to his stomach a contraction of fright. In his imagination, the floor of the lift became transparent, and he gripped the metal struts of the door as he began to visualise the drop into the blackness beneath him. His heart was hurting his chest. Then he recalled his dream: the spread-eagled flight, the youth with his spinning tray manifesting an unworldly glow. And as he pictured these fragments, the images became a diversity of tone, and a tender melody filled his heart and returned it to its normal tempo.

The Rose was feeling good. He had successfully completed an operation on a patient's neck – removing what was virtually a dewlap – and the day lay before him. An appointment with his new shrink, an afternoon swim, and home to change for Fleur's supper party with a new date.

'A follower of R.D. Laing, are we?' asked the Rose, shaking an extended hand and seating himself in the patient's chair. 'I must say, I'm sorry I didn't get to meet him.'

'Admirer,' said the psychoanalyst. 'Shot in the dark, or have you been talking to someone?'

'Colour of the walls,' replied the Rose. 'I hear he was a great one for green.'

'That was sharp. Call me Jack.'

'I shall.'

'Ever read any of Laing's stuff?'

'A bit. Interesting fellow he must have been.'

'Yes, met him a few times when he was in Glasgow. Like a cuppa? I'll get the girl to bring it in now, then we won't be disturbed.'

'Sounds terrific.' Jack pressed a button on his intercom.

'Miss Grey, a pot for two, please.' He lifted an eyebrow in the direction of the Rose.

'Biscuit?' The Rose shook his head politely.

'No? Okay,' and back to the intercom, 'a few gingersnaps for me then, please, Irene.'

'You met Laing, then?' the Rose asked.

'Yes. Well, actually only sat down with him once – we talked about academics. Heard lots of stories about him, of course. Lots of things he did I saw with my own eyes.'

'Like what?'

'Well, when he first came to the clinic in Glasgow . . .'

'By "clinic" you mean asylum, I take it?'

'Yes. He was qualified of course, but he was young. At any rate he, uh, bought this carpet – nothing special, just a cheap old thing, actually – and laid it out in his room. Left the door open. Naturally all sorts of certified loonies began waltzing in, sitting on the carpet, having a chat. Reputedly the "old guard" didn't much approve, but they couldn't do anything about it. On his own time, you see. Of course, after a few months, there were more sane loonies wandering around than loony ones. Laing said most disturbed people were only adjusting to the environment, they just needed someone to talk to and be interested in them. He had such a great mind. It might have been the effect of being in his company – their recovery, I mean. "Satsang" they call it in the East.'

'What's that?'

'Satsang? "Noble company", I believe.' Miss Grey knocked and came in with the tray.

'Shall I be mother?' asked Jack with a smile when the nurse had left. 'So tell me about yourself.'

'Oh, brilliant student, brilliant surgeon. Developed a bit of a booze problem. Until one of my superiors turned me on. Then I had a bit of a drug problem.'

'Really. Turned you on to what?'

'A subtlmayse – Fentanyl. "Pop a little of this under the skin," he told me, "we're men of medicine – alcohol's no good for the kind of pressure we're under." Surgeon to surgeon talk, don't you know. But this was a new league – like going from stock cars to Formula One.'

'And?' Jack picked up a snap and dipped it into his tea.

'Suppose I was at it a year. Started to not recall ops. Then, in the middle of one, I fixed up with the wrong stuff. They found me in the scrub-up room, stiff as a zealot.'

'What happened?'

'Not much. Head of the hospital told me to clean up my act. I

68

promised to go to a rehab centre, and he put me on the "impaired" list.'

'Which means what?'

'Business as usual, really – didn't even have to take regular urine tests.'

'My God.'

'Don't look so shocked. Signing the oath nowadays is like becoming a member of the royal family.'

'You got away with it, in other words.'

'Nothing to get away with. Drugs are our game.'

'Do you feel guilty – for your profession?'

'Not really.'

'Did you have pressure before you went into medicine?'

'Did I drink, do you mean? No, I felt pressure, but I ran, I was sort of an athlete.'

'But you're cured now?'

'No, I'm not cured, I'm clean – I have a few years of being sober. I'll never be cured. I take life one day at a time, like everyone else in recovery.'

'Do you still do neurosurgery?'

'No, wrong environment; too many people "at it". And don't forget – I was forgetting operations.'

'I see. And now?'

'Cosmetic. Face-lifts, breast-remodelling, that sort of thing.'

'Mainly women?'

'Yes. Something happened to me at the clinic.'

'Your clinic?'

'No. The rehab, when I was cleaning out.'

'What happened?'

'I was seduced.'

'I see.'

'It was like when I took that first drink.'

'Tell me about that.'

'The drink? Boring, really: ate a lunch – trifle with booze in it,

69

you see. Got drunk on port straight afterwards. The funny thing was – and this was how they knew at the clinic that I was a natural – when I was in the lavatory throwing up, I was thinking, This is great, now I can start all over again. Genetic, you see.'

'Parents drink?'

'No, nothing serious, but it can skip a generation, I believe. Gran had a bit of a problem.'

'Interesting. Tell me – and this is a purely hypothetical supposition – if you were, say, about to be born – you are a ray of pure spirit, your sex is undetermined, and you have yet to choose a mother to give you physical birth – what kind of woman would you choose?'

The Rose, sensing where this question was leading, yet never one to pass up a debate, said, 'She would be dark-haired and mysterious. The sort of woman who ages well. The kind of mother I could go running with.'

'You like athletic women?'

'Yes, but not masculine. I like my women friends feminine.'

'Can you imagine a situation in which you could desire a woman?' The Rose considered.

'If I'm honest . . . It's best to be honest, isn't it?'

'Well, you're paying – you can be what you like.' The psychoanalyst smiled. The Rose could see him sitting on R.D. Laing's magic carpet.

'And with your fees – such as they are.'

'Such as they are. More of a bargain, to be honest.' The Rose then sensed that Jack was still waiting for an answer to his previous question.

'Honestly, I can't.'

'OK. Let me see. You have no physical deviations – hormonal imbalance, that sort of thing?'

'No.'

'I only ask because, well, obviously you are in good physical shape. Most surgeons are athletes, are they not?'

'The serious ones train as though they are.'

70

'You see, in the study of embryogenesis – the study of embryonic development . . .' The Rose lifted his chin, indicating he understood. '. . . before the foetus knows whether it is male or female, scientists have discovered that only certain parts of the genes will signal it to become one or the other. What I'm saying is, far back enough down the line . . .'

'. . . the penis is structurally similar to the clitoris,' the Rose offered, finishing the psychiatrist's sentence.

'No, not similar – the same. Just influenced by different parts of the genes.'

'Does the gene attract the certain parts which influence its development, or do the parts decide?'

'We don't yet know. But the matter we are speaking of is so fragile – ephemeral, you could say – that it can be influenced by something as intangible as the preoccupations of the mother . . .'

'Desiring a daughter, for example.'

'Precisely.'

'But this is conjecture,' offered the Rose.

'Yes.'

'Yet, for the sake of hypothesis . . .' The Rose pulled his lower lip and stared at his teacup. 'This ray of . . . something – looking for a suitable mum – could be equally influenced by a mum looking for a daughter?'

'Did she?'

'What?'

'Your mother – did she crave a daughter?'

'I don't know.'

'I see.'

'And I can't ask her, because she is no longer with us. Life was tough for that generation.'

'True.' Jack took a sip of his tea. 'What did you really come here to discuss?'

The Rose leaned forward, the pale strong hands gripping the edge of the table. 'I have met a man – a youth, really.'

71

'You like him?'

'Yes, that's my feeling.'

'Is there a problem? He doesn't feel the same?'

'I don't know. It's delicate. He's "normal" – he's ambivalent, I believe.'

'Is that a problem for you?'

'It's something I have to live with. I'm drawn to normal men.'

'But you're responding differently with this one?'

'Yes.'

'How?'

'Well . . . this is silly, really . . .'

'This is a psychoanalyst you're talking to.'

'When I can't get what I want . . .'

'With this young man?'

'. . . I sulk. Actually I don't – but I feel like I want to sulk.'

'You feel like sulking?'

'It's probably nothing.'

'On the contrary. I think we should talk about this.'

'You think it's . . .'

'Look, we now have a theory – our group, that is – which we call "the child within". It isn't really that new: I believe Jung termed it "our trueself". We use the term "child within" because we have noticed that this part of us – this unconscious part that feels things – is undeveloped. It is often cut off sometime during childhood and, because it is cut off, it appears to retain the character of a child, a spoiled child, often working against our best interests.' The psychiatrist paused, and then continued. 'So this is who sulks – your "child within".'

'You think this is important?'

'My dear chap, this child – this sulking child – may be the key to your whole heritage: your genetic imprint if you like. Your life, your interactions with others, how you earn your living – these are conditions by which the spoiled brat can be brought to maturity. We are discussing using the conscious to join with the unconscious.'

'Is this a common problem?'

Jack ignored the question. 'Let's discuss this infant. You wouldn't let some spoiled kid drive your new car would you?'

'Motorbike.'

'You are the guardian of this child, and you can see it acting against its best interests. What do you do?'

'I'm not sure.'

'Look, this isn't an intellectual exercise. You start by consulting this little person. You discover what its interests are – its aims: what it wants for itself. Basically, it needs to be acknowledged. It is the feeling part of you. It needs to be appreciated, loved – not by another, but by you. Then it will grow. When it acquires stature, it will give you stature. There is balance required here. Your mental centre has matured, but at the cost of your emotional centre. Its sulking – or any other childish show of emotion – is its way of drawing your attention to its plight. You must start to listen to your child. It will enrich your life as an adult. Believe me. Can I tell you a story?'

'Are you changing the subject?'

Jack loosened his tie. 'Not really.'

The Rose leaned back in his chair, and the psychiatrist told a tale of fear. A man had contracted multiple sclerosis. As soon as it was diagnosed, he had consulted every specialist in the street. Someone told him of a fellow sufferer who had cured herself – he should contact her. Yet, curiously, he resisted – until he began to lose his sight. He looked her up while he could still see.

'Why are you here?' she demanded.

'I have multiple sclerosis, and heard you could help.'

'We don't call it that here,' she replied.

She massaged him, a brutal investigation of his spent body; painful, but at the same time exquisite. He was forbidden to scream or even cry out. If he wanted to vocalise his agony, he was told to put it into words. By the second visit, his wife's name had surfaced more than once. The healer diagnosed the root cause of

73

his condition. His wife evidently saw herself as a saintly figure and needed a mate she could direct her selfless attention to. He had become a cripple and was staying a cripple in order not to lose her.

'Did he recover?' asked the Rose.

'She explained that fear, although a natural emotion, when uncontrolled can close down life. Life being a whole keyboard of emotions, if you like, confined to the keys one hand can reach without effort. Instead of responding to life's opportunities, the mind says, "We can't do that – it's too dangerous, too fearful." So the body, which is programmed to follow the mind's directives, closes down. In the case of MS, the nerves simply atrophy.'

'Did he recover?' the Rose asked again.

'He did. Ran out of there, as it happened, after six sessions.'

'And the loss of sight?'

'It receded with regular visualisation.'

'So he recovered completely?'

'He works at it. A bit like yourself. Lost his missus, of course, but he continues to restructure his mental patterns – no easy task.'

'Does he pass his knowledge on – cure others?'

'Not many. One in ten, maybe.'

'So it's not foolproof, the system?'

'My dear chap, most folks love their disability – they don't want to be well. That's the point. They hobble in here with their silver-topped walking sticks. They bejewel their bloody indolence.'

'In here?' The psychoanalyst smiled. 'Well, I'll be damned,' said the Rose.

'Not if you grapple with your fear, your denial that nothing is wrong. But it has to be every step of the way, I'm afraid. See many shrinks, do you?' he asked.

Caught with his guard down, the Rose replied, 'I suppose.'

Jack stood and stretched himself.

'How much do I owe you, Doc?' asked the Rose, colouring a little.

'Let me see . . .' He pulled a pad from his drawer and wrote a receipt which he pushed across the table. 'Was it worth it, do you think? You must only pay me what you think it's worth.'

'That's no way to do business.'

'I know, but it was something Laing did. Rather nice, too, I think. Childlike, not to let the money thing run away with you.'

The Rose pulled out a roll of notes. 'By the way, what did he say about academics?'

'Well, we were comparing the types of books we read, and Ronnie said he never read books by academics. I asked him why, and he explained that academics spent their whole day either studying a book, or writing a book about the books they were studying. Occasionally they would take a little walk to rest their eyes while they thought about what someone had written or what they were writing. So they rarely experienced life first-hand. And R.D. was a great one for engaging life first-hand. See what I mean?'

As the Rose was about to mount his bike, he noticed a patch of oil beneath it – a characteristic of his Harley-Davidson, if it wasn't ridden regularly. But the spill lit a touch-paper to a memory buried alive in him of coming upon an old woman in a drunken stupor, lying unconscious in a pool of her own urine. He made a mental note to jot down the details when he got to his club.

Since the days of Aleister Crowley, and before, the high ground north of Holland Park – now postcoded W11 – had been considered good soil for witches, and in more recent times, when the planet was in transit, the modern-day necromancers of the Sixties gravitated, knowingly or unknowingly, towards the emanations of the vicinity (or so it seemed to the established order).

Aromatherapists, reflexologists, occultists, acupuncturists, astrologists, group therapists and many other 'ists' of the 'inner growth' movement were available for consultation within the 'miracle mile', as it was known in the flower-bedecked community. Patchouli oil and hashish fumes barely disguised by French tobacco thickened the air, and love was free for all the young witches and warlocks who selected their flying fish from the stall opposite the Electric Cinema, and purchased multigrained bread still warm from Ceres, the goddess of tillage and corn, who presided over her children from the north end of Portobello Road.

It wasn't until the saturnine Seventies were long past, when these apprentices of charm had been driven further afield by rapacious landlords, that Fleur, in search of that culinary centre Books for Cooks, stumbled upon the area and fell for the remnants of its charm. With her second fortune – recently inherited from her deceased husband – burning a hole in her bank account, she purchased the grandest property vacant that weekend: an imposing house on Stanley Crescent which circumambulated the hilltop of West Eleven. Fleur's sole exercise then as now was swimming, and it was this which finally prompted her to 'ink the deal', as the residence had a basement pool.

For a spell, Fleur saw herself as a latter-day hostess of 'les soirées artistiques', and launched a series of gatherings, summoning the doyens of alternative society still hanging on in the neighbourhood, most of whom did not appear too interested in Fleur's 'evolvement'. They simply consumed the splendid food she provided, and ran.

After a suitable period of mourning for her prematurely deceased, high-rolling husband, Fleur came to the conclusion that the sort of men she dreamed of possessing her were rarely interested in either her wealth or her lifestyle, and she settled for the type she needed, rather than the type she imagined she wanted.

Fleur had met Zeno towards the end of his reign in the rock-and-roll raj. She was working, briefly, for a women's glossy. There had been little physical tension between them, and they had quickly become relaxed with each other. She admired Zeno's eye, and tried to interest him in opening a jewelry shop in partnership with a maharanee and herself; a three-way split. Zeno wisely

76

declined: he correctly surmised his situation vis-à-vis the two voracious ladies.

Fleur continued to court Zeno, her interest only waning when he married. He preferred not to come to parties without his wife, and this lessened his desirability; he became less valuable as bait for ladies of socially acceptable pedigrees. Fleur, unlike other hostesses, was always short of suitable females.

This continual craving of Fleur's to give better and more sumptuous dinner parties knew no bounds. It knew no cause either. Or rather, Fleur never gave thought to any, although some of her earlier guests speculated that the cause was Fleur's deep-seated need, not only to be in company with the rich, famous and beautiful, but also to make them beholden to her.

Most egos of an unrefined nature find all that is above or below their own standards agitating, and cannot resist showing it. Fleur's ego, however, had become so inwardly crushed from not expressing these irritations that, by the time she reached maturity, she held herself in perilously low esteem. To be constantly acknowledged by individuals she judged to be superior to herself had become her only hope of salvation.

By the time of her carefully put-together full-moon party, her choice of man and the party games she planned were all that remained of the small girl prematurely despatched to boarding school. The house on the hilltop crescent reflected the attempt of Fleur's psyche to erect a canopy which would deflect the jarring effect life had had on her soul.

The decor was not strictly her own taste, but more how she imagined discriminating people lived. However, her own particular style did manifest itself in the form of the books and magazines which cluttered most of the horizontal areas, discs for the CD equipment, and trays of comforting delicacies which rested close by every television set and their video decks. Within false fingernail reach of Fleur's own bed sat a lacquered box filled with Halcyon, the elliptical lavender personality nicely bridging the potentially revealing moment between the day-long patchwork of distractions and the oblivion of sleep.

She kept a suite of rooms which she referred to as the 'boy's part' for, despite the fact that no serious relationship had come her way since the departure of her husband, she did not make a move without the consideration that a man would soon form part of her life. Hotel and flight reservations were always made *à deux*.

The 'boy's' quarters were above her own, and comprised a bedroom – equally spacious, but manly – and a bathroom/lavatory which had been equipped with an eclectic array of masculine devices and tools gleaned from her varied experiences in the field: a wooden bowl containing Comptoir Sud Pacifique shaving soap, and a bottle of Pinaud's Elixir Shampoo, both from Paris; a Simpson size 3 best badger brush, barely used. And amongst the more ornate objects used for seduction purposes, a folding leather clasp of cut-throat razors, seven in all, individually named for each day of the week. Behind the door, on a hexagonal brass hook – which Fleur hoped would one day soon serve a permanent butch dressing gown – hung the accompanying leather strop.

To the psychologically minded, the room at the top of the house – which Fleur thought of as the games room – also said much about her. It was not as expansive a room as the others in the house and may have served in more formal times as a servants' room or pantry.

Its dimensions did not do immediate justice to its contents. A dealer in the trade of antique toys, dolls, games, books and comics would have felt a definite increase in heart rate stumbling across this hoard. No gift or present that Fleur had ever received since her initial rattle had been thrown away. From the age of three until she went away to board, she had been given a present each day that she managed to get through without crying more than five times. Even without that the total would still have taken some tallying. The room was not visited regularly. It was saved for those occasions when a depression incurable by her other 'toys' over took her. She would put on an old track suit, lock herself in the games room, and re-catalogue her childhood playthings. Dusting some, fondling others, looking at her Rupert annuals or reading her mother's treasured Dimsie omnibus, she would recall her deepest childhood fear; returning home from school to find the house deserted, her parents gone. The seed of the Midsummer's Eve party had been sown during a consultation with a clairvoyant. This was a fairly regular practice, as she often found the present tedious and hungered for details of an incident-filled future. She shopped for Pythians with a zest women usually reserve for shoes. In a way, Zeno could be held responsible in part for the gathering, because on 22 September of the previous year – knowing Fleur's penchant for astromancy, to say nothing of the 'lady Virgo's' delight in being surprised – he had arranged for the most impressive seer (employed by Heads of State) to pay her a call.

When the seer arrived at her residence and rang the bell, Fleur opened the door and found herself looking into the salty eyes of a seeming wayfarer.

'I'm Colin,' he said and, as an afterthought, 'Colin the clairvoyant.' Fleur's eyes rounded, a reflex when caught unawares.

'Oh,' she said, verbally echoing her expression.

'I'm your birthday present.' He smiled, which buckled his broken nose even more. 'From Zeno.'

'From Zeno . . . what a dear. How wonderful.' She was still somewhat uncertain. 'Would you like to come in?'

'I would,' said Colin, and did. He sat in the needle-pointed armchair, and explained a little about himself while Vanella fixed him a double espresso on the machine in the ground-floor kitchen. No clairvoyance was offered immediately, and Fleur felt that perhaps Zeno's investment had been misguided. Yet, upon returning from the lavatory, where he had briefly 'spent a penny', he announced that the custodian of the house had revealed himself.

'Where?'

'In the loo, while I was washing my hands.' This was new

territory for Fleur, who had not received a soothsayer at home before.

'What was he like?'

'Old, Tibetan-looking. He's the doorman here, sees that no one who shouldn't be here gets in – or stays too long, at any rate.' He had a rough-hewn way of speaking, and the tenses he used often didn't make sense. But his manner was so direct, his confidence so weighty, that this lack of grammar went almost unnoticed.

Fleur became a little flustered, and Colin sensed the atmosphere about her change. He leaned forward and picked up the single stem of freesia in its tall glass which Vanella – frugal with her housekeeping – had noticed was not withered and set in its own vase.

Colin casually related the path of her life, reading from the characteristics of the single stem. Having laid his metaphysical credentials on the table, he replaced the vase and said, 'A flower reading for Fleur.'

His subject was astonished by the accuracy with which he had reviewed her past, and she sat extremely still. The Wiz paused for a moment, and when he began speaking, the words were inter-mittent, as though relaying a message from someone on a telephone. He told her that, befitting a house under the influence of five (the sum of the numbers on Fleur's front door), there had been many social activities, but much loneliness also. This was hard for her, but could be good – good for growth. Yet it had to be understood – that is to say, viewed – differently. There was going to be an occasion – not soon, later; next year, in summer – an auspicious gathering. A full moon close to the Earth, a special moment in the stars for two souls who were trying – longing – to come together. Something was owed to them. It could be repaid between sunset and sunrise, but they needed an appropriate place to meet. When Colin stopped speaking, Fleur still didn't move. The atmosphere thickened, and beams of sunlight working through the louvre doors created a staircase of light, each step a

80

swirling mass becoming invisible as it passed into shadow. With her head resting against the padded back of her chair, and eyes slightly out of focus, Fleur perceived, correctly, that the atmosphere around her was teeming with life.

The sailor eyes of the star reader were also out of focus, but he was seeing altogether different things. He rubbed the space between his eyebrows with his middle finger and said, 'If we take consideration for the moment of your birth – eleven o'clock today, thirty-nine years ago – a message all your own was written in the sky. Like Fata Morgana, it appears and disappears. We have said "written" because it is written and – as nothing ever actually disappears, as every spoken word and every feeling re-echoes for ever under this here canopy we call the universe – so the positioning of the planets on their motorways across the heavens were fixated in a matrix of the precise moment baby Fleur entered this physical plane. And from the situation of these silent masses, we contrive a symbolical insight into the "major" for this lifespan.'

He then went on to explain to Fleur that a 'major' is much the same as that created upon college entry. She had chosen her place, time and date of birth, parents, marital partners, and people around her as much for the problems their nearness would present, as for the pleasures given by them. In truth, it was from the difficulties brought by these interpersonal frictions that her greatest experiences and toughest tests would emerge and therefore the highest 'earning points'.

Vanella padded in on bare feet. She had not worn shoes until she was fourteen, when she had left Madagascar, did not like them even now, and slipped out of them whenever she could.

'Mister, would you like another coffee?' she purred.

Fleur flicked a disapproving glance towards her maid. Colin was not perturbed. It was not often that he was offered coffee this good. He picked up his cup and handed it to her.

'Thank you, that would be invigorating.' He caught Vanella's eye. 'And what is your name, young lady?'

Vanella took the cup and accepted the compliment in his steady glance. 'Vanella. It's Vanella.'

Colin smiled. 'That's a nice name.' He turned his smile on Fleur, inviting agreement. In fact, he was measuring by her response whether she had understood what he had said to her. If she had, she was not putting it into practice, for she was still looking askance at Vanella's neat retreating bottom. The fact was that Fleur had not taken in much of what Colin had said beyond his reference to the two souls.

Vanella brought another Blue Mountain special and placed it in front of the medium. He inhaled the aroma of Jamaica through his uneven nostrils. He had the impression that Vanella would have liked a reading, too, and actually picked up some interesting things on her as she dallied in the room, wriggling her toes across the silk pile of the carpet. She finally wilted under Fleur's stern look, and sloped back into the kitchen whence no further sounds came. When Colin spoke again, he took a different tack.

'You were born when the sun was in Virgo.'

'Yes, that's it. I'm a Virgo native.'

'You are, but by progression . . .' He saw immediately that she did not understand, but pressed on. 'Although you had your arising when the sun was in its final degrees of Virgo, you are for the last thirty years or so, by progression, a Libra. And these are your last years as a Libra before you move into Scorpio, which can also be beautiful, because your Venus . . .' Fleur's ears perked up. '. . . which is in Scorpio, but unaspected – albeit your problematical love life – will be finally reintegrated into Scorpio. We can expect wonderful results from this. Yet it would be the greatest pity if in this last year you cannot become the essence of a super Libra.'

'I will . . . I will,' squealed Fleur, galvanised, and reaching for a cocktail Sobranie.

'The Libran is the epitome of diplomacy, of tact – the perfect personality for the consideration of others. Remember, Fleur . . .'

'Would you like some more coffee, Mr Colin?' The kitchen door peeped open.

'Not now, thank you ' It closed again.

'That was delicious, but I must now be going. I promised my wife I would take her to the pictures.'

The earnest expression on Fleur's face faltered. She hadn't expected such mundanities from a person of this calibre. The big man stood up, and Vanella appeared in the kitchen door. Fleur felt she had somehow failed a test and, wanting a second try, said, 'How much do I owe you?'

Colin raised a firm palm.

'It's your birthday present, remember . . . from Zeno.'

'Yes, so it is.'

'My pleasure, and many happy returns.'

'Can I see you . . . I mean . . .?'

'Zeno knows how to contact me.'

'Yes.'

She walked him to the front door. He stood a moment tracing the polished brass numerals set into the wall with his thumbnail. When he looked at her, the sunlight caught his eyes, and Fleur felt curiously unnerved by his examination. He held her glance as he spoke. 'And don't forget, Fleur – the folks that distress you are also on a mission. To help you bring change, to remind you to bring change inside yourself. True change is inward, and this will reflect outward – to feel like a Libra, a super Libra.'

Again his engaging grin. He waved to Vanella, who was hovering in the background, stepped down the steps on to the pavement, and strolled off. Fleur stood on the doorstep and watched the back of his head bob from side to side until the curve of the crescent took him out of sight.

Zeno also had an unaspected Venus. It differed from Fleur's in that his fell in the eleventh house, the house ruled by Virgo. Had Fleur known this (her knowledge of astrology was limited to whichever monthly magazine she was reading), she might have assumed her meeting with the ex-pop star to be made in heaven. She believed, like most romantics, that Venus is the planet that rules the love nature. What she didn't know is that an unaspected Venus is more akin to a box of Swan Vestas on the loose.

When Zeno discovered this, he burrowed like a gerbil until he unearthed the facts of this influence. Because Venus rules our sense of appreciation as well as the love and compassion we feel, to be cast with this planet unaspected meant he was not subjected to the same structures as others who had their Venuses well aspected. At first this made him sad, as he realised that the occasions on which he thought he had felt great love were little more than overblown desires triggered by a response to beauty he found aesthetically pleasing.

The other blow to his ego was the discovery that, from an astrological standpoint, he had been born without innate charm and, on reflection, saw that he had learned from the others the ways of charm. The ultimate statement of his affection he felt to be on hold, as though awaiting someone or something worthy of perfect love.

He often viewed himself as others must see him – a receptacle of charm, bits and pieces, odds and ends, the sum total of years of using his ability to attract the charm of others, to collect and use it as his own. His persona had become a quirky remnant of his interaction with people he found pleasing. Yet beating away beneath it all his heart pulsed with unexpressed passion.

The solution he eventually arrived at spoke well of the optimistic side of his nature, for he decided to make the best of his lot by becoming charm's willing servant. He developed a manner of friendliness, using his affection in the form of attention, and tried to respect others without expectation of return. The odd friendships and relationships he struck opened him up like a house with wings continually being added, all the while feeling the underlying sensation of being one step away from a new reality. An impending . . . something that drove him on.

Colin the clairvoyant had arrived in Zeno's life in much the same way as he had arrived in Fleur's. On his fortieth birthday, a chum younger than himself – a carpet expert and lover of things oriental with whom he had exchanged exotic birthday presents – had hired Colin to announce himself at Zeno's front door. The two men had taken to each other, and the sensitive had encouraged Zeno to cast his own chart, which he assured Zeno was as essential to a seeker as a self-administered haircut was to a narcissist.

Zeno, who knew the date and time of Fleur's birth before she became edgy about revealing it, had consulted his ephemeris and seen that the condition of her Venus was similar to his own and, borrowing an example of his chum's charm, paid the clairvoyant to repeat the novelty.

It was not particularly strange that Colin did not report back to Zeno on his visit to Stanley Crescent, for genuine sensitives are as aware of the in-built responsibilities of their gifts as priests are of their stations. Perhaps more so: priests do not necessarily lose their holy orders if they abuse them, while sensitives inevitably lose the gift that gives them theirs.

What was curious was that Colin did not have any inkling of the identity of the two souls he had advised Fleur to be hospitable to.

Zeno took a seat on the near-empty Northern Line. He had opted for one of the vacant doubles facing his destination. In front of him, to his right, was a couple. He assumed they were a couple, until he scrutinised them closely. The lady – an impoverished aristocrat, he guessed – was reading *The Times*, held delicately between gloved hands to prevent the printer's ink from soiling her genteel fingertips. The man was wearing shell-shocked dungarees over a battered tee-shirt. He was looking at something that passed for a comic, which was also clutched between a pair of gloves. Rubber industrials, orange in colour.

Zeno smiled to himself and wondered whether they had knowingly sat alongside each other, or if they had been grouped

85

by the law of like kinds that attracts things of a similar nature. Since Zeno had read about it in the Marylebone Library, he saw it everywhere – from types of flowers that grew together to buses of the same number that travelled in twos and threes. Perhaps it was the couple's gloves that had drawn them together – or was a deeper attraction at play? If they stopped reading the papers and looked at each other, would she fulfil his dream of perfumed gentility, or he her fantasy of hot working-class steel?

He found himself thinking of another incident that had happened on the same line. He had been wearing a leather suit and was on his way to Camden Lock Market. At Euston, a seat became vacant and he took it. He found himself sitting next to Jim Morrison, also in leathers, chocolate-brown. The definitive voice of rock and roll looked like a cherub who had slipped through the pearly gates for a night on the town. They compared leathers, spent the day together, dropped some Purple Haze, and became friends.

The recollection of Jim may have revived some residue of LSD still in Zeno's system, for as the train slowed to pass through the darkened, frequently closed station of Mornington Crescent, Zeno, who was looking out of the window, had a brief acid flash. Sitting on a bench alongside his chum from the Doors were Hendrix, Lennon and Janis Joplin. A tab of rockers, Zeno thought, and they waved as the train passed by without stopping. He waved back, but found the hallucination unnerving. One time on the road, he had been keeping a tab of Owsley's Windowpane under his wristwatch, and found his feet melting into the ground beneath him: the acid had leeched into the skin of his arm. And though he knew there were no Merry Pranksters around these days to sew tabs of acid into his shirt collars, he was nevertheless relieved to surface into the brightness of Hampstead High Street.

He had unwittingly timed his arrival to coincide with the lull between the early caffeine-drinkers and the afternoon shoppers ready for a sugar fix. The tea-shop was quiet, empty save for a fine big girl occupying two seats on the banquette nearest the entrance. As Zeno entered, the waitress, in a neat black frock, was placing the display tray in front of her. The size of the tray – carrying some thirty samples of Louis's handiwork – and the girl were in perfect proportion. Zeno slid into one of his favourite seats, the corner of the padded banquette farthest away from the street, where the traffic noise was muted and he could view the room and listen to the gurgling of the coffee machine in the serving galley at the back. The smell of fresh coffee mixed with that aroma peculiar to pâtisseries that bake their own wares soothed him, and he inhaled deeply. Every day was Christmas at Louis's.

For some time now, Zeno had been working at sharpening his sense of smell. Zen would blindfold her dad and fetch him things to identify, first holding herbs and spices under his nose, then different types of tea and condiments, progressing to brass and wooden objects. They were currently working on Zeno's collection of books, starting with books he read and sniffed regularly, like his *Book of Runes* and the Agenda into which he jotted countless notes. Zen was ahead of her father, and could already differentiate between tap and mineral waters. Zeno accepted her superiority with good grace. It was natural, he told his wife, for a child to be more evolved than its parents.

Zeno had planned to order only a glass of hot milk, but he felt his resolve slipping as he inhaled the seductive fumes and, when the owner's wife came through from the kitchen and made a fuss over her male visitor, he submitted, opting for a pastry.

'You – such a long time. So nice to see you.' Warmth oozed from her.

'How are you?' Zeno asked. 'You look great.'

She pulled a face. 'And what about you? Always handsome – and so slim. How do you stay so slim?' she asked.

'It gets harder every day. You know – less grub, more exercise.'

'Tell me about it,' she said, her face pantomiming remorse.

'Business good?'

'Just as usual.'

It was the usual that Zeno loved about the place. Ever since he had cast his own horoscope, he had known that his horror of modernisation was related to the position of Mars crossing the orbital path of Uranus, but this insight did not ease the dismay he felt, with so many things being transformed around him.

'Shall I fetch you a nice poppy-seed slice and a coffee then, Zeno?'

'A poppy-seed and a glass of hot milk, please. You didn't ask Louis about making the slice with rice flour, I suppose?'

'You!' She waved her hand like a wet-nail-varnish actor. 'A little of what you fancy does you good – you'll get so rare you'll float away.'

Zeno chastised himself. You must stop doing that, he told himself, smacking his forehead. Trying to heal himself he had been pushed into the byways of alternative medicine. It all appeared simple now, but he remembered the nightmare nights of ulcerous agony, and was frequently prompted to share the knowledge of his cure. Having taken a swallow of his milk, he was about to tuck into his treat when he heard his name spoken by an unfamiliar voice.

'It's Zeno Studd, isn't it?'

Zeno paused, his dessert fork full of poppy-seed pulp equidistant between his plate and his mouth. When he looked up, his face bore that expression of prepared saintliness usually reserved for royals and ruthless politicians. In front of his table stood two youths; one callow, the other homely. They had a glow about them, as though they had recently discovered it was biologically possible for boys to love each other.

'My name is Stanley,' said callow – apparently the Arthur of the species – 'and this is . . .'

Zeno somehow expected 'Martha', but the spotty one was evidently an 'Eric'.

'Would you mind awfully if we share your table?' Zeno's eyes flickered to the many vacant tables. Stanley confessed, 'We recognised you when we came in . . .' He half turned to Martha – who was perhaps Arthur after all, for he prodded Stanley to stick to the story he had obviously concocted – '. . . and it isn't often that one gets to meet in the flesh anybody who's been there, all the way. To the top, I mean.'

He stopped, out of breath, forgetting the text or just overcome by feminine modesty. Zeno, who had not worked for years, could not understand how these babes, unborn when he was scorching the charts, could possibly know him. Unless the network had revived his old potboiler on morning TV. The companies must be desperate for fodder to feed the monster they had created: soaps from Australia, black-and-white pops from a bygone era. Perhaps he had been resurrected and given icon status.

Stanley had overcome his awe, and with a sunrise of a smile said, 'We'd just love to talk to you.'

Zeno managed a lopsided grin.

Phyllis journeyed home across London on the Underground. She had two more trips before she could be home in bed. She did not like parties, and although she did not find it difficult to hold her own in a group, she preferred her discussions one on one. It wasn't that Phyllis was anti-social, but her train of thought was often laboured, and in company she was frequently considered slow, or moody. Actually, the opposite was the case; it was the very passion of her mind that made social pleasantries difficult.

Her flatmate had sensed this about her, and it proved to be the factor which helped her most in the initial seduction. Julia was ranked amongst England's tennis players – which did not mean a lot in terms of world classification, but it did mean she was invited to Wimbledon. It was there she spotted Phyllis. Their relationship wasn't strictly physical, yet it wasn't particularly emotional either. In giving herself, Phyllis felt that she had at last unravelled some of her confusion. Relief rather than exaltation. Yet she enjoyed the companionship, and being with someone gratified instincts she had long held at bay.

Julia stopped competing professionally soon after they met, and had used her money to open an élite health club. Phyllis had sidestepped an offer to be a partner in the venture. However, the club had flourished, and the two saw less of each other.

'As in marriage,' Phyllis had commented matter-of-factly when Julia announced business was briskest in the evening and she would often be home late. The invitation to supper that Julia had accepted on their behalf was something new; Phyllis usually declined invitations made via Julia, as the gatherings were inevitably all-female.

'Just because we're gay doesn't mean we're freaks that have to stick together – it's not like we're lepers.'

This was different, Julia assured her. A sophisticated woman impressed with her know-how had invited Julia to advise her on the refurbishment of her private gymnasium.

'Come to supper, and bring your friend. I'll show you the space, and we can talk about it,' was what she had said.

Julia had told Phyllis, 'I'm sure it's going to be fun. She has a pool in her house. Come on – let's sparkle a bit.' Phyllis had allowed herself to be talked into 'sparkling', but as usual, now that the occasion was imminent, she felt herself withdrawing, preferring an undemanding evening at home with Winston.

She strap-hung until Holborn, where she changed trains and a well-dressed older man offered her his seat. This unexpected comfort relaxed her, and she gazed absentmindedly through the window at an advertisement posted on the curved wall. The automatic doors finally closed and the train moved off.

As it did, Phyllis saw the illustration on the advertisement change – or thought she did. It was as though she had slipped momentarily into a dream. What had been a seascape selling a cruise line became a night scene with a group around an open fire.

Phyllis blinked to clear her vision, but the train was already entering the dark tunnel.

It might have been her imagination, but she could have sworn that the aroma of burning leaves accompanied the wanderings of her mind.

'Hello, hooligan.'

'Hi there, bubble bum.' When she had heard his key in the lock, she stood up and moved to the centre of the room to show off her new dress. He greeted her, running his hand down the well of her back and over the exercised cheeks of her backside.

'The best,' he said, 'the best.'

'The dress?'

'That too,' he smirked, kissing her flat on the lips.

'You're in a good mood. Had a result, have we?'

Nicholas grinned. 'We have.'

She sniffed at the shadow on his upper lip.

'Hmm, a redhead?' she enquired.

'Gosh, you're good.' He gripped her shoulders and straightened his arms, appreciating her at a distance before confessing. 'Strawberry blonde, actually.'

'Come on, then.' He kissed her again and let his head drop on to her shoulders, inhaling the darkly odorous tuberose.

'What?' he asked, deftly appreciating both her cheeks with the palms of his hands.

What he particularly appreciated about his wife's bottom was that, no matter how many hours she pumped away on her Stairmaster, the thin top layer – the subcutaneous tissue – remained spongy. The combination of iron-hard muscle and sapid skin never failed to rouse him.

'What?' he murmured again into her ear, running the edge of his serrated tongue over the single white diamond earclip. 'Why don't you wear your pearls tonight? I love you in pearls.'

'Can't – already put perfume on.'

'Pity.'

'Come on, you rat, give me the scoop – share her with me.'

Nick gazed out through the deep open windows on to the street. One side of Tregunter Road was in shadow, and the early evening breeze sent the fragrance of privet into the room.

His wife spoke again. 'Come on, we have plenty of time. I only dressed early because I wanted your seal of approval on my little black dress.'

'It is little.'

'I know – such a slut.'

'That's true, but with the best of taste. I'm already feeling sorry for fellow guests *ce soir*.'

'Don't keep changing the subject. You're like an eel. Tell me about your scene.'

'Have I time for a bath? I didn't shower.'

'Plenty of time – we're not expected till eight. You know what Fleur's like – champagne and a game before vittles. Now, come on.'

'I'll tell you if you run me a bath.'

'Okay.'

'In your room, with your favourite oil.'

'You're such a queen.'

'I know. Is it a deal?'

'Deal.'

Miranda poured him a drink from the cocktail shaker and gave it to him. She walked upstairs, Nick following, alternately sipping his drink and trying to sink his teeth into her buttock. She opened the faucets of an old cast-iron tub that she'd updated by having it silver-plated, and tipped a few beads of carnation oil into the water as she watched him undress. He appeared to have plenty of strength left in him.

'Want a quickie? You don't seem short on energy.'

'Energy's not my problem. You know that,' he said, lowering himself into the water and resting his neck on the curve of the rim. 'It's the blue veiner I'm looking for.'

'Don't say that – it makes you sound like an Australian.'

'Errol Flynn was an Aussie,' said Nick, knowing she admired the actor. Miranda seated herself on the loo.

'Tasmanian, actually,' and twisting her legs, 'the numero?'

'Pinned her on the train. Must have been in Brighton overnight. Pretty little thing, worked for British Rail. Cute cockney accent. Mid-twenties, I should think.'

'Single?'

'Married.'

Miranda wrinkled her forehead. 'Game, then?'

Nick went on. 'The usual: husband screwed her blind for the first eighteen months and then lost interest. Course, she was as horny as all get out. I don't think she was actually on the lookout in Brighton.'

'No, just sea air and a plate of cockles,' Miranda snorted.

'Anyway, I dialogued her.'

'I bet.' Nick was soaping under his arms with his wife's iris soap. 'So how did you put the make on her?'

'Told her I'd show her how to make up her eyes.'

'Her eyes . . .'

'Did, too – bought some cosmetics in the Hilton.'

'Classy.'

'Took her to the café on the top floor, settled her there with a coffee.'

'With cream, I bet.'

'Hot milk, actually. You know how these girls are.'

'I wish I did.'

'She stayed quiet as a mouse, looking out over the park. I nipped downstairs, booked the room, and scored the eye make-up. They didn't have much of a choice, so I improvised. Took her down two floors, put the "Do not disturb" sign outside, and asked her to take her blouse off so as not to get it spotted.'

'Spotted?'

'From the mascara.'

93

Miranda gave him an old-fashioned look. 'If she believed that . . .'

'Well, I think she realised she wasn't there just for the demonstration.'

'Not with make-up, anyway.'

'Did the eyes though. Worked beautifully. Took about ten minutes. I gave the impression that I'd lost interest, then, when she thought that was all she was going to get . . .'

'You dropped on to all fives and crawled towards her.'

'How d'you guess?'

'That was chancy.'

'Not really. Her breath smelled nice, and I could tell by her skin tone that she was healthy.'

'Did you do everything?'

'Almost – she only had an hour and a half.'

'Did you turn her over?'

'I didn't, but I could have. I really worked her over while she was coming the first time.'

'Did she suck you off?'

'Of course.'

'Really off?'

'Really off.'

'How many times did you come?'

'Just the once. Didn't want to get caught short later.' He grinned, showing creamy teeth.

'D'you fancy a cuddle?'

'Later.'

'Not up to it, huh? Real studs provide at home – whatever they've been up to elsewhere.'

'Like who, for example?'

'Warren Beatty, I imagine.'

'Spare me – he's priapic. It's like cheating at cards.'

'Do you want me to look it up in the *OED*, or are you going to tell me?'

94

'What?'

'Priapic.'

'Medical condition. Guy whose joint stays erect after he's shot his wad.'

'You never introduce me to boys like that.'

'She liked my crocodile shoes, the strawberry blonde,' said Nick, finding the exchange arousing and changing the subject so as not to allow his wife to get her way.

'Did she?'

'That's what she told me. Obviously had an eye for a shoe.'

'Or a system of relating size of feet to size of member.'

'Thought it was hands – you told me it was hands.'

Miranda let some more hot water into the bathtub. 'Want me to give your back a scrub?'

'Like a rub, if you're in the mood.'

'You're the boss.' Miranda continued her barbed inquisition. 'So what effect do you think you've had on the life of this ticket collector?'

'I didn't say . . .'

Miranda waved him on. 'Did she want more – did she ask for your number?'

'No, no, I was what you'd call "the one that doesn't count".'

Nick looked at his wife, now preoccupied with buffing her nails. He looked at her legs, slightly apart as she sat, felt energy centring within him, and wondered if she was truly like him. You never really knew with women. He had never been able to exhaust her – unless you consider cystitis exhaustion. He enjoyed seeing her taken by men or women; it excited him, renewed his desire for her. Was it really the same for her, or was she just his creature?

He wondered who would be at Fleur's. Fleur – they had hit on her in the Soda Bar at Fortnum's. Miranda had pointed her out. 'She's a goer,' she'd said.

'Now?' he'd enquired.

'Listen, chum, when a girl's in the mood, there is only now.'

Fleur had left with them before they had ordered. Nick had driven, and Miranda had her hand up Fleur's skirt before they made Knightsbridge. What a natural: that freaky clitoris. No wonder she wore loose outfits. Another centimetre or two and she could have been piggy in the middle.

Who would she have found for tonight? Would the couple that he had seen at her Christmas party be there? What were their names? Odd name, the chap had. Good-looking devil, with those printed lashes he liked; she was delicious too. He had quite fancied both of them. Zeno, that was it. And what was the missus called? He wondered why he had not made the move; she was quite delectable. She was something, this Mrs Zeno; a piece – like Miranda. Why had he been so cautious? He had chatted to her, watched her mouth, waiting for her to speak. When she had, he found that she was thicker than peanut butter. A vacuous-looking model had cruised by and waved hello.

'Who's that?' he had asked.

'Her? Oh, somone I used to know.'

'She on the loose? Got good legs.'

'I'm not sure. But you wouldn't like her – she's dumb.'

How would she know, Nick wondered. Someone must have told her. She was a natural, though; he sensed that. She could be had, caught at the right moment. But mentally, that was different. It was the dumb ones that snapped when they tried to think about it.

'Are you ready for that rub, lad? The water must be cold.'

Miranda had slipped out of her new dress and into a linen kimono. Nick dried off, followed his wife into the workout room, and stretched out on the massage table. Quite a few massages that top had seen; and quite a few masseurs, too. Miranda lubed up her hands, and Nick continued his mental dissertation on the Studds.

Now the guy, Zeno: he could handle it. Probably had. Fella like that wouldn't be short of opportunities. He was a lot like himself – near the line. That magic line that divides men and women. He would know how it is to be all things to all people. I'm certain I could have him if I put my mind to it.

Nick recalled the shape of Zeno's head, the sense that informed his glance. There was a clearness about him which was not simply good health; an intelligence of someone who accepted life as it came and took responsibility for it. It always showed, sooner or later. I know how to make a pilgrim like that. Fuck with his mind. Too much command over his body. Yeah, he'd be open to something new.

Miranda's mind was also not one hundred per cent on what she was doing. She was thinking about the first time Nick had introduced her to his views on sensuality; how the same set of genitals that were pushed to make love to a wife or regular girlfriend more than twice a day could rise to the occasion a dozen or more times, given a selection of willing partners; he claimed to have gotten off fourteen times at the stag party of an old school chum.

Not always believing everything her husband told her, she had arranged a surprise harem party of her own the year after their marriage, inviting a selection of her raunchiest chums, and offering him a chance to prove his point. Twelve left smiling, and only two admitted that they would have preferred to have caught him nearer the start of the proceedings. When quizzed, Nick answered that he would probably have done better if the company had been mixed. He later added, probably to tease her, 'Guys give guys the best head, you know.'

Miranda was working on his traps. He could feel the weight of her breast through the linen on his back. What kind of nipples did Mrs Zeno have? he wondered. Modest pert daggers that stiffened if you looked at them? Or large ripe fruit that needed to be pinched into response? Now that would be a novel game to introduce at Fleur's.

He looked at the silent TV set placed in front of the climbing machine. Why don't we have our own porn channel here in

Britain, when every house and third-rate hotel across Europe can tune in? 'It's been debated in Parliament, mate,' the cable mechanic had informed him. What was it about the British and sex? Hadn't the delectable Louise Brooks proclaimed that the English were the best cocksmen? So where was the evidence – hardcore porn on television? Mary Whitehouse would ride a white cart-horse to Downing Street, where the soft-cock Cabinet would be manning a barricade. None of them had ever attended a party; nobody would ever consider asking them. Maybe that was the problem.

His wife rolled him over and began to rub the muscles of his stomach. He opened his eyes a fraction and glimpsed the glint of her earring through her sheet of black hair. She was perspiring. He could smell the natural gardenia odour of her body through the chemical tuberose. She'd be hot to trot tonight. He wondered if there'd be anything worth trotting out for.

Then a provocative idea for a game floated into his head, just as his wife said, 'By the way, Turk, thought of a good opener for tonight.'

THE EVENING

PRUDENCE COULD HEAR murmurings as she passed the second-floor bathroom. She didn't stop; it was a weekly ritual, one of the many that Zeno still indulged in with his daughter. This particular routine had started soon after Zen was born. Bath night was something her husband had brought with him from his working-class boyhood; showers sufficed for most of the week, but Friday was bath time. The high-pressure alternating shower that Kenny Wisdom had bought for them in America still functioned perfectly and was used by Zeno religiously every day. But Prudence felt sure it was only to give 'tub night' its sense of occasion. She had often said that their daughter was getting too old to still be bathing with her father, and Zeno had promised to change the routine when she was nine. Zen had celebrated her ninth birthday this week (a high tea had been given, with Zen's two best friends, Karma and Alleluiah, in attendance), and Prudence waited to see if Zeno would keep his word.

Inside the bathroom, bevelled discs of glass cast prisms on the walls. The windows were misted up, and the condensation had been used by father and daughter to practise freehand circles drawn with their fingers. Some were quite perfect. Those less good had been made into faces, with the names of Zen's schoolteachers written underneath.

The tub itself had seen better days. An important feature of the house when Zeno purchased it, the bath was deep enough to cover his shoulders when he sat at the wide end. Zen admired her dad's shoulders. Lately, she had started taking note of the boys at PE lessons, on the lookout for a similar pair.

'Who's this Miss Davidson you don't like?' asked Zeno, pointing to one of his daughter's mist-drawings.

'She's horrible and she hates me.'

'Does she? Are you sure?'

'Well, she always picks on me.'

'Why do you think that is?'

'I dunno.'

'Maybe she picks on you because you don't like her.'

'Oh, don't be soft, Dad.'

'It could be true. I bet she doesn't get up the noses of the other kids who don't mind her. It's your resistance to her that she pushes like a button. If you could lose the button she wouldn't have anything to push. Now wouldn't that be a smarter way of dealing with her?'

Zen considered a moment. 'It would, if I could do it.'

'Of course you can do it. Just look at her eyes the way you do the sad animals you like so much, and then you could touch her.'

'Touch her?'

'Sure, she doesn't even have to know. Bump her, or touch her when she isn't looking.'

'Would that work?' Zen asked, unconvinced.

'I think so. It doesn't hurt to try.'

'Okay.' Zen changed the subject. 'What's this present you promised to give me when I was nine?' Zen enquired, newly nine and with presents still on her mind.

'Are you sure you're grown up enough?'

'I'm nine. Time's passing. I'll be in double figures soon.' She swept up her hair and regarded herself in the distressed mirror on the wall adjacent to the window. Zeno wondered at the constant preoccupation women had for the passing of time. He had never really thought about it until his eyes started to back up on him.

'It's in two parts you see, this present,' his delivery slowing as thought added weight to it.

100

'Oh, come on then, Dad,' said Zen, who could smell pro-crastination a mile off.

'The first part', began Zeno, not allowing his daughter's impatience to influence him, 'is that from now on you can have the bath to yourself on Fridays.'

'Okay, that's the bad part. Now what's the other?' She stuck out a lower lip, which Zeno knew from previous jarring was often accompanied by a gnashing of teeth.

'The exciting part is that now you're nine, we are going to teach you how to breathe.'

'I already know how to breathe,' said Zen, snapping her jaws and rubbing her clenched teeth from side to side with that unnerving grating sound. 'And who is "we"?'

Zeno dipped the sponge, the size of a rugger ball, into the water, and sponged the conditioner from his hair. It fell smooth and straight almost to his shoulders.

'By "we" I mean all the people who have taught me, whose combined knowledge I am the sum total of. You won't have to attend any extra classes . . .'

'But I know how to breathe,' she repeated, realising the surprise was not going to be the roller-skating boots signed by Raquel Welch that she was convinced would fit her now, and which Zeno still cherished.

Her dad reached out for one of the selection of towels which hung on heated brass pipes that almost covered the wall behind him, and, lifting his hair, twisted the towel into a turban with a practised movement. It was a gesture Zen usually relished. She liked the look it gave her dad, and signified the water part of their evening was at an end. To be followed, if he was in the mood, by a massage of her feet – 'zoning', he called it. Today she was impervious to the twisted towel, and made faces at her own reflection.

Zeno pressed on. 'There is a mystery about breath which few are aware of. As a matter of fact, I'd say about . . .' he mentally counted, watching her face in the mirror to see if he had captured her attention, '. . . one in eight million.' He had.

'Of course, I regard you as special: you have a proper diet like me. But if you don't feel up to it . . . I mean, you are only nine, perhaps if we wait . . .'

'A mystery,' she said, watching from the corner of her eye as he climbed from the bath and wound himself into an outsized flat linen towel – towels purchased at auction from the hoard of a maharajah, bought from Harrods in the Thirties when chauffeurs were sent to fill their travelling trunks with them, and never used, was the tale he had told her.

'Have you ever wondered where breath comes from? Or where it goes to, for that matter?'

Zen had a foot out of the water. She was studying her toenails, one of which was varnished. 'Well, it's just there, isn't it?' Zen was now staring intently at the painted toenail. 'Do you think this is a good shade for me? It's Chinese Red.'

'I suppose so, if you see yourself as a wanton dragon-lady type.'

'What does "wanton" mean?'

'Oh, it means a girl who is unrestrained, who wants everything. There are girls like that – they go shopping all the time.'

'How boring.'

'Exactly.'

Zen swivelled around to the end of the tub that Zeno had vacated, and pulled the plug. 'So what's the mystery then?'

'The secret of life is hidden in the breath, because when the breath leaves the body, the body, for all its marvellous ingenuity, goes back to being dust.'

'Eaten by worms.'

'Eaten by worms if it is buried. Let's rinse your hair.' He unwound the coiled handshower, and let the water run through her hair. When she wasn't paying attention, he changed the gauge and finished her off with cold.

'Ugh, you're horrible – you always do that.' She leaped out of the bath and scrambled for a towel.

'Good for your circulation – gets the blood to your head, so you'll understand what we're talking about.' Zeno had one towel wrapped around his midriff, another draped over his shoulders, and was flexing his hands.

'Want me to zone your tootsies?' he asked.

'Yes.'

She finished drying herself, put on her bathrobe and, spreading a dry towel along the bath mat, lay face down on it. Zeno kneeled down and took her left foot in his hands.

'In the East, the Brahmins teach their children rhythmic breathing when they're nine.'

'What's the Brahmins?'

'The ones who don't eat meat.'

'Like us?'

'Like us.'

'Why do they do that?'

'Well, they understand that the most important thing in life is health, and, as health is absolutely dependent on breath, they figure nine is a good age to teach them awareness of it. Like eating food that's good for you.'

'Because you are what you eat?'

'Well, your body is what you eat, so, bad food, bad body. But bad breathing can make for bad everything. And as they don't teach it in schools, we thought we'd teach you at home.'

'Will it make me run better?'

'It will make you everything better. It may even make you able to see ghosts.'

Zen lifted her head and screwed it around to look at Zeno. 'Ghosts?'

'Ghosts, or spirits. Yes, spirits would be a better word.'

'My friend Karma saw a ghost.'

'Did she?'

103

'It was after her grandad died. She saw him walking in the garden where they lived.'

'Was she scared?'

'I don't think so. She went to tell her gran, but he'd gone by the time she fetched her.'

'Well, he wasn't actually there.'

'She saw him.'

'I'm sure she did, but the only way you can see spirits is from the inner space.'

'There was a video called that,' offered Zen.

Zeno pressed on. 'Like when you dream. You often see loved ones who have passed on. But they aren't outside of you, are they? Not really.'

'You mean in the dream?'

'Yes, all the people in the dream are inside you – are part of your inner world. When you see a spirit and you're awake, it's almost the same thing.' He finished the narrow left foot and started on the right, gently rolling his clenched fist into the arch.

'But Karma saw her grandad outside. In the garden.'

'Look, when we go to the pictures, we see the film on the screen, but really the images are in the projector – on the film in the projector. It's the same with ghosts. We only see the reflection.'

'So it's like dreaming when you're awake?'

'Kind of. Breath is like the light in the projector. In fact, it is light – the light of the senses: seeing, hearing, touching, smelling, tasting all happen by the light of the breath. What happens when you go to sleep is the senses turning their backs on the outer world and beginning to focus on the world within.'

'I'd like to see that,' said Zen.

'Well, that's what I thought. And the first step is to learn about the rhythm of the breath.'

'Miss Davidson says my rhythm is not very good.'

'That's absolutely not true. I distinctly remember you waving your little arms and legs in perfect rhythm as soon as you were born. You see, no one teaches us rhythm – we bring it with us.'

Zeno paused and gave his attention to a tight achilles tendon. He caught his reflection in the mirror and saw the patch of greying hair on his chest. Perhaps she really wasn't that interested in what her old dad had to say. In a few years he would be losing her to another man.

'Did you know that when you are hurrying, if you lose the regularity of your breath, you can't think properly? Now if judges knew that, they'd have a few more breathing teachers and a lot less prisons.'

'Dad . . .'

'Oh, yeah,' Zeno said, remembering something else he wanted to say. 'I was wondering – if you wore a thick pair of socks, do you think Raquel's skates would fit?'

Zen squealed with delight. 'Oh, Dad . . .'

The sun wasn't yet low, and the street – its houses uniform, save for personalised front doors – was hot and empty. Phyllis and Julia had chosen to live where families had lived for years, sons and daughters staying on when they married. People here considered their houses extensions of themselves. They were as houseproud as their ancestors, for whom the working cottages had been built. Phyllis and Julia adapted accordingly.

Julia hesitated at the front door. She was a handsome woman, and the paper-thin boiler suit she wore today emphasised the rolling ease with which she moved. She stopped to assemble her thoughts and consider a way to break the news. The sign-off whistle blew from the nearby Volkswagen depot, and the silence that followed ensnared her. She was still appreciating the moment when something caressed her leg and miaowed.

'Hello, Winston,' she said, as she picked him up and wrapped him around her neck. 'Now that you've arranged a rendezvous for later, I suppose you want a snack.'

Julia was intrigued by line breeding, and asked the cat about his heritage as she fondled his anthracite coat. But Winston only offered his inscrutable gaze. His genes were a mystery, but from his musical soirées in the early hours, he was obviously leaving his mark on the neighbourhood.

Julia, who never carried a bag, reached into her pocket and drew out the keys with a slow intake of breath similar to the one which preceded her eighty-mile-per-hour serve, and plunged the key into the lock.

Phyllis, in a cotton slip, had her head bowed in front of a steaming kettle, reviving her curls. Had she been witness to an incident earlier in the day, she might have been in need of more serious resuscitation.

The flower seller outside Green Park was not particularly imaginative in his choice of flowers, and Phyllis, rather than walk to the stall in Bond Street and add fifteen minutes to her journey, had taken it upon herself to educate him a little. He was not unresponsive and his selection of wares soon took a more adventurous turn.

The evening of the dinner being a Friday – the day Phyllis treated herself – she was leaving the office in Stratton Street when a man in a green linen suit pushed past her, without apologising, into the building. Phyllis, knowing the manners of the young English and preoccupied with denying the urge to pull the after-work cigarette from her bag, paid no heed. She also missed the upward-looking group on the pavement opposite her building. She brightened a little when the flower man produced the bunch of cream anemones he had put by for her. At the precise moment that Phyllis rummaged in her purse for coins, the man in the green suit reached the eighth floor, and made a desperate lunge for a friend who was just about threatening to toss himself over the balustrade. The suicidal man moved slightly, and the crowd below watched green-suit's rugby tackle become a swallow dive. Phyllis had just handed over the money, with instructions to keep the change, when the florist's thanks froze on his lips. The flash of green caught his eye, and a 'Gawd' escaped his lips on the thud of impact. Phyllis gave the florist an odd look – it was only a twenty-pence tip, she thought as she joined the throng heading down into the station. Wrong Man Leaps From Building was how one paper headlined the incident the next day.

Julia was admiring the anemones placed alongside the framed snap of Miss Sage when Phyllis came in from the kitchen.

'They're probably grown under glass, but they are nice.'

'Like you,' said Julia, turning to her.

'You're cutting it a bit fine for eight, aren't you?'

Julia took Phyllis's face between her hands and kissed her.

Phyllis, already suspicious, said, 'You going like that?'

'Listen, Red, I've had three of my staff let me down tonight. I'll have to work the evening shift myself. I left the day girl on till I get back. I wanted to explain face to face.'

Phyllis considered her response. 'I see,' she said.

'I had to pop in to tell you. Sorry love.'

Phyllis put down the hairbrush and walked back into the kitchen to switch off the kettle. 'No problem. I'll go for a jog and have an early night.'

'No, no,' said Julia. 'You've got to go. I promised to plug you into the glitterama.'

'I can't go on my own – I don't know anyone.'

'Oh, don't be soft. You'll knock 'em dead. Look, I want you to go.'

'Jools . . .'

'Listen, she probably wants me to re-equip her gym. If neither of us shows . . . well, it could be a big order.'

Phyllis looked down and Winston, who was still imitating a fox fur, caught her eye and said 'Go.'

Julia went on. 'Now, wear something sensational and have fun. You can tell me all about it in the morning – give me something to look forward to.'

'Okay,' said Phyllis grudgingly.

'Thanks, love. I'd better be getting back.' She went into the kitchen and was helping herself to a peach from a bowl when the cat decided he had waited long enough for his snack and jumped to the floor. His movement startled Julia and she upset the bowl, peaches rolling across the floor.

Phyllis, who had followed them in, said, 'Don't make yourself late, I'll tidy up.' Julia, the peach forgotten, made for the door. 'Count ten,' advised Phyllis.

Julia counted six under her breath. 'See you when I see you. No perfume on your knees tonight, okay rooster?' Phyllis nodded.

As soon as she was alone, the delayed response caught up with her. She picked up two peaches and slammed them together.

'There's a girl in my class who's got six toes.'

'Has she?' said Zeno. 'That's nothing. I've got eleven fingers.'

'You do not.'

'You wanna bet?' They were coming down the stairs, both in their bathrobes. Zen was trying to look at her dad's hands, but he had them deep in his pockets.

'You're on,' said Zen finally. Zeno, displaying his right hand, counted backwards starting with his thumb: 'Ten, nine, eight, seven, six.' He pulled his left hand from his robe and held it up: 'And five is eleven.'

Taken aback, Zen began to count his fingers herself. By the time they entered the ground-floor living room, she had caught on. 'Look, Mum, I've got eleven fingers,' she announced, her face shining.

Her mum's wasn't. 'The sitter can't make it, Zeno,' she said.

'Christ, she left it a bit late.'

'It wasn't a she. It was Danny the Nanny from the hairdresser's.'

'Oh, yeah,' said Zeno, glancing down at his Afghan goatskin boots and getting himself together.

'Mum, I've got eleven fingers,' repeated Zen.

'You'll have to go on your own,' Prudence said, ignoring Zen and chewing the inside of her cheek.

'Can't we get that German kid?'

'Ya, ya, goot. I like her,' chimed in Zen.

'It's too late. I don't mind. I wasn't really looking forward to the games anyway.'

'Just put *Space Draculas* on the video and lock me in,' said Zen, sliding her arms up over her dad's shoulders and jumping into a piggyback position, as if to enforce her point.

'Come on, Pru, at least try to get someone. You haven't been out for months. And she serves great food.'

'She always forgets we don't eat meat.' Prudence dropped her head into her chest. Her hair, which she had hennaed only that afternoon, looked harsh. The submissive posture reminded Zen of a friend's king poodle.

'Please go on your own. They're not interested in me. It's not nice, all that smoking and drinking.'

He shrugged. Her 'please' was plaintive. 'It takes all sorts, Pru,' he said.

'Oh, Zeno . . .' She actually wrung her hands, just like her mother did.

The sun was right in front of the window, causing a low-level bank of cloud to give the impression that London had gained a range of hills to the west whose tops were as red as coral. But in the middle of it all – the chimney; the eyesore that infected every sunset.

'That bloody chimney,' Zeno said in a rare display of pique. 'One of the biggest stacks in London, and it has to be in our view.'

Zen, still riding piggyback, said, 'Looks okay to me.' He unclasped and slid her around in front of him. Her presence cooled him, like looking at a sweet pea on a hot day. 'Dad.' Zen gave him a nudge with a small elbow. 'You okay, Dad?'

Zeno felt guilty that she had witnessed his show of temper. He smiled. 'Sure, sausage.' Turning to his wife, he said, 'Okay. This chapter is entitled "Zeno Braves Fleur's Den Alone". Is the shirt to my blue outfit clean?'

'It's clean, but it's not ironed.'

Zeno had pioneered a look in the Sixties, when he was still touring. Figuring that fans would expect their pop idols slightly larger than life, he had addressed the problem by putting together a series of monochromate outfits. He had kept these costumes for a long time and sometimes wore one when he felt in need of a boost. But charity auctions increasingly delved their ubiquitous fingers into his wardrobe, and of the original six outfits only the midnight blue was still in his possession.

He shuffled off to dress, returning in a few minutes with the first unlined linen jacket he ever owned over a tee-shirt. 'My Dirty Harry look,' he announced, clasping both girls to him. 'Wish me luck,' he said to his wife. And to his daughter, 'Don't forget to sit quietly before getting into bed.'

The long case clock struck 7.30 as they walked him out into the hall. Outside, leaning against a war-zone Citroën, was an unshaven minicabber. The sounds from his two-way radio bounced around the cul-de-sac.

'Motor ordered for half-past. You . . . er.' He peered at a scrap of paper, '. . . a Stud?'

Zeno grinned at Prudence, and Zen ran indoors.

'Well, yeah, that's me.' He turned to look at his wife. Her face in the direct sunlight looked worn. If it hadn't been for the regular dyeing, her hair would probably be quite grey. In spite of all his nutritional devices, Time was leaving its footprint. 'See you later, then,' he said.

'Sorry about the shirt, Zeno.'

'My fault – should have given you more notice.'

She blinked a couple of times, went in and closed the door. As Zeno turned to go down the steps, there was a knock from inside. He pushed open the letterbox, and little fingers pushed through a square of thin silk, which he put in his pocket. Amid squeals of laughter, Zen said, 'Don't do anything I wouldn't.'

The minicab took some time to swing into High Street Ken from Victoria Road, so Zeno knew the weekend crowd had joined the daily commuters. If you can't do anything about it, don't worry about it, he said to himself as he relaxed in the back. The driver had a tattoo – a blue line around his neck, with the letters CUT HERE. But his choice of radio station was interesting –it sounded like Radio Four.

'Observers of the astrological sky will know that tonight brings the beginning of a most unusual configuration. The great planet Pluto, ruler of the subconscious, tonig' t makes a very close aspect with Venus and Uranus. And this occurs on the occasion of the longest day, when the sun is nearest in orbit and marked by a beautiful full moon. Everyone must have been feeling the unusual emanations today, and tonight Water and Earth natives may be swept away by a tidal wave of long dammed-up passions. If abroad tonight, life preservers will be in order.'

Zeno recognised the tell-tale tremor in the broadcaster's voice as he deviated from his script with a daring ad lib.

'Adepts will surely know that the esoteric name of Pluto is Minerva, symbolising the wisdom of seeing things as they really are. During this . . .'

The cab driver had spun the car around, and was going to take his chances through the park. They had caught a red light at the Exhibition Road entrance, and Zeno was absentmindedly gazing out of the window when a bus drew up alongside and a child sitting in the front seat disturbed Zeno's reverie by pulling a length of folded-up paper straw from his nostril.

'. . . brief period, the Venus aspect can provide an opportunity for revelation, the moon triggering this process. More directly, you can either drown in your emotions or plumb the secrets of your own depths. Either way, it is safe to say that many of you out there will never be quite the same again. In the language of the ageless wisdom . . .'

The driver twirled the dial, and a standard from *West Side Story* filled the car. Zeno, who had lately been pondering what effect if any this massive release of astrology into the collective consciousness was having on the individual, asked the driver, 'Do you follow your stars, then?'

'Me? Naw, me missus was listening to it. I was dropping her off when your booking came through. I was miles away, to tell you the truth.' The silence broached, he openly regarded Zeno in the mirror. ''Ere, I know you, don't I? Don't you do that Durex ad on the telly?'

The car had turned right into Porchester Road in an effort to sidestep the crush in Westbourne Grove. It had crept its way level with the Queensway corner when a fire alarm sounded on the wall of the Turkish baths. From the baths' curved entrance poured a wave of pashas – some red and steaming, others British white, some wearing underpants, most covered only by blue-check loincloths. Between two of these pale scrawny men a statuesque black man squeezed so tightly that, from Zeno's point of view, the group resembled a liquorice allsort. The smaller of the white gentlemen suddenly whipped the loincloth from the black man's waist. Unabashed, he snapped his fingers and did a few bumps for the stunned late-shoppers. Zeno and the driver acknowledged the black man's proportions. Zeno passed his hand through his hair in a recognisably feminine gesture, and the unusual signet ring he wore on his little finger caught the driver's eye. He turned to his fare and snorted, 'Blimey – give a week's wages for a tool like that.'

'A week's, huh?'

The Citroën engaged gear and began to thread its way forward through the traffic. The sun's rays were lower now; they came raking down the adjacent streets and, as they motored past, the shimmering hot tarmac surface seemed to be momentarily paved with gold.

An unexpected chill of excitement ran through Zeno as the car neared Stanley Crescent. He hadn't felt anything like it since he had first slung his guitar over his shoulder and prepared to meet his public.

Phyllis sat alone in the end carriage, travelling west to an appointment she didn't want to keep. What she did want was a cigarette. She fingered the pack of cigarettes through her clutch bag, knowing how much better one would make her feel and not sure why she continued denying herself.

The train stopped, the doors slid open, and a black youth entered shouldering a ghetto blaster with radio blaring. A BBC voice was telling the world of a weird astrological configuration happening this very night. The teenager soon tired of this glimpse of the stars, pulled a cassette from his shirt pocket, and put it in. Mindless rap filled the carriage. Phyllis was outraged. 'Shit,' she said to the carriage. As if in response to the insult, the train slowed and halted in the tunnel. The lights flickered and went out. 'Let's fuck, let's fuck, let's fuck,' the ghetto blaster advised in the darkness.

Phyllis wasn't frightened; she wasn't even nervous. The fact that her fear of performing had over the years compounded itself by soaking up all the other elements in her life that were worrisome created an impression of stoicism. And as she didn't care much for the use of the usual feminine tools of make-up and high heels, she might have been considered dowdy – if she hadn't been so striking to look at. In truth, apart from her satin underwear, her only feminine luxury was perfume, which she always carried – mainly because her nose worked as well as it looked, in spite of the years of nicotine abuse. And many of the aromas that she encountered in her daily life were as offensive to her nose as the almost constant city noise was to her ears.

She thought for a moment about how luxurious this dark, almost empty, carriage would be if filled with a Scarlatti fugue or

113

Cole Porter's 'Night and Day' instead of 'Let's fuck'. Phyllis finally settled on 'Aria' from Suite in D by Bach. She got out her Vent Vert, sniffed it, put a dab of perfume behind each knee, closed her eyes, and began to play the piece in her head.

She was unaware how long she had been sitting in the dark; the combination of Bach and Balmain turned her mind inward, and the contemplative mood she had awoken to that morning returned. Her body seemed to tilt forward and, although a part of her knew she was safely seated, she went with the motion, floating gently above her seat. Suddenly, the train shuddered, the sense of consciousness holding on to itself vanished, and Phyllis felt her back against the seat and a dryness in her mouth.

The blaster fell silent, and the train moved off. In the quiet between the end of the rap music and the train surging forward, Phyllis heard a refrain. It was not a melody she recognised, and odder still was the actual quality of sound, which came from beyond the ear.

The train stopped and started between stations without explanation. By the time it reached Gloucester Road, a number of passengers had joined Phyllis and the musicologist, including two gypsy ladies who had come through the interconnecting doors, apparently working the train. Both were dressed in black. The older of the two had a frieze thrown over her shoulders, in spite of the heat. They clutched bunches of heather, each tuft neatly twisted in silver paper. Most of the commuters stared fixedly ahead or turned away as the gypsy women passed. The elder of the two wore her dark hair in a single plait and, as she neared, Phyllis saw that the roots of her hair – a good two inches – were quite white. She reached into her purse for change. As the elder neared her, Phyllis had smelled, or thought she smelled, baked fruit – not exactly apples, not quite pears; something in between. When she looked up, the woman's steady eyes were looking into hers. The nose was fine, and shaped not unlike Phyllis's. In her hand she held two sprigs of heather. 'For you,' she said. 'For good fortune.'

Phyllis handed her a fifty-pence piece, and as the silver changed hands the elder woman leaned towards her. She smelled of old-fashioned lavender.

'A gift, Rawnie, for your journey.' And passing the bits of heather into Phyllis's hand, she and her companion moved on.

When Phyllis emerged at Notting Hill Gate she knew she was late. The sun was low in the sky, and red. She looked around for a cab. There were none. She set off on foot down Kensington Park Road.

Fleur could not always trust the men she fancied to do what she asked. Most of them gave her a bad time and, as it had been happening most of her life, she made allowances for it. Being a devoted hostess, she knew that nobody liked to be the first to arrive, so she had tried getting her dates to arrive early. All promised, few complied. Captain Toby, her latest, she knew would let her down, so she asked the Rose to come early and help. He seemed like a gentleman and, if she guessed correctly, also liked to trade a little on the rough side – and knew the price.

The surgeon arrived early as promised, at 7.30. Fleur, on the advice of her wine merchant, had decided to serve Château Giscours '64 with the main course.

'It won't get any better,' he'd told her; and she had a great deal.

The Rose admired the ground-floor proportions of Stanley Crescent. He found Fleur's interiors a bit garish, but the way the drawing rooms opened on to the garden via floor-to-ceiling sliding glass doors – allowing the eye full vantage to the end of the plot – never failed to impress him.

'Who helped you design the exterior, Fleur?' he asked.

'Oh, a wonderful man did everything – even bought the statues for me.'

'It works perfectly.'

'Would you be a dear and help me get the vino from the cellar? I've left it a bit late – should have been uncorked by now.'

And so the first task of the evening for the reformed alcoholic was to fetch the wine from the basement and let it breathe. He uncorked three and decanted two. Fleur planned to greet her guests with a bottle or two of bubbly, which she preferred quite old, when it was a comfortable papery colour. The Yquem '67 – with dessert – was spending its final hours in the freezer, and the Rose, who had dined with Philippe de Rothschild at the château in Bordeaux, suggested that she freeze the glasses as well. He washed his hands in her double butler sink, selected a bottle of Badoit from the refrigerator, and joined Fleur, who was having a cigarette and fussing with the table setting in the garden; she hoped to have her guests all seated by the time the sun went down.

He poured himself a glass of water and studied his handiwork; she was looking remarkably well, and bore witness to her own theory that plastic surgery worked best for women who started early – the younger the better.

Inhaling the fragrance of an old-fashioned powder-puff rose, he said, 'They're wonderful this year.'

'I take a gardener once a week, and try to do a bit myself. Do you like being called the Rose?'

'I do.'

'Why is that?'

'I was always a great believer in the mystery of flowers. You grow beautiful flowers, Fleur – you must have a rose somewhere in your heart.'

Fleur came over all unnecessary and fiddled with a napkin. They were her best, inherited from her mother – old heavy linen, cut as large as tea towels. The Rose leaned across the refectory table and squeezed Fleur's hand. 'Enough of that. Tell me the gossip. Who's coming this evening?'

'Well, there's one absentee already, I'm afraid – tennis player, smart cookie, rang to say she couldn't make it. Her girlfriend's coming, though. Supposed to be a delight. Then there's Miranda and Nick. They're nice. He's wealthy, powerful. She's a mouthful

– a bit wicked. They're sort of on the lookout, if you know what I mean.'

'I do.'

'Then there is an old chum of mine, Zeno, and his wife. She used to be ravishing. Quiet, though – haven't seen her for a while. He's interesting – you might get on with him. And then there's my date.'

'And what's he like?' asked the Rose, pointing a steady finger at Fleur. 'Is he going to be inspecting my handiwork first-hand?'

'Oooh, I wish. But tell me about yours first.'

'Okay.' The Rose paused a moment, considering how to adjust from surgeon to confidant.

'I belong to this club near Berkeley Square. And when I stopped drinking and started swimming, I saw all these interesting chaps reporting to the fencing academy – same level as the pool, you see. So I joined up. Rather good at it, as it turned out, or so the swordmaster said. Natural eye-arm coordination, I suppose. That's how I met him – fenced at the club where he trains.'

'So what's he like?'

'Gorgeous. In the films, I believe. And he has a tattoo.'

'Oooh, I like tattoos.'

'You must ask him to show you. I haven't seen it myself, yet, only heard about it.'

Fleur smiled sympathetically. 'Let's hope tonight's our lucky night.'

The Rose held up his glass in a mock toast. 'I'll drink to that,' he said. 'Now tell me about Mister . . .'

He was about to say 'Right', when the doorbell chimed and Fleur went to let in the first of her guests. When they came through to the garden, they were already holding glasses of champagne. The woman was saying to Fleur that she would have only one glass, as champagne made her breath smell. The man acknowledged the Rose with a vague smile, and appeared to be waiting for his companion to finish speaking. The Rose assessed the couple.

The woman was taller than the man, and wore a short tube of a dress, simple and black. Her hair was up, twisted into a bun, giving full expression to her neck. And the face. More handsome than beautiful; the mouth was wide, but also deep, like a walnut. The hands were slender, the nails finely shaped. Every feature that could give sensual pleasure was aesthetically appropriate.

The Rose's trained eye spotted a curiosity, for though the hands were well cared for and manicured, the nails of both middle fingers were cut short. The shape of her body left only details to the imagination. The Rose could detect no line of underwear, and deduced that, if she wasn't wearing a g-string, she must be naked. With a dress this short, it showed a brazenness he had not come across before. She made a profound visual impact on him. He thought she was perfect, save perhaps for a feverishness about the eyes.

He realised that his appreciation of the woman was being quietly observed by the man, who had emptied his glass and moved across to the tables bearing food. The Rose could tell by the aromas that wafted across him that the man was lifting the various tureens, but all the same the Rose knew he was being watched. When the surgeon turned to him, he appeared to be savouring the smell of Fleur's summer curry, waving the fumes on to his nose. The Rose looked away, having already discerned the man's considerable power. He felt drawn, wanting to step close, yet not daring to; one infringed the territory of such a man at one's peril.

A gravelly but cultured voice said, 'Those girls are never going to stop gassing. I'm Nicholas.'

'Sorry, darling,' said Miranda almost immediately. 'I've been hogging Fleur – girls' talk, you know.'

Her voice was also well-to-do, but the Rose sensed an undertone, as though her delivery was a learned pronunciation. Nick was reaching for the Rose's extended hand.

'My friends call me the Rose,' he said, looking into dark eyes which lowered to inspect his grip. He's going to make me work to know him, the Rose thought.

The bell chimed once again, and Fleur received the Rose's friend. And although he was well turned out in an obvious sort of way the Rose was made ill at ease by his appearance – not that he was ashamed of him in any way, but the man he had just shaken hands with would know much about him by his choice.

The Rose's date had been asked to guess how many pearls were sewn into Fleur's blouse (an obligatory game question, prize to be announced later), he had made a meal of answering, and was duly escorted into the open with his glass of fizz. Fleur introduced him as Flick.

Trick, Nick said to himself, and grinned as he shook hands. Strong boy. A young Steve Reeves; the last of the non-steroidal Mr Universes. Like all bodybuilders, better viewed without clothes than with. Bet that jacket'll be off and sleeves rolled up before he sits down to eat. Actually, it happened sooner than Nick had guessed. Flick had only downed half his glass when the coat was festooned across the back of a chair. The short sleeves were pre-rolled. Miranda slid past Nick with Fleur in tow. Fleur was saying, 'Did you see his too?'

Nick had. Just above the rolled-sleeve line of Flick's arm he had glimpsed the end, or the start, of a tattoo – big work by the look of it. Nick, who knew all about the bleeding, and the addiction to the pain involved, filed it under 'Trick'. So the knifeman liked his boys inked, did he?

He grabbed Fleur the next time she floated by, and asked for a cognac, which took them back into the house, leaving Miranda putting sand down with the Rose and his escort.

Captain Toby and Zeno arrived together and were let in with a beatific smile from Fleur. 'What a dangerous combo,' she said. They were ogled by a short man holding a brandy balloon. 'That's Nicky,' said Fleur, gripping an arm of each arrival and propelling them towards the garden. The sun was almost down, and still a guest to arrive; this wasn't going according to plan at all.

119

She deposited her charges in the garden, anticipating that the sun would set in another fifteen minutes, and went back to the drawing room to round up Nicholas, who had made himself cosy on the settee. His glass was empty.

'This is a good drop of cognac, Fleur – have to hand it to you.' Realising she could not shoo him out like the others, she sat down on the corner of the sofa and twisted her body towards him.

'Glad someone appreciates it – it's pre-phylloxera.'

'Whatever it is, it goes straight to my balls.'

'Wherever your treasure is . . .'

'Are there any girls – any other girls – coming tonight?'

'Is that how it's taking you at the moment?'

'Mmm. Had a piece of strange this afternoon – didn't do everything to her that I wanted to.'

'Got you at it, did it? Just like Christie when he came upon his strangler's rope unexpectedly after a lay-off.' Nicholas lowered his eyelids a fraction and observed Fleur. 'Have you ever been taken with a rope around your neck, Fleur?'

Fleur, momentarily unnerved, replied with a smile, 'Someday you'll be served your heart on a plate, Nick.' When he didn't respond, she added, 'I did invite Zeno's wife, but he showed up without her – some crap about a sitter letting them down. Daughter's almost grown up. Feels out of her depth, I suppose.'

'Silly goose.' He reached out and lifted the decanter, placed it within reach, and poured himself another. 'Met her actually. Gorgeous, but dumb – limits things a little. Not like you, flower.'

'Taken tonight.'

'Have been, or about to be?'

'*Inshallah*, as we say in the desert.'

'Scarborough's not the desert, flower.' Fleur giggled. 'The Captain?'

'Dishy, isn't he?'

'Is he?' I suppose he is, thought Nick, What's he a captain of, I wonder? Fleur stood up and arranged her toile blouse; it was white and, in the sidelight, transparent. Showing her new bosom, thought Nick, no wonder she's asking everyone the number of pearls.

'What about Flick? He looks like he swings.'

'Your type, is he? The Trick. Looks like he's anyone's. I'm just in the mood to see Miranda with another chick – been thinking about it all afternoon.'

'I know the feeling. There is supposed to be a young woman. Can't imagine where she's got to. She's gay, I think. Haven't actually met her but . . . she's a redhead, I believe.'

'Really? Curious.'

There were footsteps outside and the bell chimed. Fleur whispered, 'Probably her now,' and went to the door. Nick downed his cognac and stood up. Zeno wandered into the room through the open sliding glass doors, and from twenty-five feet away watched Fleur open the front door. A slim figure was framed in sunset light, and then the man moved across the room, hungrily, his arm outstretched. In silhouette he saw her put out her hand, after which his vision became fogged, and his legs felt unsteady like the first time his mum had taken him to St Paul's Cathedral.

Fleur watched Nick take the proffered hand and place it on his crotch.

'I'm Nick,' he said.

There was a second when nothing appeared to happen. Then the girl looked down at her hand held by Nick's, felt around a bit, and looked up into his eye. 'Small to middling,' she said. Fleur, who'd done nothing except open her mouth to ask how many pearls were on her blouse, was still holding the door. For a moment it seemed that the late fairy might walk straight out, but she turned to Fleur with a composed expression and asked, 'Is there a bathroom? I need to wash my hand.'

Zeno hadn't stirred. Watching the little drama at the door, he had a mental picture of cream cascading into dark melted chocolate. Fleur walked ahead to the top of the staircase where it sectioned into a gallery running the width of the room. She switched on a light, and Zeno caught the girl's profile before she disappeared. He felt his heart accelerate, and put his hand to his chest. It took him a moment to realise he was holding the right side of his chest.

Alone in the bathroom, Phyllis was taking stock of her evening so far. An overly made-up woman had opened the door and invited her in, when a short prematurely balding man with alcohol on his breath had practically put his cock in her hand. Was this the famous glitterati that Julia was looking forward to hearing about? She didn't know if she felt outraged, ready to fight, or both. And who was the little twerp with the semi-permanent hard-on?

She was still analysing her mood and running her wrists under cold water when the door opened, a woman peeped in and, seeing another female, entered quickly and closed the door. With a brief 'Excuse me' she hitched up the few inches of her dress, sat on the pedestal and started to take a pee. Obviously not a great one for briefs, thought Phyllis, noticing the legs.

'You all right? You look a bit fazed,' said their tanned owner, gracefully wiping herself with a tissue and wriggling her dress back down over her bottom.

'Some overgrown kid with glaucoma made a sort of pass at me.'

'Oh, that's my husband. You shouldn't mind him. He goes over the top when he's had a few drinks. Quite charming otherwise. Probably instantly taken by your looks.' She gave Phyllis the once-over.

'Bloody infidel. You should keep him on a leash.'

'I do, most of the time. Dirty little sod. Anyway, I apologise for him. Come on, let's join the others. Fleur wanted to seat us before sunset, romantic thing that she is.' She gave Phyllis a peck on the cheek, but Phyllis, wary of physical contact, was aware that the softness of the other's lips stayed in contact a moment too long. 'I'm Miranda, by the way. That's nice perfume. Unusual.'

'Thank you.' Then Phyllis looked Miranda squarely in the eye and said, 'What are you two, anyway – a team playing away?'

Fleur steered Zeno over to Flick with a 'just you two boys stand close' number and, with less expertise than David Bailey, pushed them together and produced the common polaroid. 'He's in the industry, too,' she added, loosely lining them up in the view-finder. 'There,' she gasped. 'A flash of stars.' Fleur was fond of the collective noun. 'How many pearls on this top?' she asked, turning sideways.

Flick blinked. 'You asked me before. I've no idea,' he said.

'Well, guess, silly.'

'Hundreds, I should think. Er . . . two hundred.'

Fleur, who had a sticky square of paper stuck on the back of the camera, took a pencil from her skirt pocket and scribbled Flick's guess. 'How about you, Zeno?'

Zeno, who had played Fleur's game before, waited a moment and said, as though he had actually thought about it, 'One hundred and twenty-seven.' He was considering Fleur's commitment to her games when he realised that she had gone, and Flick was standing alongside him with the polaroid smile still on his lips. Zeno breathed deeply and said, 'So you're in the industry?'

'Er, sort of.' He faltered, and swilled down the rest of the champagne in an effort to fill the silence. Zeno took the empty glass from his hand and parked it on the food trestle nearby. Flick's hands were no sooner empty than he reached for a cigarette. 'D'you mind?' he asked Zeno.

'No, used to smoke myself. Reckon it's the hardest habit to break. More difficult than the Peruvian diet.'

'The what?'

'Cocaine.'

'Oh, is that right?'

Zeno nodded. 'You were going to tell me about being in the business.'

'Was I? Oh yeah. Well, do a bit of stunt work, you know.'

'That's great. Tough cookie, eh?'

'I'm mainly in the crowd,' confessed Flick, his voice in descent, and suddenly intrigued by how his Silk Cut was burning.

'You don't say. I started in the crowd.'

'You didn't.'

'Sure as I'm standing here,' said Zeno with a warm smile. 'They were shooting around the old Queen's Theatre in Poplar. We lived over that way, and one of my mates told me they were looking for local colour – crowd, you see. So I went along. Turned out it was a Gary Cooper movie. Eric Portman was the English star.'

'Wow! Did you meet him? What was he like?'

'Coop? Oh, a prince. He was ill at the time – spinal cancer, I believe. Of course nobody knew it then. I made a right fool of myself and asked for his autograph. He was great. Made the stills guy take a snap of us. I still have it.' Zeno chuckled unselfconsciously. 'One of my treasures now, of course.'

'Wow! I'd like to see it.' He outed his cigarette.

'I understood something watching Coop. I was only on the set for three days, but it made me realise that the stars – the real stars – well, frankly, the bigger the star, the nicer they are. It's part of what makes them special. Modesty is beautiful when it's natural – don't you think?' Flick was far too comfortable listening, so Zeno went on. 'I mean, modesty is a beauty in itself because its action is to veil itself – it veils its own vanity. I find that beautiful.'

'What was Portman like?' asked Flick, getting back on to more familiar ground.

'Portman, he was the opposite. Never spoke to any of us. Sent his dresser to ask me if I'd like to go and see "Mr Eric" in his trailer.'

'Wow! What did you say?'

'Well, I was full of myself at the time.'

'Yeah.'

'About your age, maybe younger. Anyway, I said, "You tell Mr Eric that if he gives me an Austin-Healey I'll give him a good hiding." '

'You didn't!'

'I didn't, no. I mean, I said it, but didn't do it.'

'Right.' A look of discomfort passed across Flick's face, and when he spoke, Zeno realised he must have been giving the question serious thought. Actually, he was waiting for the half Valium he'd taken to take effect. When he finally spoke, he asked: 'You a Buddhist, Zeno?'

'No. Why do you ask?'

'Well, you're sort of easy to talk to. I am.'

'That's terrific, Flick.'

'But you're not?'

'No.'

'I, er, go to meetings. I chant and that for everything I want.'

'Inner peace?'

Flick's pained expression returned.

'You chant for inner peace,' Zeno repeated.

'No. New car. Better gear. Stuff like that.'

Zeno allowed this new use of the prophet's philosophy to sink in before he spoke.

'Great soul, the Buddha. The traditions,' seeing the pain on Flick's forehead, Zeno added, 'the teachings . . .'

'Oh, yeah,' said Flick. 'But you're not a follower.'

'Nope.'

'Why not?'

'I'm my own man. I have a problem with translations. Jesus, Buddha – all these guys have been translated. The Buddha only spoke the Maghadi language, yet his teachings were translated into Pali or Sanskrit, which must have been done many years later. And I can't put my life on the line on the strength of some translator who, odds are, never ever sat with the man.'

Fortunately for Flick, the hostess summoned them to the table before Zeno could get started on the misrepresentation of the Naz and the flaws in Christianity.

Flick had done her placement giving a clue to her bourgeois spirit; Captain Toby and Fleur sat at either end; Zeno, his back to the sunset, with Nick on his right and Miranda to his left.

He knew he had been sounding off a bit with Flick. He only realised why when he sat down opposite Phyllis and became fully aware of the effect the girl was having on him. It was the feeling that every man trying to hold a marriage together both dreads and longs for. He felt uncommonly hot, and feared that his ears were shining red – something that had not happened since he had first become interested in girls.

Zeno had held the rush in check by gossiping to Flick, yet sitting across from her, he felt like a schoolboy at his first dance, unexpectedly paired with the class beauty. The sexpot on his left was demanding his attention, and when he didn't respond sufficiently, she read his name aloud, picked up his napkin and draped it across his lap, her hand somehow brushing his groin in the process.

Fleur served the starter herself – a chilled cherry soup – and announced it was everyone for themselves from here on in. The white wine on the table was something amusing she had discovered in Alsace. Nicholas raised his glass and said, 'Cheers.'

Captain Toby extracted what looked like a propelling pencil from his blazer pocket, and dispensed a saccharine into the wine with a 'Tally ho'.

Miranda, who apparently now remembered Zeno, enquired after his wife, and asked why she wasn't here.

'She's at home with our daughter.'

'So you're a father. How old is she?'

'She's nine.'

'Quite mature then?'

'Some of her is – part is still very much a little girl.'

'Been married some time?'

'Afraid so,' said Zeno, doing his old-codger voice.

Miranda, missing the attempt to lighten up, or ignoring it, pressed on. 'Still fancy her, do you, or are you feeling the strain a bit?'

Fleur was explaining to the Rose how they served curry at room temperature in classical Indian cuisine when she remembered Zeno was a vegetarian. 'I'm sorry, Zeno,' she said across Miranda. 'It completely slipped my mind.'

'Oh, I'm sure there's plenty of . . .'

He was getting to his feet to go and look when Miranda said, 'So you're a vegetarian – for how long?'

'Must be fifteen years now.'

'I'm a real cannibal, I'm afraid. Hope it won't offend you, watching me eat.'

'No, of course not,' said Zeno, going out of his way not to make waves. 'Is not all one, after all?'

Nick was already piling the aromatic pieces of lamb on to a plate when Zeno started trying to make his plate look respectable with the side effects. He was no stranger to the situation now. When he'd first become a vegetarian he would often eat at home before going out to dinner. Tonight was easy: wild rice, mango chutney, yoghurt with cucumber, pine nuts and raisins. No one would have noticed if Fleur had not announced it.

'What did you mean by that?' asked Nick. He had loaded his portion and was watching Zeno tap-dance with his.

'All is one? Well, everything lives on everything, doesn't it? Sounds disgusting, I suppose, but it's a fact.'

'If you say so, old chap.' Nick delicately extracted a chunk of lamb from his curry and popped it into his mouth. He licked his fingertips, but made no move to return to his seat.

Zeno took up his theme again. 'This piece of baby lamb you're chewing, for example. I bet if it had known it was going to become a well set-up smart fellow like yourself, married to a terrific wife like Miranda, it would have leaped into the old stewing pot.'

'Why did you give it up then?' asked Nick, seemingly focused on his next morsel.

'Oh, I liked it, but it didn't like me. The choice wasn't philosophical: dicky tum – too much mischief in the Sixties.'

Phyllis had been rather intrigued by the vaguely familiar-looking man with the winning smile, until she heard the 'all is one' remark. Then she dismissed him as simply another casualty of the Sixties. She remained seated and was taking her time with the delicious fruit soup, having decided that the best way to cope with the small octopus was to be all sweetness and light. But she was not inviting another close encounter, and planned to wait until Nick returned to his seat before going for the main course. The pale man on her right turned to her and introduced himself. 'My name's Clement. Shall we get some more food?'

'Are you sitting in someone else's place?' asked Phyllis, indicating the place setting which clearly said 'The Rose' in Fleur's italic hand.

'It's a nickname,' he said with a smile. 'Never was too fond of Clement.'

'The Rose.' Phyllis savoured his very British pronunciation. 'It's a nice word. To tell you the truth, I've never much liked Phyllis, but it hasn't occurred to me to change it.'

'Why ever not? Think of the difference it would make to your life.'

'Did it change yours, then?'

'Absolutely. I only really noticed how much I missed it when I left the hospital I was in and had to start telling strangers my real name. I feel there's a great mystery hidden in a name. Not only does it mean something to others, it has an essential influence on its owner. Why don't you think about a name you really like, or maybe imagine what you'd call a daughter if you had one. The change might surprise you.' He paused. 'I think the trough is clear now. What about that curry?'

'That's a stylish dress you're wearing. Alaia isn't it?' said Zeno, tucking into his rice and salad.

Miranda tossed her head. 'Is it? I can't remember.'

'I think so. Bought my wife one from him. He's Tunisian, isn't he?'

'Does she wear it?'

'Not much actually. I think she feels it's a little young on her.'

'Did you put your hands up her legs when she wore it?'

'No.'

'Well then.'

'I don't see . . .'

'If the next time she wore it, you groped her – say, while she was serving your veggy burger – she would be doing the housework in it.' While Zeno was thinking what to say, Miranda lost interest and turned to Fleur. 'Scrumptious curry, darling. Hot and slow.'

Fleur giggled. 'Like you.'

'Zeno doesn't think so – do you, Zeno?' asked Miranda, peeling her walnut lips back over her teeth. But Zeno was otherwise occupied watching Phyllis and the Rose. He was becoming aware of subtle changes in the atmosphere whenever he focused on the girl. The sun had finally gone, and in the twilight her skin had taken on the delicate texture of a magnolia. If he looked at her without listening to the conversation, he could see the lights and shades each of her movements produced. A sense of well-being accompanied the focus of his look, not dissimilar to the sensation he had felt years before when composing songs for the B-sides of his records.

At the other end of the table Nick was taking stock of Fleur's fancy man. There was something he found disturbing – disturbing only because he couldn't nail it down. He began separating what he saw into categories: the man's dress was conventional, perhaps a bit too conventional – the blazer well cut, but hard to say if it was made to measure or Marks and Sparks, as he was sitting down; his shirt was dark blue with a white collar – a style Nick had always found irritating – and matched by a tie almost the same temperature blue, with black diagonal stripes. A club tie, perhaps – but from which? He also noticed that the man ate hastily, and had the habit of laughing before any humorous sentence was finished, as though half consciously aware that every pleasing experience soon passes, but instead of savouring the experience by retaining it, became over-anxious and, in hurrying, hastened the pleasure. Nicholas felt Fleur's interest might be misplaced. He wondered if the man had been a prisoner of war, concluding that he could possibly have taken part in the campaign in Korea if his rank had been earned in combat. His chin was shadowed, even though he was close-shaven. One of those poor chaps who needed to shave twice a day. The timbre of his voice was keen and powerful, but not immediately noticeable because his accent was a little off – a voice that had started life speaking one dialect, tried to move to another, and fallen somewhere in between. And, finally, there was the signet ring on his pinky, a custom which in Nick's experience generally indicated sexual deviation.

Nick's subject appeared to be daring Flick to do something, while blowing his nose into the generous napkin. Flick, whose Valium had begun to work, enquired of the table, 'Does anyone mind if I smoke?'

Extending his chosen role for the evening, Nick replied, 'Does anyone mind if I fart?'

In the awkward silence that followed, Flick's face went a bit red and the Rose, coming to his rescue from Fleur's end of the table, enquired, 'Did you know that the five principal gases that make up a fart are odourless?'

'That's correct,' added Zeno. 'It's the traces of other constituents that give the aroma. Mercaptans, I believe they're called. And, of course, hydrogen sulphide is the main culprit.' Phyllis wondered why the English were so preoccupied with flatulence.

Flick, receiving no direct rejection, and receiving additional prodding from the Captain, reached below the table and withdrew from somewhere – Zeno assumed his sock – a rather dog-eared hand-roll. 'It's not tobacco,' Flick squeaked by way of introduction. He placed the hand-roll demurely on his salad plate, as if awaiting the verdict.

'What it is precisely?' asked Nick.

The would-be executor of stunts, encouraged by the glimmer of interest in Nick's voice, patted the reefer and extolled its virtues. 'A bit of Thai stick. Not as lethal as Nick's fart, perhaps, but a lot funnier.'

'Well then,' said Nick, pulling a worn gold lighter from his pocket and pausing to sniff the petrol on the wick.

'Ooh, lovely,' squealed Fleur, squeezing the Rose's arm in anticipation of a general loosening of inhibitions. And, as if wanting to extend the zenith of the moment, 'Now who's brought a new game?'

Nick, who now had the reefer, said, 'Never fear, Flower, Nicholas is here.' He twirled his Dunhill and fired up. After he had inhaled, and with a big smile to Flick, he said, 'I don't know about Thailand – this tastes like Maida Vale WB to me.'

'WB?' asked Fleur.

'Window box, I should think,' said Zeno.

Nick continued. 'My game is called statistics, and all parties contribute.' He hesitated for effect. 'First, we all have to guess how much of our lives we spend in orgasm. Not foreplay, not making it – orgasm only.' His voice cast something of a spell over the table and no one save the Rose noticed he was holding on to the reefer.

'What's second?' the Captain wanted to know.

'When we've made our guesses and written them down, I collect the answers, being as honest as possible' – a wicked glance towards Fleur – 'more possible for some than others. We each write down when we started, how many times a week we did it, how many times we do it now, and how long it lasts. When each of us arrives at a total, we add them together and divide by eight. Whoever's total is nearest wins. The one who is farthest out pays the forfeit. I decide what the prize and forfeit are.'

The Rose looked across at Miranda. 'What does your old man do for a living?'

'He puts his hand to many things.'

Nick finally passed the joint to Zeno. 'Right. Everybody game?' asked Nick, splashing some claret into his glass.

Zeno was about to pass the joint to Miranda when he saw Phyllis watching him. 'Don't you smoke either?' were her first words to him.

'Not now, no – tried everything though.'

'And now?' Zeno shrugged, but the unwavering eyes held his. 'Surely you don't begrudge a little weed the chance of becoming a hip, laidback chap like yourself?' Not feeling up to explaining, and wanting to impress, he gave a resigned smile, inhaled fully like an old head, and pointedly passed the smoking stub across to her.

Nick's assessment of the marijuana being homegrown was probably accurate – if not Flick's own window box, then some other local horticulturist's, but certainly a stranger to the longitude of Thailand. Phyllis, accustomed only to nicotine – and missing it – inhaled deeply, and found the effect unexpected. As the smoke entered the bloodstream, its molecules bonded with the brain receptors which triggered the hypothalamus, giving rise to a momentary blackout. She didn't actually faint; in fact, there was no outward effect at all. Yet inwardly, a second passed when she was aware of . . . nothing. A sensation too intense to be registered.

She was facing Zeno and, in the moment which preceded the absence, she saw not Zeno's face, but another. Then . . . blank. And then Zeno again, turning slightly to his left, apparently unaware he had been away. Phyllis was still staring at what the surgeon next to her would have termed the non-hair-bearing area in front of Zeno's ear when the Rose took the butt of the joint from her fingers and passed it to Fleur.

'Thank you,' she said absently to the Rose, and half turning towards him, 'another non-indulger?'

'Can't,' he replied apologetically, 'I'm an alcoholic addict.' She looked directly at the Rose to make sure he wasn't pulling her leg, and by the time she turned back to face Zeno, his chair was empty.

Fleur passed behind her, lighting the candles on the table, which burned straight up in the still evening air. Phyllis found herself watching them. Then a worrying feeling began nagging at her, followed by a jolt of nausea, and she guessed she was experiencing the predicament of the man who had left the table.

Fleur, on her way back to her seat, was conferring with the Rose, everyone else was busy calculating on the back of their place-cards. Phyllis located her bag, stood up, and left the garden unnoticed.

She was making her way to the bathroom she had used earlier when something prompted her to turn right, into a short passage with two mahogany doors. She opened the first door and found herself in an elegant masculine bathroom, all polished wood, brass and marble – even a fireplace with a small club fender. Zeno was slumped against a wall, his long hair looking silver in the overhead lights. Although visibly distressed, he managed a smile when he saw her.

Phyllis entered and closed the door. She spotted the cut-throats, selected one, deftly sharpened it on the leather strop hanging from the door, and eased the razor through a curl of her hair. She took her lighter from her bag and set fire to it. Then she blew out the flame and, while the strand was still smoking, held the burning hair under Zeno's nose. The acrid fumes acted like smelling salts. He coughed a bit as she guided him to the Victorian fender and sat him down. He closed his eyes and placed his palms over them.

Phyllis studied him afresh. She put him in his mid-forties – yet there was a boyishness about him that he would probably carry with him all his life. He looked well cared-for, as though loved by a good woman. But then, this type of man would look clean even

133

if he'd been shovelling coal-dust. His hair fell into strands, as though combed with the wide end of a comb. She was suddenly overwhelmed by two distinct sensations, one the root of the other, the way emotion is the depth of thought. Part of her felt maternal towards him; the other part felt like an unsure child.

He was still crouched on the fender, a dazed boxer in a neutral corner. Then his hands dropped, his eyes opened, and he looked up at her. His voice sounded shaky. 'I'm sorry to be . . .'

He was about to say 'a bore' when Phyllis raised her hand, which still held the singed curl. With a 'Sshh', she placed it in the sink. 'Tried everything, huh?'

He grinned. It brought spots of colour back to his face. 'Thanks. Your first time too, I guess.'

'I've smoked before. Trying to give it up actually.'

Zeno continued to gaze at her. He said evenly, 'I meant, in a female body.' Under most circumstances she would have scoffed, but she didn't. She didn't move either. Zeno unwound his legs and stood up. 'We've been together before, haven't we?'

Phyllis's mind splayed out into itself. She recalled the end of her dream, just before she had woken. But she hadn't woken – she'd dreamed she'd woken. The dream had continued. She had heard a strange noise – music – and seen a face, the woman whose face she had seen imprinted on Zeno's. This person had changed during the dream. She had become remarkably like the man who stood before her now. Zeno reached out his hand and laid it on the side of her neck. The touch was uncluttered by thought, motive, or sexual overtone, yet it sent a tremor through her. She heard herself sigh, and restrained an almost irrepressible urge to touch the space in front of his ear.

There followed an instant in which, in the future, whenever either of them gave it any thought, neither would even guess how much time passed. There came catcalls of anticipation from the garden, and Phyllis shivered. 'Let's get out of here,' she said. She saw Zeno's glance waver. A 'we can't just leave' expression crossed his face. 'You going to make waves for them – or for us?'

134

As if in answer to her question, more screams came from below, and Nick's strident voice announced, 'Eleven hours, seventeen minutes,' followed immediately by Miranda's, 'Can I have mine all tonight?'

Phyllis and Zeno left the house – where they had finally made contact – without so much as a look back.

In the haste to discover the precise total of life's foremost pleasure, the absence of Zeno and Phyllis was not immediately noticed. However, once it was, a search in the manner of hide and seek was instigated before the announcement of the winners and losers. Nick, already devising special forfeits for them both as punishments for abstaining, and anticipating coming upon errant love-making, took the less conventional settings – basement, cupboards, cellars and the coal bunker – whilst Miranda scoured the bedrooms. Captain Toby investigated the gymnasium, the Rose and Flick had second helpings of summer pudding.

Fleur was momentarily anxious in case Vanella had forgotten to lock the toyroom. She was zealously hospitable – with the exception of this one department. When it was certain the prey had not gone to earth, but had run for cover, there was a desultory post-mortem over coffee in the garden. The enormous orange moon rose unnoticed. Miranda and her husband were the only couple to take visible umbrage. She cornered him and hissed rattily, 'I can't believe how unsubtle you were.'

'Thought I'd nudge her towards you – it's worked before.'

'It worked on a dyke with fried-egg tits – this numero had class.'

'Just a nudge.'

'Nudge? Chuck would be more accurate. As soon as I mentioned we were married, she assumed we were in tandem.'

'Fleur told me she was gay. You sure she got a good look at you?'

135

'Outside of doing a can-can. Perhaps she wasn't in the mood. The full moon doesn't affect everyone the same. Or perhaps she had PMS.'

'Didn't stop that fairy, Zeno – did it? Vegetarian, my arse.' Miranda giggled. 'What's so humorous?'

'You whingeing. You who can get anyone. But the one that gets away drives you crazy. You boys . . .'

'Just in the mood, that's all,' said Nick, petulance still in evidence.

'Hold on to that mood, boy – I may check you out later. Come on, lover, smile for the camera.'

'Zeno Studd. How could she leave with a guy called that?'

'Put your nose out of joint, that's for sure.'

'If it were only my nose . . .'

Scenting bitchiness, Fleur sailed over. 'Bad upbringing, that's what I say – leaving without so much as a "by your leave".' And then, 'Come on – let's open some more champagne.'

They did. But later, when Toby discovered the singed curl in the sink, it made them curious again, and set them wondering anew.

They walked down the incline towards the Bayswater Road in silence, yet in their silence there was unceasing communication. Her monogrammed slippers and his Cuban heels accentuated the difference in their heights; nevertheless, there was an easy rhythm between them, and their bodies touched as they strolled. Gaining distance from the house, the feeling of 'at one-ment' became so strong that even a word would have jarred – a breach neither wanted to risk until they reached the Friday-night clamour and lights of Notting Hill Gate. And then it was her reason that began to question the recent events.

'Perhaps it's the stuff we smoked,' she said. It was more a statement than a question.

Zeno listened to the inrush of her voice. Although it was true

136

that the spoken sentence obstructed the energy of the silence, the obstruction of a flow of electricity produces a light – and the quality of her voice lit a beacon within him.

'I've smoked some deadly weed in my time,' he said, accustoming himself to the sound of his own voice. 'Even used to put THC under my tongue at night so I'd wake up stoned . . . I don't know what this is, but it sure isn't dope.'

'What shall we do?'

Zeno grinned. 'Speaking for myself, I could just stand here with you for a day or two.'

The large, almost loose mouth widened, the motion bringing dimples to her cheeks. 'Zeno Studd. Is that your real name, by any chance?'

'Zeno is. I became Studd when I got my break. Don't you like it?'

'It does have a ring to it. Someone in the family?'

'Who, Zeno? No. Mum wanted a Zena.' He grinned lopsidedly without thinking about it. Phyllis opened her bag, and Zeno caught a glimpse of the heather. 'What's that?' he asked.

'I bought them from a woman, a gypsy. Well, she pushed them on to me, actually – on the train coming here.'

'Real gypsy, not a didicoy?'

'Didicoy?'

'A traveller, a tinker – they're different from the Romanies, who are real gypsies.'

'They looked real to me. She called me Rawnie.'

'And she gave you two sprigs. You didn't ask?'

'I didn't say anything – just gave her some change.'

'Okay.' Zeno considered. Every time he stopped speaking he was aware of a current pulsing in him. 'Rawnie. Well, she was right there. It means beauty, or lovely. Listen, I'd like to take you to meet someone. I have theories about everything, but I would like to get some back-up on this. It's not far – we can walk if you like.'

Phyllis put her hanky back into her bag. 'Who could say no to someone called Zeno?'

The air was warm, and the full moon cast a mantle of shadowless light around them as they walked west. When they were nearing Shepherd's Bush she linked her arm through his, and at her touch he launched into the opening phrase of Johnny Ray's hit 'Such a Night'.

The first thing she saw as they neared the encampment under the flyover was the flickering fire. This age-old site had been set aside for the Romanies when they travelled the length of Britain, supplying ponies for the coal-pits. And today they still behaved as if the new flyover – which trapped the woodsmoke beneath it and covered everything with soot – did not exist. The spot was theirs by right; they hung on with strong nails.

Phyllis had never known of its existence, though she must have sped over it countless times. Yet when they stood on the threshold of the site with its smoke, dogs, haphazardly parked vehicles and the general debris of life in semi-transit, it didn't feel alien to her.

A shoeless child sidled up to them and slipped a small grubby hand into Zeno's to lead them into the camp. Phyllis stayed abreast of him, breathing the smoky air and looking about her. The child passed them on to a middle-aged woman and dropped back a few paces, to be joined by other small ones who followed the outsiders from a distance.

There was order within the seemingly random configuration of cars and trailers, which became apparent as they were escorted deeper into the encampment. They finally arrived in front of a hand-painted caravan, the type traditionally associated with wayfarers, carved with the care of a bygone age, witness to an aesthetic of necessity long since discarded. Phyllis approached the caravan at eye-level, surprised to see it perched on a trailer.

They waited while their guide climbed aboard and entered the caravan through a door between the horse's shafts. A short moment later, the top section of the door opened and they were summoned.

The person who greeted them from the candlelight sat among her possessions, which included a cream cockatoo who displayed a pearly comb when they entered and said, 'Hello travellers.' The dukkerina smiled, revealing a sliver of gold set between her middle front teeth.

'He's very old, like me, and he likes visitors,' she said in a crackly voice. 'He will talk to you if he likes your voice – won't you, Manushie? Come, sit and have something to drink.'

She sat, propped by cushions, at the far end of the caravan on a bench built into three sides of the oblong interior. In front of her the table was set for tea with a padded tea-cosy and three cups. Zeno came through the split door and went to sit down straight away, making his greetings to the elder. Phyllis hung back and made friends with the parrot, whose cage hung near the door. Her voice apparently passed muster, for Manushie was soon showing off his songs and vocabulary.

Zeno introduced his new friend, and asked if the old woman had anything to tell them. She produced a bowl of wax from a shelf above her head, and a small primus stove from beneath the bench. She lit the stove, which smelled of methylated spirit and burned with a blue flame.

When the copper bowl was placed on the stove, she asked them to hold out the hand they favoured. Both offered their left. The old lady dipped a spoon into the melted candlewax, let it cool for a second, and then poured the contents first into Zeno's palm, and then into Phyllis's. Zeno looked at Phyllis, Phyllis looked at her palm, and Manushie looked at the proceedings, blinked and closed his eyes.

As the wax solidified it curled up at the edges, taking the shape of a shell. The dukkerina took one of the lit candles and set it directly in front of her. From her skirts she pulled a device like a pair of chopsticks, joined at one end, which she used to lift the wax matrix from Phyllis's hand. She then repeated the procedure with Zeno's.

'My, my,' she clucked, as she placed the imprints together and lifted them to the flame.

After a time she moved the candle so that Zeno and Phyllis could see the doubled outline for themselves. Neither of them knew what to look for, yet could not miss the fact that the lines of both impressions appeared to complement and complete each other; the map of their destinies could be read as one.

'Please take each other's ghost palm and roll it into a ball while I talk to you.'

She poured more liquid from the teapot into their cups. Phyllis did not know what it was, but it smelled of lavender and was pre-sweetened with honey. Zeno later told her it was a herb called Echinacea mixed with lavender flowers. As Phyllis rubbed Zeno's wax, it slipped between her hands and fell on to the table. The dukkerina picked it up and returned it to her. While Zeno moulded Phyllis's imprint into a ball, it crackled as though giving off sparks. Both listened as the old lady began to explain.

'This is a fine, strange thing we have here, very . . .' She paused, trying to find the right word in a language which she probably didn't speak too well. '. . . rare – of the first water.' She moved her glance to Phyllis. 'Have you heard of the twin soul, docha?' she asked, peering into Phyllis's eyes, which were inky in the candlelight. Phyllis immediately turned to Zeno. 'I did not ask him,' the dukkerina continued.

The theme of Isolde's 'Love Death' floated into Phyllis's head, but it did not occur to her that the music was a response to the question.

'As I say, this event is rare – two souls sharing a ray of spirit. Been together for a lifetime, perhaps more. Maybe brother and sister, or man and wife, maybe lifetimes of not meeting, only looking, lonely for each other. Of this I can't speak, not mine to know. If you can understand how difficult for soul to find its way through the spheres to even get body, you understand a little the chance of a spirit divided to come together. Million, millions to

140

one. This night,' she jabbed down, jolting the table with a rigid finger, 'this very night is special – special for you, because tomorrow . . .' She flashed a ringed hand in front of her as though rubbing away the word. 'No, I will not talk of tomorrow, because this night you can do something for each other, make tomorrow different.' She paused, looking again into Phyllis's eyes. 'Look, listen to me. You have old knowledge of each other. Not strangers. You can . . . complete each other. I make sense to you? Must be tonight. If not, opportunity lost, not happen again, maybe. Sure.' She stopped speaking and blew out the candle.

Zeno spoke. 'Grandma, could you point a way for us, we've only just . . .'

'No.' The word cracked the ambience. Manushie opened an eye.

'You connected deep. Not for stranger like me to point way for you. Go now.'

Zeno pulled out the wad of notes he always carried, a habit from his antique-dealing days, and pushed two twenties across the table. Grandma took them.

'The honour is dukkerina's. But it's bad luck for Romany to refuse money offered.'

Zeno smiled, and leaned over to shake the elder's callused hand. She grasped his and rubbed it between hers.

'Put ghost palms back into the pot, please. If not, and someone take them, whoever it is will own your soul.'

'Is that true?' asked Phyllis, quickly dropping the ball into the pot.

'I don't know, docha,' said the old woman, giving Phyllis a kiss for the road, 'but made you do it, didn't it?'

Away from the smoky atmosphere of the encampment, life went on as usual. Back on the main road, a bus stopped at the lights. It had a cream roof, and the word 'General' stencilled on the side. It was freshly painted, without advertising, and empty save for a smiling conductor on the running board. On impulse, Zeno said, 'Let's grab this.'

141

They jumped on. First they sat opposite each other on the bench seats, and listened to the cheery conductor.

'All aboard? Good. Fares, please. Sorry, no HP. But American Express and Visa cards accepted,' cooed Mr Woo.

When they no longer had the bus to themselves, Phyllis took Zeno's arm and led him to the left-hand front seat.

'Now just you tell me, Zeno Studd – or whatever your name is – what made you say this was my first time in a girl's body?'

Zeno hunched his shoulders and scrunched her further into the seat.

'Blimey – the way you wielded that cut-throat, it didn't take much working out.'

At Stanley Crescent, the candles had burned out and the garden lights had been switched on, but the guests and hostess had moved inside. Two bottles of champagne were empty, along with the decanter that had hosted the distinguished cognac. The robust Sauterne in the freezer had been overlooked, and lived to please another day. Some port was open and everyone was merry – or drunk, depending on how sober you were. Only the Rose was sober. He would have judged Miranda, Nick and Toby to be merry, Flick and the hostess to be drunk. During the cracking of the port, they had unsealed the envelope giving the prize that Nick had obviously meant to win (his time of twelve hours, forty-five minutes had been edged out by the Rose's eleven hours, twenty minutes). The prize read 'The winner has the honour of deciding the next game, which will be obligatory'.

It was the right moment for a real zinger and everyone waited while the Rose decided. The Captain sloshed some port into his brandy glass.

The Rose paced the length of the drawing room, paused between the open glass doors, and with the moonlit garden framing him, announced: 'My game is entitled "Statues".'

'Not a good omen,' said Miranda.

'I won the privilege, did I not?'

'Tell us about the game,' encouraged the hostess. The surgeon placed his hands in his pockets and unveiled the discipline. At any one moment during the evening, he would shout 'Stop'. On this command, everyone else would freeze, holding the exact position they were in when they heard the order. As they might not all be in the same place when the game began, everyone would be on their honour to come back into the sitting room if their posture faltered.

'Honour!' trumpeted Nicholas.

'I'll trust you,' the Rose said. 'You look like a man of your word.'

'What's the prize?' Fleur wanted to know. She was obviously goal-oriented.

'The winner or winners . . .' The Rose paused to give the moment a little relish.

'. . . will choose their own prize,' interjected Miranda.

'As I was about to say . . . will choose their own prize,' said the Rose.

'Oooh,' chortled Fleur, giving the Captain a once-over. Miranda caught Nick's eye and winked.

'When does it start?' asked Flick.

'The second I give the command. Oh, yes . . . the eyes should stay fixed as well; you remain looking at whatever . . .'

'But what do we do now?' Flick wanted to know.

'Whatever you like, I guess,' said the Rose, breaking his headmasterly stance and coming into the room again. 'Nobody said the evening had to be non-stop entertainment. That right, Fleur?'

Fleur smiled her accord. And Miranda, who was feeling the heat, said: 'How would a swim grab you, Flick?'

Flick, who had been wanting to unveil his tattoo since his first cognac hit the residue of the Valium, yelled his assent, and Fleur, who had just the tonga in mind to compliment her new figure, led the way. Miranda didn't have as much inhibition and, having

143

unpeeled her little black dress, was the first in. Flick followed suit in his navy jockeys, which looked colour-coordinated with his considerable inking. Nick remarked, 'The fellow's turning himself into a Ming vase.'

It was almost true. The upper half of Flick's torso was a tapestry which encompassed his chest shoulder to shoulder. Areas that were not completely finished were indicated in spidery turquoise guidelines. In the past twelve months, Flick must have attended the tattoo parlour as frequently as the renowned tattooist's cleaning lady.

'Did Bone ink you?' asked Captain Toby when he saw Flick stripped.

'He didn't do this first bit.' Flick indicated his left bicep. 'Heard about him after I'd started. Here, then – how'd you guess?' he added as an afterthought.

The Captain just grinned. He wasn't up for a swim, being more interested in constructing a stovy from the remains of his after-dinner cigar and a lethal looking cube of hash compound he had produced. Nick was also viewing the proceedings from the sidelines. He had watched Fleur emerge from the little changing area in her yellow tonga – a butterfly, as her maid called it – and thought it a tactical error on her part. When the Rose slumped down in the canvas chair alongside him, Nick voiced his opinion.

'If she wants to snare that guy, she should have let him see what he'll be getting.'

'I don't know – "what's half revealed is twice as tempting", isn't it? What do you make of him, anyway?'

'Cumbrous. What about you?'

'He's a bit off, don't you think?' asked the Rose, with a nod towards the Captain, who had completed his patchwork of cigarette papers and was looking around for a light.

'I did push him on the captain bit. Seems it's a Boys' Brigade rank.'

'My God – do you think he's one of those diary people?'

'Professional gossipmongers? Why? We're of no interest.'

'Wasn't that Zeno chap a pop star?'

'For about twenty minutes. Dead as a dodo nowadays.'

'I'm surprised you and your wife haven't become an item.'

'Most of the time you have to want to be featured. I know folks who actually cultivate them, invite them to functions, that sort of thing.'

'Never thought about it like that.'

'What intrigues me is the columnists themselves. What a way to spend your life, eh? Trying to look up other people's arses. I mean, I'm not averse to looking up a great arse myself, but not for clinkers.'

'I suppose they regard what they're doing as transitory – hoping to become editors, own their own paper.'

Nick slipped out of his shoes and silk socks, and paddled his feet one at a time. He watched his wife and Fleur fooling around at the shallow end. They had caught the tattooed wonder's eye, and even the stoic Captain was showing interest now that his spliff was fired up.

'I don't live my life as a rehearsal,' Nick said finally. 'Some people do, and that's their privilege – good luck to them. But all I know is, I'm here once and that's now. I think it's too precious to spend pissing down my own leg. Can I get you a glass of Badoit, pilgrim? I need one myself.'

'Aren't you worried about keeping an eye on that exquisite creature of yours?'

'I was leaving that to you, squire,' said Nick with a wink.

They had left Mr Woo's bus at the bottom of Regent Street and taken the short cut through Man in the Moon Passage, past the secret bottle banks to Vine Street. Opposite the police station a builder's skip had been parked, a solid five-foot-high affair, with its contents accounting for another eighteen inches. Some local gentry must have used the occasion to dump the contents of an old wardrobe or two – as they passed by it they could hear whoops of excitement coming from inside its metal walls. Zeno drew Phyllis across to the far side of the road and they watched the show from the steps of the station. Two bag-ladies, up to their waists in rubble, could be seen pulling on and off old clothes and parading for each other with more flair than models on a catwalk.

As they crossed Piccadilly, the ornate clock on the front of the building struck ten-thirty, and Mr Fortnum and Mr Mason made a brief appearance. The street was enjoying a moment of quiet, which was fortunate for the driver of the Jaguar who came joyriding up Jermyn Street against the advice of a one-way sign, and powerslid around the corner into Duke Street St James as Phyllis and Zeno were about to enter the Soda Fountain. The car's headlights flashed on to the glass of the doors, momentarily transforming them into a mirror. In the reflection, Phyllis thought she saw a dark exotic woman and a flaming-haired youth. The brakes of the Jaguar squealed, and the car slid on to the pavement, narrowly avoiding a Ranger Rover that had filtered right from Piccadilly. As the Rover passed, Zeno, seeing the driver's white face and Toad of Toad Hall eyes, said, 'She looks like she needs a coffee more than we do.'

'If her roots weren't grey this morning, they'll need a touch-up tomorrow,' Phyllis added. She opened the outer door of the Fountain and stood aside for Zeno to enter, as a young woman dressed completely in orange exited backwards between them. She passed, waving as she went. Inside, a man with long hair and a beard, in a similar orange outfit, was returning the goodbye by holding his hand in front of his heart and blowing on it as if to cool his passion.

The Fountain wasn't empty but the few customers there sat around the perimeter of the place, as though lacking the confidence to take a table in the middle of the room.

Phyllis did not lack such confidence. She strode in and sat down at a table on which a plump, pretty waitress had just laid a fresh pink tablecloth.

'What can I get you, miss?'

'Cappuccino, please.'

'And you, sir?'

'Do you have herbal teas?'

'I'm afraid we don't, sir.'

'Okay. A pot of Lapsang and plenty of hot water.'

Zeno looked around the room. There was nobody sitting at the bar, but behind it stood three waitresses elbow to elbow, like back-up singers at a concert. Phyllis slipped off her jacket, revealing arms and shoulders to touch a strong man's heart. She leaned back in her chair and looked at the bearded lover.

'Why's he wearing all orange?' she asked.

'He's a disciple – obeying his guru's instructions.'

'Why such a bright colour?'

'It's the colour the monks of old wore in the East. It was thought to help them imbibe the energy of the rising sun. As if it were that easy . . .' The waitress brought their order on a tray. Phyllis drank and Zeno poured.

'If what were that easy?'

'If consciousness could be expanded by growing hair or wearing robes. People have been trying all that tomfoolery for ever.'

'Are you okay?'

'Sure am.' Phyllis looked across the room. A Moslem couple sat alongside each other. She was in total purdah, with a grille for a face. He had a turban tied neatly over one eye. He lifted his head to eat, and she pulled her visor aside to pop in the straw of her milkshake. Two nuns sat facing one another like blackbirds, one obscured by a Knickerbocker Glory, the other hunched forward over a large Scotch with ice.

Nobody noticed Phyllis's stares, save for a gent sitting at the far corner table, which had a 'Reserved' sign on it. He was late middle-aged, and also wore a rather quaint outfit. It reminded Phyllis of a costume in a production of *Don Giovanni* that she had seen at Covent Garden with Imo Sage. The man was smoking a cheroot. He smiled at Phyllis when she looked at him.

'Are you okay?' Zeno asked.

'Fine. Do you want to let your wife know where you are?' Zeno gave her a questioning look, so she added, 'These ears don't miss much.'

Zeno grinned. 'I'll give her a buzz now.' As he made his way to the public telephone, he passed their waitress, who was quietly singing 'You May Not Be An Angel' to herself. She sang in tune. Zeno picked up the receiver of the telephone in the lobby above the powder rooms, dialled, and found that he had dialled a crossed line. One voice said, 'So she wants to be a pop singer, does she?' The other answered, 'Yes, but she hasn't the backing.'

'You could advertise in the *Melody Maker*,' Zeno said helpfully.

There was silence. Then one of the voices said, 'Hang up, you nosy bastard.'

Zeno did as he was told. He redialled and heard his own voice on the answering machine. He left a message to say he was checking in. When he returned to the table, Phyllis was chatting to the waitress. When she saw Zeno, she made a move to leave, but Phyllis introduced her. 'This is Jackie, Zeno.'

'Hello. That's a lovely face you've got there.' Jackie smiled and looked to Phyllis, who smiled back.

'I suppose lots of guys tell you that?'

'You're not the first, sir.'

'She has a lovely voice, too,' Zeno said to Phyllis.

'Have you?' Phyllis asked.

'Well, they say the Irish like to sing.'

'Come on, then, let's have a song,' said Zeno.

'Now, sir?'

'Come on. You're among friends. The Super's gone. What do you know?'

'Oh, mostly songs from the shows.'

'Give us something from *West Side Story*, then.' Clasping her hands in front of her, and emboldened by the harmony around Zeno and Phyllis, Jackie started to sing. Shyly and softly at first, she grew in confidence as the room turned and listened to her. The trio in black behind the counter moved closer together and swayed in harmony. As Zeno listened, he watched Phyllis. She flushed and closed her eyes. Customers began arriving for after-theatre suppers, and waited, stilled, at the entrance.

Jackie ended wonderfully. Phyllis and Zeno clapped, and everyone joined in. The waitress was blushing, but loving the response and attention. The reserved man continued clapping when everyone else stopped, but no one noticed. Phyllis said, 'That was thrilling and . . . Brava!'

'What's your other name, Jackie?'

'Kelly, sir – Jackie Kelly.'

'Thank you, Jackie Kelly. It is always a special moment when one hears a new voice.' He turned to Phyllis. 'Isn't it?'

'Yes,' said Phyllis, suddenly preoccupied with her coffee cup.

'And wonderful to use it – eh, Jackie?'

'Yes, sir.'

'Not so much of the "sir" – Zeno and Phyllis will do fine.'

'Happy to meet you both,' she said with a bob, and went off to seat the newcomers.

'How did you know she could sing?' asked Phyllis.

'Oh, you can tell.' The tables around them were starting to fill up. A couple were shown to the table in the corner – the reserved man was gone. Phyllis saw his cheroot still smoking in the ashtray, but the waitress didn't appear to notice it.

'Do you think I could have another cup of coffee, Zeno?'

'You can have anything you like, if you keep saying my name like that – I'm a sucker for a beautiful voice.' He caught Jackie's eye and mimed 'one more' for Phyllis. 'You know what I mean?'

'I do.' Jackie zoomed up with the coffee, which she had made herself an extra helping of Akbar. Phyllis drank some.

'It's good coffee,' she said with a foam moustache to prove it.

There followed a long moment, and when it became clear Zeno wasn't about to speak, she said, 'Two souls sharing a ray.'

Zeno poured himself half a cup of tea. He finally voiced his thoughts. 'My feeling is that we shouldn't fret about it. It's true we've only met a few hours ago. Yet the feeling I have that I've known you for ever is also true. Reincarnation can't be proven. I choose to believe it because it makes sense to me. Makes more sense to me. There is no reason to worry unnecessarily, because whatever has been working to bring us together will show us what to do, if anything – don't you think?'

Phyllis studied the face opposite her. The eyes looked greyer in this light, and she could see that there was something sad, unfinished about them, even framed by the dark lashes and laughter lines of a lifetime. She wondered if the sadness was self-imposed.

'It's hard to apply any rationale to it at all. You're married – in a situation. I'm in a relationship. What I'm saying is, the implications don't fit well with how I feel right now. If I could somehow just appreciate . . .'

Zeno poured another cup that passed for tea. 'Why not do that, then? We'll simply behave like we met at a dinner party we didn't like, and left so that we could get to know each other better.'

'Can we do that?'

'We can try.'

'Okay – you first.'

'Come on, I've been nowhere, done nothing. I'm sure you've been everywhere.'

'You've never been anywhere?' Phyllis asked with a laugh.

Zeno finally spoke. He said self-consciously: 'Flying – I have this fear of flying. Heights, actually. Only left the island once – went to India.'

'You've only been away once, and that was to India?'

Zeno nodded. 'Yup.'

'You're kidding?'

'I'm not.'

'Tell me about that, then.'

'My trip east? Well, wow! First you have to know about the task I set myself, which was and is to discover the meanings of some philosophical puzzles posed by my namesake – which as I've said was a mistake. My name, I mean – me mum wanting a girl.'

'You don't say!'

'You see, I hadn't had much of an education. I sort of understood stuff – carpets, antiques and such – and then I went on the road with the rock show. I used to be a pop singer.'

'You went on the road singing? For a living?'

'Well, I wouldn't go so far as to call it "singing", but I did tour theatres, cinemas. Bought and sold. In my own time made a lot of bread, took care of business.'

'Sort of a didicoy?'

'Precisely. I married, and when the honeymoon was over we found that we weren't that suited. I started this, er, refinement project, trying to refine my mind.' Phyllis nodded, seeing for a moment the earnest young Zeno in the face in front of her. 'I never did unravel the puzzles, but I did realise that there was a definite similarity to what most of the great thinkers had laid down. The big stumbling block was always the translations. For example, the Naz – Jesus – was always saying, "I am the way." And you know what? In Aramaic, the verb "to be" doesn't exist. What I needed was a heavy I could talk to, someone alive to explain things to me.'

'Did you find anyone?'

'I fell upon a book – or rather a book fell on me. I was in one of the weird shops on Museum Street, and this book fell to the floor as I passed. Well, the words that were looking up at me – I think it was a translation of a Chinese poem – said, "Who will prefer the jingle of jade pendants if he once has heard the stone growing in a cliff?" '

'What does that mean? Did you understand it?'

'Not really, but as I went to replace the book I saw this face

151

staring at me from the cover of another book. You know how things suddenly become clear and stand out from the background? And this was some face. So I read a few pages. It was only a small work – printed cheaply in India by the look – but I knew this was the man. My hands shook when I read the flysheet and realised he was alive and living in Bombay.'

'So you just went?'

'Not exactly. I first organised myself. Even my daughter was impressed. I went home, found the telephone number of the publisher, and rang them. It took hours, but I eventually made the connection. It turned out that the book was published by a bookshop, and the chap I spoke to said the Sage was still alive.'

'The Sage?'

'That's what he called him. Said he was alive and living in a suburb of Bombay. He couldn't put his hand on the address, but would locate it and send it to me. So courteous, Indians. I told him not to bother, just to get the address and I would come by the shop and pick it up. Do you know what he said?'

'Tell me.'

'Good idea, sahib – Indian posting isn't what it used to be.'

'You went alone?'

'Yes.'

'And the fear of flying?'

'I went from terrified to petrified, and vice versa. I had bought a special flower potion designed to ease trauma and acute distress. Rescue Remedy it's called. Three or four drops is supposed to do it. Must have downed half the bottle. Got me on the plane though. My missus thought I had lost my head – I suppose I had. My daughter kind of understood.'

'She sounds like good news.'

'She is.'

'So what finally made you overcome the fear?'

'I knew he was old – it said on the book cover that he was nearing ninety – and I had this feeling that if I didn't make the effort and face my terror quickly, I'd miss him – that he'd die on me.'

'I know the feeling.'

'This'll make you laugh. When I eventually arrived. India! I can't tell you what a culture shock it was.'

Zeno stopped speaking, his face reflecting his dilemma in trying to put his feelings into words. He finally gave up, but Phyllis thought that watching his face was like seeing a silent movie. He finally settled for, 'It was so different, so completely different. The plane landed about three in the morning. Anyway, I couldn't sleep – it was right out of season, as it happened, pre-monsoon. By seven it was like being in a pressure cooker. The bookstore was a five-minute walk from the hotel. You went through a Chinese restaurant to get to it. It was normally closed on Sundays, but the chap I had spoken to on the phone was in doing a bit of stocktaking. That's when I started feeling okay.' Zeno paused and fixed some more tea. 'Have you ever met anyone really fine? I'm not boring you, am I?'

'I have. No you're not,' Phyllis said, and she laid her hand over his, so he would know that she meant it. The palm of her hand touched the signet ring with the square stone on his little finger. It felt warm.

'The bookshop wallah made me repeat the name of the district. Taught me phonetically. Said nobody would take a foreigner there unless I pronounced it right. Cat district, you see – local hookers lived there. Gave me the street and name of the building.'

'You found it okay?'

'Sure, I found it. But nothing could have prepared me for what it was like. Open sewers running along the street, and directly opposite the building I was looking for was a public gents' restroom. I was pretty tense by the time I located the building, and when I saw this lavatory I thought I'd take a leak while I had the chance. Big mistake. If I say it wasn't clean, I mean it hadn't been cleaned for years. The toilets – you know, the pedestals – weren't

153

visible at all, just heaps of excrement behind open doors. And the urinals themselves were filled as well.'

'You mean with crap?'

'And what crap. Arse high – higher. Customers must have been jumping up to relieve themselves. I almost vomited from the smell. Couldn't have been out of there quicker if the place had been full of vipers. As I hit the street, I looked up to check the name of the building – I was sure I'd made a mistake. A person of quality couldn't be living here. But he was.'

Zeno paused. This was the first time he had ever spoken of his trip, and the images in his mind were undiluted. Yet it was hard to put them into words even now. 'This tenement I was facing when I bolted from the . . .' he smiled, 'convenience, was about three storeys high, with a central entrance for the apartments; not unlike the Trust buildings here, but smaller. The flat where he lived was on the ground floor, first door on the right. There were pairs of shoes and sandals outside the door, which was open. I knocked and went in. There were two main rooms, quite small, but with high ceilings. In the room to the right – the one that overlooks the public lavatory – an extra room had been built by constructing another floor half-way up. This was the Sage's quarters. It was reached by a ladder, which went to a trapdoor. More sandals had been scuffed off at the foot of the ladder. Without my saying a word, I was ushered up the ladder by a youngish woman, who turned out to be his daughter.

'As soon as my head passed the level of the opening, I found myself being stared at by the eyes that had so impressed me in Museum Street. The old eagle motioned me up. The irony was, he couldn't speak English.'

'After all that.'

'He only spoke Marathi. And apparently used a kind of street Marathi usually spoken by poor people – like Cockney, I suppose. There were always translators when he received people, guys who made my English feel inadequate, but the day I arrived being a

154

Sunday, he was there with his mates. Reading the Sunday papers actually. On the face of it, he seemed to understand my condition, and straight away motioned me to sit near him and close my eyes. I assumed he was reading my aura, but in fact he went back to reading his paper. Then one of his cronies turned up who spoke a bit of English and explained that Maharaj – that's what they called him – made himself available weekday mornings. If I could stay a day or two, I should come tomorrow.'

'Which, of course, you did.'

'I did.'

'What was he like? What did he sound like?'

'He looked fragile, but he wasn't – although he was well nearly ninety. He mostly wore white cotton – very thin, so it always looked rumpled. His voice could be absolutely imperious, but he was also very funny and, of course, his timing was magic.'

'Did he confirm any of the theories you had?'

'The early visits were spent stripping away any preconceptions I had. It was unnerving, to say the least, and I sometimes found it hard even to go see him every morning.'

'Why? I mean, you'd gone all that way . . .'

'A lot of the time I just wanted to come home. It's hard to explain. He would always have me ask a question – which sounds simple now, but faced with the authority of this fella . . . The first morning, for example, he wouldn't speak until I asked a question. So finally I told him that I was finding my life a bit complicated because I'd married young, and now I was interested in spiritual matters and she wasn't – she didn't understand. And he said, "Well, wake up and where is the family?" '

'What did that mean?'

'Exactly. And when I asked, he said, "Who is asking?" and I said, "Zeno Studd." He asked, "Who is he?" and I said, "Me." Then he asked, "Who is me?" When I couldn't answer, he said, "Go and find out." And that was just the first week. Now you see why it was hard to keep going back?'

'So why did you?'

'There was something about him. I've often thought about it. It was like . . . the perfume of his personality got to me. Because he was never unkind, and deep down I was certain that he was taking me somewhere. The second week, I finally confessed I didn't know who or what I was. He asked, "What were you before you were born?" "A glimmer in my father's eye," I replied. Which made him laugh.

'He had two translators who did alternate days – both were excellent. But the funny thing was, he always knew if they didn't translate precisely what he'd said. This time, when I made him laugh, he said something in Marathi and the translator – it was a Mr Sapre that morning – translated it as "Do you think you came from your father's penis?", and Maharaj immediately interrupted. Mr Sapre corrected himself and said, "Do you think you come from the thing your father urinates with?" "Not really," I replied. "Right then. Tell me what you were before you were born." That was the second week.' Phyllis pulled a face.

'What was going on inside you all this time?'

'I felt I was on to a good hiding to nothing, and just when I was ready to pack and split, he asked me how did I know I was at all, and I said I had a feeling when I woke up, and he said . . .'

'Who had a feeling?'

'You got it. And I screamed, "All right, there is a feeling of 'am'-ness when sleep ends," and he laughed and clapped his hands. "This is your capital," he said. "This is the money in the bank, this is what attention has to be paid to. It is the witnessing that is constant – everything else is subject to change." "You mean, that's all there is – this feeling of 'am'-ness?" I asked. "We can call it 'I am', now that we are clear that there is no such entity as 'I'. No, that is not all there is, but this feeling 'I am' is the cloth with which we clean the mirror, the point of the pen with which every book is written." That was our last meeting at his place.'

'You didn't see him again?'

'Once, the day before I left. I had heard he liked the Taj Mahal Hotel where I was staying, so I invited him for tea. He came wearing a red woollen cardigan, and it was so odd to see him stompin' up the stairs with his stick, and the other guests just passing him by like he was another old codger. He didn't behave any differently, naturally, but I was less inhibited – no other devotees. My home patch, so to speak. I asked him about himself – how he'd got started. He confessed he hadn't been promising material. A friend of his had taken him to meet his guru, and he'd been impressed by the man. The guru told him he wasn't what he imagined himself to be, and to hold on to the feeling "I am". Everything had happened naturally. He told me not to worry. He, Maharaj, had given me the push. I no longer needed him. The sadguru was inside, and it would draw me to itself. He told me just to hold on to the "I am" – not to let myself get bored. He said he would give me something to say to myself – a mantra, a remembrance. Mr Sapre had his tape recorder – Maharaj recited, Sapre translated and recorded.

'Mr Sapre offered to drive me to the airport, and I took him up on it. Sapre remembered my first query about my wife. He suggested that, until I reached the exalted state hinted at, I do my mantra and breathing exercises in private so that my wife would not feel intimidated, which often happened. On the other hand, he said, if you are doing something secret, mysterious, she may be attracted and want to become part of it. We shook hands on it.'

Jackie suddenly appeared beside Phyllis. She had the bill in her hand.

'I'm sorry to disturb you, Zeno,' she said, 'but we're closing the till.'

'Of course,' said Zeno, rustling up a tenner and handing it to her. 'You keep the change – okay?'

'It's not necessary, sir.'

'We've occupied your station all evening. And you've sung for us. If anything, it's too little.'

'It's true,' said Phyllis.

As they were leaving the restaurant, a man cycled by with a big sow strapped to the case rack, wriggling as she passed. Phyllis had another look to make sure, and looked at Zeno, who warbled, 'None of the guys go steady, cause it wouldn't be right, to leave your best girl home on a Saturday night.'

They strolled across St James's, with Phyllis not questioning Zeno's lead in spite of the fact that she had worked in the area for some time. He appeared to have an innate knowledge of the district. He turned right into Blue Ball Yard, and through a subsidiary door of the Stafford Hotel, which opened directly on to a cocktail lounge. He sat her at a vacant table. 'Won't be a minute – got to see a man about a dog.'

'I'm new to these isles, remember.'

'It's something my dad used to say. In this case, it means I need to take a leak.'

He disappeared into the hotel. While Phyllis was looking in the direction Zeno had gone, a young woman came directly towards her. She had her hair in a bun and was wearing an amber necklace with large cut beads. She glanced distractedly in Phyllis's direction. She was lovely in an old-fashioned way, and Phyllis smiled. The woman paused, looked at her watch and went into the ladies' room. A civil-servant type in his mid-sixties was sitting at a table on the other side of the lounge. In his lap was a brown bowler hat. He clutched his bowler, got up, and walked over to Phyllis.

'Travellin' alone?' he asked. Phyllis looked him over.

'That depends,' she said.

He lifted his hat and allowed Phyllis to look inside. An unusual, lewd drawing was fastened to the wall of the bowler. Phyllis took a moment to decipher it. The civil servant grew in confidence. 'Well, my dear?'

'Give me a break.'

Zeno reappeared, and saw the man scuttling out the back exit. 'Everything okay?'

'Sure – just someone who watches too many movies.' She shrugged but her attention was drawn by the woman with the amber necklace, who was exiting the ladies' room, and who appeared to have aged forty years.

'Did you slag him off?'

'Who?'

'Colonel Blimp.'

'Oh – sure.'

'I wish I could. I'm such a softie – wind up in the most embarrassing situations sometimes.'

She took his arm, and they started to walk through the hotel. 'I always figured it was easier for guys.'

'Well . . . when it's difficult, it's more difficult – if you get my drift.'

A duvet-soft blonde was leaning on the reception desk, chatting to the night man, her pampered bottom prominently displayed. Phyllis noticed Zeno staring. And then Zeno noticed Phyllis watching him. They both giggled, and the doorman opened the front door for them. 'Good night, sir. Good night, madam.'

'They have a great restaurant in there,' said Zeno as they headed towards the passageway that connects the boundaries of St James's with Green Park. As they emerged from the covered lit section to the open dark half, Phyllis saw a pair of tawny eyes watching them, and nudged Zeno. They slowly continued walking. In the clearing, at the end of the passage, an urban fox waited. Zeno stopped a yard or two from her. Satisfied that they were only night creatures like herself, she turned and padded off into the darkness of the park.

There was a paling missing in the fence, and it left a gap through which the fox went. Zeno ducked through, and beckoned Phyllis to follow. The air in the park smelled of cut grass. A flock of geese flying overhead honked unseen as they passed, their wings cutting the air.

'My kid's mad about ducks and geese. We can't get her to eat chicken eggs. She says she'd prefer to be like a duck than a chicken. The other day I asked her why duck eggs were blue. Do you know what she said?'

Phyllis smiled, her teeth luminous in the moonlight. 'Tell me.'

'Because ducks were sad – sad they weren't people.' He paused. 'This generation of kids are really amazing. But I suppose all parents say that.'

'What's she called, your daughter?'

'Zen.'

'Really.'

Zeno smiled self-consciously. 'We've told her we won't be uptight if she wants to be called something else, but there's an Amber and a Tao in her year – to say nothing of her friends Karma and Alleluiah. She's already got ideas about forming a group.'

'Called "The Love Junkies", no doubt.'

'I wouldn't put it past her.'

'You must love her.'

'Closer to her than Prudence most of the time . . .'

'Your wife? Why's that?'

'Oh . . . you know.'

'We're not going to have our first row, are we, Zeno?'

'God I hope not. Why?'

'Well, you were about to say that your daughter is more of a friend to you than your wife, and you didn't trust me enough, so you stopped.'

Zeno reflected. 'That's true. I'm sorry.'

'I'll let it pass.'

Zeno put his hands deep into his pockets. Phyllis had noticed that the English are great ones for pockets.

'I fell for my wife, but we've never become chums.'

'You didn't make her your friend?'

'No. And it's a pity.'

'I've heard marriage is more about friendship than romance,' said Phyllis, slipping her arm through his again.

'I guess so.'

'What did he mean, your Mr Sage in Bombay, when he said "wake up"?'

They had moved under the big plane trees, and the atmosphere was warm and still. The only light came from moving traffic, filtering through the privet hedges of the Piccadilly boundary. If she looked straight ahead, she couldn't see him, she could only hear the sound of his voice.

'I think he meant "wake up from the dream".' Realising he was talking to himself, he added, 'I've thought about it a lot and it seems part of a view they have in the East that the world of appearances is maya or delusion. Putting together a lot of the things he talked about, I came to the conclusion that the consciousness which is mirrored in each of us by the feeling "I am" is all-inclusive, and that whenever we see ourselves or others independent of that reality, then it is unreal or a dream.'

'That's rather frightening,' Phyllis said after a long moment. 'Do you see the world like that, Zeno?'

'Not really. But I can understand it.'

They had reached the high ground of the park, when Zeno stopped and leaned back against one of the giant old trees. 'I experienced my first real carnal knowledge on this very spot,' he said.

'I dread to think.'

Zeno smiled. 'It was quite normal – well . . . if normal is a Catholic girl who'd do anything except lose her virginity before she was married.'

'What do you think is normal now, Zeno?'

Zeno put his hand to his head. 'Either that's the second time I've been asked that today, or I'm suffering from *déjà vu*.'

'Why? Who asked you?'

'Two boys I met in Hampstead – having their first mad fling. Feeling guilty for having so much fun, I suppose.'

'Did you know them?'

'No.'

Phyllis moved alongside and leaned back next to him. 'They asked you to tell them if they were normal?'

'You'd be surprised at some of the things people ask me.'

'I wouldn't. Are you going to tell me?'

'Are you really interested, or are you just trying to make me feel good?'

'Both.'

'That's all right, then. I gave them my theory of reincarnation – that souls reincarnate both as men and women. When they're in the body of a man, the female tendencies are held in abeyance, and vice versa. Usually the realised tendencies seek their buried characteristics in another for fulfilment – traditional matings. When a previous lifetime weighs heavily on someone, say a girl is still seeking to complete herself with a male, although she is now a boy in actuality, more ambivalent relationships happen.'

As Zeno started his rap, Phyllis felt a certain weariness descend on him. She realised that very few people ever listened to Zeno Studd and the theories he had spent his adult life gleaning from dusty books in libraries and museums. She was listening, however, and his words created a sensation that her mind – which for years had resembled an abused filing cabinet – was having its contents magically put in order. By the time he reached his pet part, Phyllis's attention was having a symbiotic effect on Zeno, and when he paused for breath, Phyllis asked: 'Did you really tell them that?'

His face was shining, and that part of him which would always be a boy was near the surface. 'Well, something like that. I'd had a poppy-seed slice with sugar, so I was speeding a bit.'

'They must have loved it.'

'The converts? I couldn't tell. They held hands a lot.'

'And you? Do you believe that's how it is?'

'Of course. This – what's happening now – is only the coarse beginning. It's still identifying with the body. It really doesn't have to do with what undies you wear. It has to do with our Original Face, or what we were before we were pulled into our mother's womb.'

Phyllis reached out to touch the side of Zeno's face. In the second before her hand made contact, she had a hallucination of an unusual birthmark and a turquoise earring. Zeno stroked the hand that touched him. 'The carpet of the mind,' he said.

'Hmmm?'

'The skin – are you like that all over?'

'What if I were?'

'Your brain is in your head, but your mind is all over. When breath becomes its vehicle, instead of the body . . .'

She whipped around to face him, her eyes searching his. 'Who told you that?' she asked. The nearness of her made him desperate to kiss her, but something held his desire in check – his need was at odds with hers. It felt inappropriate. 'Zeno?' The voice touched him. She was close to him. 'Zeno – why did you say that?'

'Popped into my head, only my way of telling you how fine you are. I didn't mean to unsettle you.' She was still looking directly into his eyes, but the stare had softened – whatever had caused her concern had passed.

'You're good news, Mr Studd.'

'I'm not, really, but sometimes when I'm not in the way, it feels good.'

Phyllis rested her head against his neck and he held her tightly to him. Then something caught his eye – a figure moving un-obtrusively in the shadows beneath the trees. As his eyes became accustomed to the near dark, he saw a second figure, then another; a whole series of watchers spaced at intervals encircled them. They were all men, save for one woman in a ballgown. Zeno straightened his legs, drawing them closer to the tree, and Phyllis's head slid on to his chest. He could feel her breath through the cotton of his tee-shirt. Zeno, hardly ever averse to an audience, felt he ought to tell his friend. 'We have attracted a fairy circle.' There was a murmur from Phyllis, who was preoccupied with being held so closely by a man. 'We have company, love. Thought you should know.'

Phyllis, reluctant to move, said, 'What is it?'

'Voyeurs Anonymous, I should think.' Phyllis looked around. 'Shall we split, or put on a show?'

'Ugh.'

'They're only doing their thing.' Phyllis began dragging him towards the streetlights.

'You're such a freak. I hope you know some more holes in the fence.'

THE NIGHT

THE ROSE HAD chosen his moment rather well. Fleur was in the first-floor bathroom freshening up her make-up, with Flick leaning against the door jamb, still in his damp Y-fronts, explaining his tattoo. Miranda had been caught pulling a tortoise-shell comb through her hair in the main room. He didn't think she'd last the course, even though she badly wanted to, as the hand holding the yellow comb was already quite white. Nick was near by, reaching for the port like a runner before the off. And he had just come upon the Captain, crouched as though genuflecting, near the front door. As he was checking the steadiness of his gaze, there was a hell of a bang closely followed by another on the thick mahogany front door.

Thinking it might be Zeno with Phyllis, he hastily opened it and was pushed aside by an elderly man who scampered in, carrying a large flat bundle. Whether propelled by knowledge or instinct he made for the drawing room. By the time the Rose had shut the front door and joined him, he had kicked one of Fleur's Mies van der Rohe chairs into position under one of her English Romantic paintings and, banging on about what a load of tripe it was, had taken it off the wall. Miranda, in whose line of vision the intruder happened to be, remained a statue. And as she appeared to be the only one paying him rapt attention, he directed himself at her. Unzipping his artist's case, he drew out a stretched but unframed painting roughly the size of the Romantic – which was now leaning against the back of the chair – and hung it on the hook.

'Now, that's a picture,' he said with a flourish. 'What d'you think that's worth, eh?'

Nick kept his heels firmly planted and, as though moving into a different stretch, slowly swivelled his head to take in the scene. What he saw was an old man in an equally old corduroy suit standing on a chair, declaiming like Polonius, his extended right arm drawing his audience's attention to a wallpaper-type drawing the likes of which suffocate park railings the world over on Sunday mornings. The Rose was standing near by as though someone had slid an umbrella down the back of his suit. Then Miranda giggled and lowered her comb, placing both hands primly in her lap.

'Five hundred,' shouted the old boy. On getting no reply, he added, 'It's worth double,' even louder.

They were soon joined by Captain Toby. As the uninvited guest's voice rose to a howl, he began dragging more stretched wallpaper from his bag. Flick and Fleur, believing the game abandoned, arrived together. The artist focused his sell on the newcomers. Seeing Flick, he asked, 'Why's he got no clothes on?' A prude, thought Miranda.

'Who's he?' asked Flick.

'Just a bum,' said Nick.

'Bum?' echoed the stranger. 'I'll have you know I'm an artist of repute. Now which of you toffs will give me a carpet for this 'ere work?'

'A carpet?' queried Fleur.

'He means three hundred quid. Don't you, sport?' said the Captain.

'Let's throw him out,' said Nick. 'He smells.'

But Miranda, ceasing to be a mermaid, closed in.

'Listen, you. I'll give you three hundred if you drop your pants.'

'What!' The newcomer's bearded chin fell.

'That right. Now. Right now. The offer is open for three minutes.'

The intruder was gobsmacked, pale now beneath his single malt tan.

'Two minutes to go,' prompted Miranda. The man looked about him. 'Show him the money,' said Miranda, turning to Nick, who pulled a wad of fifties from his back pocket. With his eyes stuck on the roll, the man loosened his belt and let drop his ancient cords, revealing a long-tailed shirt and a very curious pair of underpants. Miranda closed in to inspect them.

'They look like demob issue,' piped up the Captain.

'Let's have them off, then,' said Miranda.

The Rose, who was quite close, could see that her eyes flickered with excitement. She moved closer. Her prey stood motionless on the chair, trousers bagged around his ankles. She tugged at the frayed elastic of his shorts.

'You said trousers,' he said.

'Off!' Miranda commanded, sensing victory. 'No show, no dough. Come on, lad, let's see your lunch box.'

'Off, off,' joined Fleur. And the Rose was surprised when the Buddhist Flick took it up too.

'Off, off,' bounced around the room. The Captain stepped forward.

'Come on, pops,' he said. 'Let's get you out of here.'

The old man hitched up his trousers, and the Captain helped him down from the chair. He saw him to the door, pressing a tenner in his pocket as he left.

Nicholas had spotted the Rose's despondency as he watched the happening. He chose this moment to test the surgeon's resolve. Gliding over and taking his arm just above the elbow, he steered him firmly but gently, as though escorting a jittery woman across a busy street, to a pair of chairs close to the garden doors. They faced each other across a coffee table, on which was placed a golden box of chocolates. Nick knew that recovering addicts almost always transfer their craving to sugar in one form or another. He'd noticed that even health-freak nancy-boy Studd sank a few before dinner. 'Don't you think it's fascinating – this gathering tonight?' asked Nick, sitting down and helping himself to a chocolate.

'I suppose so. Anyone in particular?'

'We're all such freaks, aren't we?'

'Are we?'

'All deviants in one way or another. Mmm, these are good. Elenas – definitely the best in the world,' he said, extracting the last of the dark chocolates, leaving only the top layer of fresh white cocoa-butter creams within the other's reach.

'You think that's why the other two cut out?'

'Maybe. Maybe it was a bit too close to home – didn't want to brave an encounter, even by reflection.'

'You think Flick is strange? He seems rather innocent to me.'

'Well, it's relative. He's a walking carnival act for a start. Give him another year or so and he'll be inked all over and shooting steroids to look like Conan.'

'And me?'

'A guy who likes to be called the Rose and cuts up chicks for a living?'

'They come to me.'

'Sure, because they've been brainwashed into believing they're imperfect – physically unworthy of love. The media loves you cut-and-tuck guys. A sober plastic surgeon who is too scared to fuck one, but redesigns them anyway.'

'And you, Nicholas – a man of intelligence who's dedicated his life to the pursuit of eleven hours seventeen minutes of pure pleasure?'

'Not so pure,' added Nick with a grin. Taking the loss of equilibrium in the surgeon's voice as a sign of interest, he started to talk a little about himself. He helped himself to another white chocolate. 'Do have one of these – they're absolutely mouth-watering.'

'They look it. Not too good for me at the moment, I'm afraid.

Mood-altering substance, chocolate – triggers the endorphin gland.'

'God forbid we should alter our mood. Anyway, never thought I'd marry. It's so obviously a put-up job. It's nowhere to be found in the book of nature, which is the only book I pay any attention to.'

'Some animals and birds mate for ever.'

'But no gold rings.'

'Why, then?' asked the Rose, shifting his position to see past Nick. But the room was empty.

'When I first introduced Miranda to my style, we snagged this newly-wed from his wife – he couldn't resist Miranda – and the pillock went and confessed to his good bride. The next thing I know, she's on the blower to me having a go at Miranda, who is listening on the extension. "She's incorrigible, your wife, in-corrigible," she ranted. When I got her off the phone, Miranda was already looking up "incorrigible" in the dictionary. She's worse than me, I thought.'

'Does it work?'

'It's an experiment in eroticism with all the ingredients of a successful marriage – trust, affection, appeasement of loneliness – with sex as the glue. Lots of glue. It's a universal law: when the shagging stops – which it always does after a few years – the marriage founders because the erotic isn't appeased. It's racing around looking for unfamiliar pussy or young stiff cock. But that's the conspiracy. No one ever talks about it. No, Rosy, old boy, Miranda and me are into superglue. Our orgasm doesn't feel like taking a piss. We sleep well, and we're saving the testosterone for our old age.'

'When I'm sure it will work beautifully.'

'Does now, if you're sensible.'

'There are instances of prostate cancer, I believe.'

'I'll worry about that when it comes.'

'When did this odyssey of yours start?'

'Always knew. My mother, bless her heart, told me I had erections whenever she breast-fed me.'

'Taken off the breast early, were you?'

'On the contrary – supped till my milk teeth came through. And, of course, there was the member itself.'

'Unusually large?'

'Not quite Pasolini's dream of bliss, but sufficient to deal with both directions of traffic without trouble. "It's not the size of the ship, but the motion of the ocean," as they say in the Indies. No, the texture was the clue. And this I didn't realise until I saw other boys. And then I assumed I was unique, which I believed until I scored this negro weightlifter, who couldn't wait to do the business. When I was getting dressed, he was still out for the count – I noticed his genitals were white.'

'Don't tell me yours are black?'

'Not exactly, but look.' He rolled up the sleeve of his dark silk shirt.

'Feel how delicate my skin is – like a sixth-former's, isn't it?' The Rose brushed the inside of Nick's forearm with the back of his hand. 'My prick is as dark and rumpled as the sack my balls hang in. And I came into the world with enough acid in my system for twins – which left my tongue as rough as a cat's. Now, I was never what you would call a great beauty, but my destiny was clear. I know a good thing when I see one, and I was it. Naturally amoral, all I had to learn was to become ruthless.'

'Which wasn't hard, comparatively speaking?'

'Comparatively speaking, no.'

'So besides the twelve hours and whatever it was . . .'

'The average was low – probably because of your minimal input. My total will be considerably higher. It was only a game to loosen the party a little.'

'So would you say you were approaching love of the untethered variety?'

'Give me that in plain English, Doc. I'm not a great one for poetry.'

'I wouldn't say that,' said Miranda. 'Some of your modes of expression are very poetic.' She sat on the floor next to her husband's chair and drew her knees up under her chin. With a nod to the Rose, she said, 'You were saying – is it Doctor or Mister?'

'It's Mister. Love without possession – usually impossible in a physical relationship.'

'Well, Mister Rose, love might be a bit simplistic without it,' said Miranda with a grin at Nick, who cupped her breast in his hand. 'Most men like to be given a good time and a bad time, alternately – a bit of each keeps them interested. That wouldn't work unless they were possessive.'

'No,' said the Rose. 'But you are speaking of desire. Possession isn't part of love – it's the thief of love.'

'And where has the exquisite bod been?' asked Nick, tiring of the subject.

'Giving chummy a tour of the house. Where's Fleur and the tattoo manual?'

'Showing him the sauna, I should think.' Nick looked at the Rose. 'Demonstration probably.' There was an awkward silence. It wasn't an angel passing. 'Pang of untethered love, Doc?' enquired Nick, moving off. The Rose helped himself to one of the white chocolates.

There is an arresting landmark in Piccadilly, riveted to the kerb on the south side, equidistant to the Athenaeum Hotel and the Hyde Park Corner roundabout. It stands about five feet high; sturdy planks supported by two iron legs – a bit high to vault over, too narrow to lie on. It was designed for milkmaids to rest their yokes on when milk was transported by hand; no doubt during the days when the lad Sainsbury, fresh from the country, was trying to acquire a shop of his own to qualify for the hand of his boss's daughter.

Minutes before Big Ben – visible in the distance – struck twelve, Zeno had hoisted himself on to the milkmaids' rest and was

171

contemplating the trees in the park they had just left. Phyllis was leaning against the wooden cross-section, looking at the empty MCA building on the opposite side of the road. One window was filled with a huge pair of lips. In the window to the left, an ear listened, and from the right an outsize eye blinked eerily at her. She pulled at Zeno's sleeve.

'Am I seeing things?'

Zeno looked. 'It's the work of a group of artists who shoot little films, and this is their way of exhibiting them. They cover the windows with tracing paper and project the movie on to a mirror which reflects into the window. The mirror doubles the distance that the images travel and reverses them, so we see them the right way round. Original showcase, isn't it?'

'You're so smart.' The show hadn't drawn the anticipated audience; the street was quiet – save for the Hard Rock faithfuls – and the contours of the valley that swept across it were visible.

Phyllis continued to watch the show, the hum of traffic in Park Lane supplying the soundtrack. Zeno rested his hand on the wood beside him, leaned towards her, and said softly in her ear, 'So you want to be a singer, huh?'

Phyllis didn't actually splutter, but her intake of breath was audible, and her hand was reaching into her side pocket for the cigarettes when Zeno clasped it.

'Sorry,' he said. 'Didn't mean to startle you.' Phyllis gave him her man-to-man look.

'You devil, how did you know that?'

'Oh, you know.' He slid alongside her, facing across the road. 'Feminine intuition.'

'I don't know . . . I don't . . .' She seemed close to tears, as though the revelation of her secret had torn at a part of her.

'Anyway,' said Zeno cheerfully, 'let's not change the subject. Want to sing, do we?'

Phyllis had composed herself. 'Hell, I am a singer. Trained. Studied with the best. Came to England for it.'

'So,' said Zeno. 'What's the problem?'

'I haven't performed publicly, that's all.'

'I see.'

'I doubt it.'

'Having our first row, are we?'

'Yes . . . no. We've only just met and you're digging into . . .'

'Lying to me now, I see. You remind me of a bloke I knew rather well. As a matter of fact, he made the same mistake. You see he always wanted to sing . . .' Phyllis opened her mouth, intending to stop Zeno from embarking on one of his marathon anecdotes, but apart from a delicious 'O', no sound came forth.

In distant Basil Street, the doors of the fire station peeled back. Men too young and strapping to be burned pulled on their protective clothing and struggled to find secure places on the engine as it slammed right along John Betjeman's favourite street. The driver's mate didn't hit the siren that awoke the slumberers in Trevor Square until they passed Harrods.

It was the muffled siren, along with the amorous quackophany from St James's Park, that set off the chain reaction that was to change Phyllis's life. Her hearing opened out to include the fire engine, the Chinese ducks, Big Ben's chimes, a shouted laugh from the sidecar of a passing motorbike, and continued expanding to include all the other extraneous noises, fusing them together until she became conscious of the always-present, seldom-heard drone that gave to the melody of life its line. Momentarily aware of the sound beneath the noise, she perceived the futility of fear, the affront to life of every 'No'. She heard a voice saying, 'Okay, pal, do it to me.'

The voice sounded astonishingly like her own. Zeno stuck a thumb and finger in his mouth and produced a whistle that was forever Wapping. On the grid of Down Street, a cab's diesel engine turned over, engaged gear, and swung towards the whistler and his friend.

'I know a place where we can do it. I think tonight's the night, don't you?' said Zeno, as the cab drew up.

'Let's get there fast,' Phyllis replied, relieved that she had not been asked to perform for the queue at the Hard Rock.

Once inside the taxi, Zeno slid open the glass panel dividing them from the driver to get a better look at the D.A. hairdo and velvet collar. 'What's your name, then, John?'

'Why – d'you wanna report my driving already?' the cabbie said, returning the once-over in his mirror. 'Ain't you that tea-leaf on the telly?'

'Used to be. How do you know that?'

'On the breakfast, ain't ya? My kid gets me up to watch it with 'im – which as I'm on nights is an unforgettable experience, you might say. Len's my name, mate – I'm Brixton's answer to Shakin' Stevens.'

'Pleased to meet you, Len. My name is Zeno, and this is a new diva I've discovered, the lovely Phyllis.'

Len had a quick look round at Phyllis. 'You can say that again,' he said. 'What's your pleasure?'

'There's a working men's club up Kensal Road way. No reason why you would know it, but they rent it out to a sort of travelling restaurant one night a week.'

'I do, mate – took a film producer up there last Friday. He was telling me all about it. Sort of raw-fish gaff – sounded horrible. Can you imagine?' asked Len as he negotiated Hyde Park Corner, which still had traffic. Zeno crooned a bit of Lennon's masterpiece and Len joined in.

The cab was motoring up Park Lane. Len flicked off the restrainer from his glass divide and announced, 'Just think – if he 'adn't taken off to the States, he would have been here now.'

'It's no good worrying about what ain't, Len,' said Zeno, and they sang the final verse of 'Imagine' for John.

Phyllis discovered her thumb was in her mouth. Feeling a bit silly, she jerked it out, but didn't join in the singing.

And then she noticed her other hand resting in her lap in a strange position.

Nick and Miranda were investigating Fleur's bedroom. Nick had located his hostess's collection of vibrators and was measuring one against his outstretched hand.

'No wonder she's so casual about guys.' He twisted the end of the plastic penis and grimaced at the battery-driven motor. 'That's what puts me off.'

'What?'

'The racket.'

'Perhaps she prefers the whining to the whingeing.'

Nick ignored the dig. 'Do you think the Rose is losing his trick to Fleur?' Nick said to Miranda, having found his hostess's bedside stash of Halcyon, and inspecting a lavender ellipse between his thumb and finger. 'I've heard about these – it's the designer downer they've banned. She must have stocked up. Do you think I could handle one now?'

'She's only winding Toby up. Following my advice.'

'That was altruistic of you.'

'Not really. I like it when everybody gets off.'

'You're easily pleased.'

'Which is what you like about me,' said Miranda, taking the pill from his hand. 'Although even I didn't realise the full definition of multiples until I came across you.'

' "Came" being the operative word. So what do you think about the little purple people-eater?' said Nick, reclaiming the pill.

'If you nod off on the job, I'll push ice-cubes up your bottom.'

'Promise?' said Nick. Their love play had taken all kinds of turns since the afternoon when she had inserted her necklace a pearl at a time into him as he made love to her. As he later reported to a chum, 'She whipped it out right in the throes – I didn't know if I'd pissed, come, shit or farted.'

'Go on, drop it if you feel like it. If it all starts slipping away, give me a nod and I'll scam another bottle of cognac from the cellar.'

'Do you know where it's stashed?'

'Of course. Gave the Captain the guided tour. I showed the Captain Fleur's collection of silver and gold plate, and his trouser-front lit up like Brighton's pier.'

'You're so smart.'

'I know, but am I sexy?'

'You have my word, as a scholar and a gentleman,' said Nick, placing the charmed pill on his tongue and then putting his hand on his heart. 'I hear the only side effect of this little bugger is a complete loss of short-term memory.'

'Which means you won't remember a thing from now on.'

'Probably.'

'Oh good. That means I can behave really badly.'

'I'll only swallow if you promise to tell me all in the morning.'

'If I said yes and you believed me, you'd swallow anything.'

Fleur came upon the Captain naked in the glass-roofed workout room at the top of the house. He was methodically testing the muscle-building machines, moving from one to another like a bumble bee in no particular hurry. Before she modestly faced away, she noted that his member fell into what she categorised as the 'bodkin' type – full at the base, narrowing towards the head.

'Don't spend everything on the machines,' she said coyly, clasping her hooded towel robe about her before turning back to appreciate the mass of hair that covered his body. Inspecting him more openly, she realised that he had shaved not only his chin but his neck as well, and the growth finished around his collar bone like a necklet.

She reached out to touch it and found it unexpectedly soft. He ignored her, reaching up to grasp a cross-bar above his head. He held the grip level with his groin until the veins and tendons cut through his shoulder and chest muscles. He didn't speak. Fleur lowered herself on to a low benchpress, letting the robe fall open around her legs. She stroked a perfectly waxed thigh.

'Shoes,' grunted the Captain. Fleur reached behind her and picked up a pair of black Chinese trainers with an alice band.

'Too flat,' said the Captain beneath lowered lids.

'I won't be a second – don't go away.' She skipped through the door. The Captain lowered the sectioned weights and regarded himself in the floor-to-ceiling mirror at the end of the room. He began stroking the hair on his stomach. He was thus occupied when Fleur teetered in on cherry-pink suede slingbacks. Toby took a few steps towards her and pulled the tie from her robe. Fleur raised her arms as if to embrace him, but he pushed her towards the upright machine he'd been working, and double-hitched her right ankle to the leg of the apparatus. Then he walked over to his trousers – slung over another appliance – and took from his pocket a pair of steel handcuffs. He grinned – part of the game – and cuffed her left hand above her head. Looking her over for a moment, he saw that her restrained hand was shaking. He pulled the pressing bench across the room and sat astride it in front of her.

'Let's see what you do.'

'Do?'

'When no one's around. Let's see.'

Fleur giggled, 'In the dark.'

'What?'

'In the dark, please.'

'No.'

'But I can't . . .'

'Don't like "can't". You're not doing it for you – you're doing it for me. No dark.'

Fleur nervously reached between her legs with her free hand. There wasn't any visible action. He watched Fleur's hand a moment and said, 'What d'you call that?'

Fleur flushed crimson and kept her head lowered. 'It's what I do. It's rather large. I don't want to distend it. Girls at school pulled theirs out of shape. I don't want to look like that. I can only do it gentle.'

'Large, eh? Let's have a butcher's.'

Fleur was so excited she didn't notice that Toby's shire accent had slipped completely. 'What?'

'Come on – show me the pink.'

The Captain got up, and Fleur, thinking penetration was imminent, opened her knees. He pinched the stiffened clitoris between his thumb and fingers. Fleur yelped with pain and reached out her free hand for him, but he angled his body away from her, still retaining his grasp.

'That's nice,' he said. 'But I can only get it up with slaggy old toms.'

'What's an old tom?' Fleur asked. It wasn't the right response, although if she had known, she would probably have agreed to being one. The Captain exerted more bruising pressure. Fleur whimpered. He released his hold on her and, by the time she opened her eyes, he was dressed and slipping his bare feet into his soft shoes. When she realised he was about to leave the room she said, 'Where are you going?'

'Me?' asked the Captain, buttoning his dark shirt to the neck and pocketing his club tie. 'As I said, I can only get it on with old slags. See you in a bit.'

Len's cab stopped at a red light in Edgware Road. Almost immediately, an old banger drew level. Len didn't pay any attention, accelerating on the green to get out of the night pattern of stop lights. He moved over into the left lane, anticipating the filter left on Sussex Gardens. The older car again pulled alongside, this time in the outside lane. When the light changed to green, both vehicles pulled away together. Just before the main crossroad, the older car pressed ahead, pulled over in front of the taxi and stopped. Len halted the taxi, and Zeno, anticipating a call for directions, slid down the window on his side. The driver of the other car threw open his door and jumped out. By the time he reached the cab he was abusing both Len and Zeno. As Zeno's window was open, he became the target.

'What d'you think you're doing, eh? Can't you see I've got kids in the back? Who d'you think you are, you scumbag? Hey – I know you. Seen you on the box. Think you're something, don't you? Get out of the cab, you douchebag, and I'll give you french letters.'

He was joined in the fray by his overweight wife, who began screaming at Phyllis through the other window. 'And you, you dirty bitch – don't you look down your fucking nose at me. I know your sort – think your shit doesn't stink . . .'

Phyllis regarded the wife's distorted face clamped to the glass. Her husband's insults, in almost perfect sync with her lip movements, appeared to be echoing from the woman's mechanical mouth. In the car, the children, munching on chips, were crawling against the window like stuffed toys.

Len began backing up the taxi, and the stranger, sensing retreat, squeezed his face sideways through the top of the window and renewed his attack, wheezing through uneven nostrils. 'You're nothing! Do you hear, you soapy ponce – threatening the lives of decent people . . .'

Zeno appeared totally absorbed in the contortions of the man's face. He could have been watching a play. As the cab stopped, Phyllis opened the nearside door and stepped down. The woman's 'I've got a good mind to tear your head off and piss in it . . .' evaporated on her lips.

In the secure semi-dark of the taxi, Phyllis had felt unusually composed. The hand that had reached to unlatch the door had moved by itself; as she stepped on to the pavement she heard herself speak. She couldn't remember the actual words, but the feeling that accompanied them she never forgot. The tone and quality that advised the mother to get her children home and into a warm bed was strange and compelling. Strange in that Phyllis had never experienced this particular quality before. Compelling in that it was as familiar as her own heartbeat, and closer to her than her jugular vein.

It was the sound, not the words, that created the compliance, for it touched the same chord in all present.

As unexpectedly as it erupted it subsided. The couple were back in their banger and heading for fresher fields. Len turned in the driver's cockpit and said to Zeno, 'Think he fancied you.'

'Yeah.'

'Why didn't you do anything?'

'I wasn't sure how to lock the door.'

'I was confident you could handle it,' said Len, filtering left.

'I was trying to keep my breath regular – not letting his rhythm affect mine.'

'Bit sick, if you ask me.'

'More than a bit. His breath was putrid – cancer of the stomach probably. All that rage. Still . . .' Zeno dusted his jacket, as though removing any overspill of bile, '. . . it takes all sorts, I guess. They're on a mission from God, too, like the Blues Brothers – to keep us alert.'

The men continued their chatter as though Phyllis's timely intervention had never happened, or a temporary blanket of invisibility had been drawn over it. And by the time they reached their destination, more pressing concerns imposed themselves on Phyllis's mind time.

The entrance to the working men's club was dark, the building appeared deserted. But there was light coming from the top floor. Phyllis had no idea where she was. When the cab had slowed on the curved road to check their whereabouts, she had seen a sign painted on a building. 'Camelot Studios', it said. But apart from this one cheery landmark, she was lost.

'Give 'em another bell,' said Len. Phyllis stepped up, turned the doorknob and pushed. The door swung open. She looked to Zeno. Zeno looked to Len. Len said, 'Do you want me to hang about?'

'Well . . .'

'Got nothing else to do.'

'Come on, then,' said Zeno. Let pocketed the keys, grinning at Phyllis, and all three went in. As they climbed the concrete stairs, a couple in evening dress passed them coming down.

'Action's over, I'm afraid,' the man said with a smile, happy to bear bad tidings.

'You never know, Colonel,' said Zeno with an encouraging wink to Phyllis.

The doors of the top floor opened on to the Forties, a sibling to school assembly halls the world over. The pea-soup green was still in evidence beneath the hastily added cream distemper. There was no sign of renewed design, and little of upkeep. It had an integral cosiness, and the clumps of balloons, shells and crêpe paper decorations gave it the feel of the night after a British Legion Christmas party. Tables and chairs of varying styles and sizes were scattered across the parquet block floor. Even the raised stage at one end had an improvised end-of-term air about it.

A few night creatures slumped across the tables, along with the remains of a gastronomic experience – that being the initial purpose of this travelling complement, the brainchild of a young chef seeking to win his cooking spurs without the outlay of fashionable rent. The details of this current location had been passed by word of mouth. The early endeavours were staffed by friends of the cook and out-of-work thespians. To the right of the stage was the spacious but largely makeshift kitchen where the chef was winding down with a tumbler of wine. This was where Zeno headed, although he wasn't looking primarily for the chef.

Earlier in the year the chef had been entertained and mystified by a magician hypnotist – or illusionist, as he preferred to be called. His show had been entitled 'I' and was also a new concept to Britain, being more in keeping with the supper-show cabarets of late-night Paris. London theatre critics – mostly middle-aged and set in their ways – didn't even try to change those ways to accommodate the young illusionist and the extravaganza folded. The illusionist stayed on in London, studying stage-flying techniques, met the cook who offered him a cash-in-the-hat gig that provided him a chance to keep his hand in and try out new routines.

181

And so the great Arturo entered the proceedings, altered the light plan, and encouraged the 'resting' artistes to wear full make-up and 'perform' as well as wait tables. The style of the evening increased along with the price by bringing a touch of magic to the outskirts of London.

'Don't wander off,' Zeno had ordered, while keeping an eye open for Arturo. Len settled himself at one of the uncleared tables as if he'd been there all evening. Phyllis let her body collapse into a chair next to him, crossing her arms and legs in the symbolic pose of full flight. A boy with a lantern jaw who resembled Desperate Dan caught Zeno's eye. He beckoned him over.

'Is the master about?' he enquired.

Dan's head pivoted around. 'There he is,' he exclaimed. 'At the back of the stage.' He was pointing to a tall slim figure in white tie and tails, about to disappear between the back drapes.

Zeno covered the few yards separating them and they embraced. 'Maestro!'

'Zeno!'

'*Buona notte*, maestro.'

Arturo mimed kissing Zeno's ring. 'Eminence.'

'I need a favour.'

'If I can, I will,' said Arturo with a bow, the light hitting the skin of his forehead which was made up white, like an apprentice geisha.

'I have a friend. A new friend but . . .'

'. . . an old friend, as well.' Arturo finished Zeno's sentence and looked towards the newcomers. '*Splendida*,' he crooned, never slow to appreciate beauty and essence. 'She needs a job?'

'No, it's just that she wants to sing. But she's blocked. Never performed in public, you see.'

'I see,' concluded Arturo. He looked pensive. He placed his thumb under his chin and spread his forefinger at right angles across his lips, as though motioning silence. Phyllis felt his stare, but didn't look up. 'We should prepare her for the crystal door of fear?' he asked, *sotto voce*.

'That's right. No time like the present,' replied Zeno.

'No time except the present,' countered Arturo, without taking his eyes from the subject.

'So young. So smart,' jibbed Zeno.

'You know, my princely friend, if someone is sleeping, perhaps sleep is what they need most.'

'I feel this one is stirring.'

'In that case, we shall gently offer a hand.'

The young man looked to his right, and a tall girl in an evening dress moved away from the group she was standing with and came towards them. She reminded Zeno of the female link of the fairy circle in the park. The gown was similar; dark green sequins.

'This is Cole,' Arturo said. 'She is my assistant.'

Cole acknowledged Zeno, but crossed to the table where Phyllis was sitting. Len stood up. 'This is Phyllis, I'm Len.'

Cole didn't speak. She rolled her eyes at Phyllis.

'Hello then, Chuck,' said Len.

From Phyllis, 'Hello, sailor.'

Cole gave a baby crocodile smile. 'Yeees.'

They were joined by Arturo and Zeno. 'Get this man a drink,' Arturo said to Cole, indicating Len. Cole glided off.

Zeno gave Phyllis an inward smile. 'It's okay, we can use this place.' Phyllis nodded, not quite with it. 'Your debut – we'll use this room. It's fine with Arturo. He's going to lend a hand.'

Phyllis opened her mouth to speak, but, as no sound was forthcoming, she closed it. Arturo was looking into her eyes and she was caught in the gaze. When he spoke, his voice was gentle, yet persuasive: 'I see your right hand is at rest on your knee. Good. Imagine a blue balloon with your hand resting on it. The balloon is rising, lifting your hand. Your eyelids are heavy, closing, closed. Good. The balloon is getting bigger. It is lifting your hand. When your hand touches your face, all tension will leave your body. You feel the tension leaving. Gone. I'm going to count from one to five. When I reach five, you will be in deep relaxation. One, two – deeper – three, four – keep relaxing – five.'

The back of Phyllis's hand touched her face. Her eyes stayed closed.

'You will remember the precise moment you knew you wished to perform. A wish is living – it has power, and increases in power when kept a secret. And now, tonight, we scotch the fear. In a moment you will open your eyes. We will walk to the stage. You will gather the fear – you, not me – and smash through. You will see things differently. You can lower your arm. Thank you. Open your eyes, now. Now.'

Phyllis opened her eyes, stood and started slowly for the stage.

Zeno and Len watched them go. Zeno sat in the chair that Phyllis had vacated. Len said, 'My dad offered to buy me a pair of skates once. But I had to sing outside the pub in front of everybody. No song, no skates. I couldn't do it. I often think about it.' He knocked back his toddy.

Phyllis, Cole and Arturo disappear into the wing of the stage. The light plan of the room dims to half. Some of the helpers come and draw chairs near the stage, others festoon themselves around the walls. Everyone is still. Most of them have been there at one time or another.

Arturo walks on to the darkened stage. A single white spot from the wing picks him up as he comes to the centre.

'Ladies and gentlemen, we now welcome the return of a solar angel. This is a special night for all present. And don't forget, as the art of terrorism is terror, so the art of listening is to listen. Clear your minds and truly accompany her.'

Arturo snaps his fingers. From the side of the stage, his 'sawing the lady' cabinet is carried out like a coffin. The bearers come to a halt behind him and set it down on its metal stands. It is now two feet from the floor of the stage. Arturo opens the side of the cabinet, revealing Phyllis. He starts to move off stage. Phyllis's lips move soundlessly. Arturo turns, and realises that she is still in the box. Exasperated, he clicks his tongue and motions her out. Phyllis pops her head out and sees him looking at her. She swings herself out and on to the stage, gathers herself, and sings.

From Phyllis's point of view, the hall is crowded, a multi-tiered auditorium. Some of the spectators are pale, others brim with life. Imo Sage is present, sitting between a man with a ruff and a heavy-set woman with gold bangles. Phyllis sings for her teacher the way they rehearsed it. Although Phyllis is singing 'a cappella', in her mind she is accompanied by the piano in Half Moon Street. The notes that come from her throat fill her head with the odour of violets. She sings as if her very life depends on her rendering.

She finishes. Everyone applauds. Cole runs across the footlights, dragging the house curtain behind her. The spectators continue to clap. On stage, behind the curtain, Phyllis swoons. Arturo moves from stage left to Zeno and Len.

'Is she all right?' asks Zeno. Arturo doesn't answer. Out of the darkness come Cole, Desperate Dan and two others. They are supporting Phyllis's rigid body on their shoulders. They lay her like a plank against a chair. Arturo folds her into a sitting position. A bottle of champagne arrives on a silver-plated tray. Phyllis opens her eyes.

'Are you okay?' asks Zeno. Phyllis nods dumbly.

'You were great,' Len says.

'Feel okay?' asks Cole.

'Bit punchy, I expect,' says Len.

'Hit by a fistful of stars,' agrees Cole.

'You look amazing,' says Zeno. A bottle of bubbly is popped. Phyllis finally speaks. 'I always wanted to be called Scarlett.'

Arturo offers Scarlett his baton, and as she reaches for it, it changes into a bunch of flowers. He laughs, draws her to him and whispers, 'Your voice will make you a light unto yourself. Shine solitary and bright. *Brava*, Scarlett!'

'Len,' Zeno says, 'he means "let's make a move".' Len springs to his feet, finishing his glass.

'I could dance – you know that? Dance,' says Scarlett.

'And sing?' asks Zeno.

'*Ragazzi*,' calls Arturo as they leave, 'good fortune on the road.'

Flick and the Rose were discussing Flick's career in movies when the officer knocked on the door. While the Rose answered, Flick pulled on his tee-shirt. A young policeman stood on the step, his helmet under his arm. He appeared to be offering the Rose something. It was a small key.

'Just apprehended a felon vacating these premises, sir. Red-handed, you might say – with the family silver by the looks of it.' He pointed to the Q-car in front of the house. By the light of the streetlamp, the Rose could see Captain Toby slumped in the rear.

'Sorry to disturb you, sir, it being so late, but we believe he left the lady of the house . . . er . . . incarcerated in the exercise room. Could someone make sure she's all right?' The Rose took the key and told Flick, now decent, to go and check out the gym.

'Anything I can do for you officer?'

'Don't think so, sir. Just wanted to make sure everything was all right here. Copped him cold. Lucky accident actually. Patrolling my round, saw this fellow coming up out of the basement with a bag. Looked a bit sus, so we gave him a pull. Radioed in. He's an old lag, on new territory now. Quite a well-known conman – ladies of means, usually elderly. He owned up. We can come by in the morning and take a statement, if that's in order.'

'Yes, I'm sure that will be fine.'

'And what's your name, officer?' asked Nick, arriving to view the trade. 'My God – you're the spitting image of the young Burt Lancaster. But I suppose everyone tells you that.'

Flick discovered Fleur manacled to the Paramount equipment. She had wrested one arm free from her robe, but her efforts to cover herself had not been successful. She still wore the cherry-pink high heels. She'd been crying – her Boots No. 7 was streaked down her face, and her nipples were rigid with fright. Flick paused

186

with the key in his hand.

'Christ, Fleur,' he said. As he bent down to unlock the handcuffs, Fleur slid out her tongue and ran it across the blue ink of his arm.

Phyllis had not heard Zeno's directions to Len – she no longer cared where she was going. But, as the cab moved off, an image rolled back into her mind. It had happened as the panel of Arturo's magic box had opened. She had been looking down at her feet. She hadn't seen the velvet slippers she'd left home in but a pair of leather lace-up boots which no girl had ever worn.

When the gyrations began at Manhattan's Peppermint Lounge – and in the space of a few weeks spun across the Atlantic, bringing a new looseness to the pale inhibited islanders (never great ones for inviting a stranger to dance) – it also rang the death knell for an institution that had become peculiarly British – the ballroom dance.

Even the most uncoordinated members of the jive generation could grimly manage to rotate their pelvises a little without disturbing their upper lips and 'The Twist' spread almost as rapidly as the Fire of London. The new movements ushered in new music, new faces, and new fashion – this seraglio of birds of paradise demanded fitting surroundings to execute and exhibit their wares – and entrepreneurs sprang up everywhere to accommodate them. Almost overnight, saddle rooms, discothèques, crazy elephants and speakeasys spread like fireweed after a blaze, the once-gracious foxtrots, waltzes and quicksteps taking a fall.

However, this 'fall from grace' was not instantaneous, and therefore not immediately apparent. Had not the milieu accommodated the tango, assimilated the cha cha, and systematised the jive? No, fashion changed, but ballroom dancing and its exponents went on for ever.

Nowhere was it so entrenched as in the capital, whose stalwarts believed that once the provocative contact of dance was lost, the form itself would dissipate – and they were right. Since the Twist, dancing has mainly consisted of folks jigging haphazardly about in near proximity to someone who may or may not be their partner. These twisters, however, did not mature to ballroom dancing – they abandoned it altogether. Thus, the experts of foxtrot and tango became a minority group and, like all such species, bonded together. Ballrooms and studios, whose freeholds were held by the keepers of the flame, stayed open for business. There the art-form continued to be taught and practised by the happy few.

Josephine Bradley was such a happy one. Her basement academy, amidst the Middle Eastern swirl of South Ken and Gloucester Road, was open seven days and evenings a week. Weekdays, dance instruction was offered; Saturday and Sunday were reserved for dances. On Friday evenings, a dance for beginners was held, which the instructors attended. It was to the deceptively modest front door of Ms Bradley's studio that Zeno instructed Len to take them.

As the trio entered, the strict tempo version of 'If You Were The Only Girl In The World' was playing, and they descended in Indian file down the curved staircase, into the basement ballroom. The only instructor not occupied – a man named Henry with pebble spectacles – grabbed the first of the group to reach the sprung maple floor – it happened to be Len – and started one-two-three-ing him in waltz time.

Phyllis, now Scarlett, looked around the old ballroom. The side-wall lights were shaded pink, and the reflecting globe spinning from the ceiling threw light across the room. Zeno took one look at her wonder-filled face and fell even more in love. 'Shall we?' he asked.

Scarlett stepped up into the outstretched arms and followed his lead. They pretty much had the floor to themselves. Miss Bradley had already retired to her quarters. Aside from Len and his partner and a would-be tripper of the light fantastic clutching a young blonde instructress, only a few spirited beginners were still cutting the rug.

'How did you know about this place?' Scarlett asked.

Executing a reverse turn Zeno said, 'I always wanted to dance with my mum, but I never did get round to it. When she passed away, I had the feeling she would have liked me to know how to dance anyway. I found out the best place and signed up. My wife didn't want to bother, so I came by myself.'

'You're a surprising fellow, Zeno.'

'Am I?'

Len was also enjoying himself. The minute that Henry had gone to put on a fresh record, Len had taken over the blonde instructress and was now mastering the intricacies of the rumba. 'Blimey – I've wanted to do this since I first saw George Raft do it,' he called across to Scarlett and Zeno, sitting one out. 'If the trouble and strife could see me now, she wouldn't believe it.'

'He means that his wife wouldn't believe it,' translated Zeno.

'I'm having trouble believing it myself – and I'm sitting here.'

Zeno had another look at Len. 'I see what you mean.'

Scarlett's foot was beating time to 'Say Si Si'. 'Why are we sitting this one out – don't you rumba?'

'I do, but I came over all unnecessary, holding you in waltz time.'

Scarlett turned to look at him. 'You did, did you?'

'I did.'

'Aren't men strange.'

The speeded-up rumba finally ended and Henry announced, 'Take your partners for the last waltz.'

'Come on – show me how to do it again,' she said, pulling him on to the floor. He waltzed her in slow time to Stanley Black's Band and crooned 'Just The Way You Look Tonight' in her ear.

At the end of the dance, she noticed that his eyes were moist.

*

'I was interested in what you were saying about love and possession,' Miranda said.

'Your husband wasn't,' said the Rose.

'We're not joined at the hip you know. "Thief of love", I think you called it.'

'I meant they were opposites.'

'Which don't meet?'

'Something like that.'

'So?'

'I was expressing my own emotional inhibitions, I suppose. Sometimes I don't think, I just sound off. Then I realise what I've said might well apply to me.'

'Like what you said tonight?'

'I suppose so.'

They were lounging on the second floor in one of Fleur's hi-fi areas. The Rose had selected a CD of Jobim, and Miranda was stretched out on a butter-yellow settee. She had kicked off her shoes and put her feet up. 'And?'

'It's wanting reciprocation. That's the problem area – it can't be love. Love isn't dependent on getting something in return. In my case, my obsessions and addictions all stem from being frightened of giving love. At least, that's what I thought. But what I was really denying was the fear that if I gave myself in love, it wouldn't be returned. I was wrong. You can't lose by giving love. That's its nature.'

'So how do you feel, now that you're ready to give love?'

'I don't know.'

Miranda grinned. 'How about one last game.'

'You sound like Fleur.'

'Not exactly,' she said, pulling out a packet of condoms from her bag and tossing them across to him. He caught it and read the description.

' "Unusual grooves",' he quoted.

'Come on, don't be a plonker – play. You know how to play,

190

don't you?' Miranda crossed her legs. 'I know you'd prefer tattoo, but he's gone the way of all flesh and ink, I'm afraid.'

'I'm happy he's with Fleur. She's had a miserable day – and she did go to a lot of trouble.'

'Oh, don't go all saintly on me – think of yourself. Here you are – sober, single and over twenty-one.'

The Rose smiled. There was a long silence. Miranda watched him. Just when she thought the subject was closed, he said, 'I've never been with a woman.'

'Is that true?'

'It is, I'm afraid.'

When Miranda spoke, her voice was playful. 'As they say in the ad, "You don't like it cause you haven't tried it." '

'You're so feminine.'

'I'm so everything.'

'But good?'

'The best I've met.' Again the silence. The Rose sensed that his reluctance made her unsure. She crossed her legs again, as though he was a normal man. He smiled apologetically, but she didn't react. Finally she said, 'Not performance anxiety, is it?'

'I could give performance anxiety a whole new meaning.'

'That would be my problem, wouldn't it? Look, there's no down side here. If we fall wickedly in, we fall wickedly in. If we don't, we remain chums.'

'I was just thinking that I'd never get another chance with a woman like you.'

Miranda's hot eyes shifted. 'You know, when I first saw you, surgeon Rose, my tongue went so stiff I could hardly speak. Or maybe that's the worry.'

'You're much too smart for me,' he said, unlacing his shoes and taking them off. He had odd socks on. Miranda breathed in. There was that funny sinking in her stomach.

'Shall we go up?' They climbed the stairs in silence. When they

191

reached Fleur's room, she said, 'Now – are you a lights-on person or a lights-out person?'

'Whatever you find pleasant,' he said and, as an afterthought, 'Where's Nick?'

'Scrubbing his teeth. He's become so . . . anal of late.' She pulled her dress over her head and came to help him.

'Any anxiety yet?' she asked, inspecting him and then leading him to the bed.

She settled him on Fleur's bed and turned away from him. For a moment they lay like spoons in a drawer. He began appraising her skin clinically, running his hand over her body. At first she remained passive, almost inert. But as his interest gained confidence, she began flexing the tempered layers of muscle, her back becoming hot. There was an odour which reminded him of evening gardenias. And as if in response to this new desire, his brain cooled, and for just that moment he knew that in truth there was neither man nor woman, only love and its expression.

'Come on, matelot, drive him into me,' she said, curving her body and straining open to receive him. He sensed another presence in the room, but was already sliding into her. As she closed around him and their bodies locked, he felt animal, almost rancid, breath behind him, fine teeth fastened on to his shoulder, and Nick's curiously rough flesh drove into him.

From upstairs, Fleur's moaning began.

The taxi was moving smoothly up Exhibition Road. The park gates were closed, and Len turned left heading west. Scarlett felt she had covered all points of the compass since setting out.

For the second time she became aware of her hand. She glanced down without moving. Again, its position was unfamiliar; the back of her hand was on her thigh, her fingers curved as though holding a bowl. The middle finger felt heavier than the rest.

'Can I wear your ring for a bit?' she asked Zeno.

She could hear the smile in his reply. 'And you, who never even met me mum.' Winding the ring from his finger, he dropped it into her palm. She slipped it on the sensitive middle finger and turned her hand to see the effect. It was not a bad fit. Now her whole hand felt at ease. And warmth crept up her spine. Just as they were passing Kensington Park Gardens, she saw a light deep within the grounds. It flickered like a fire. The warmth at the top of her spine stopped.

'This looks familiar. We're not going back to the party, are we?'

'It wasn't part of my plan, but we can if you want. They'd be overjoyed to see us.'

Scarlett didn't answer, once more lost in the feeling that Zeno's presence gave her. She no longer questioned it – she had come to terms with the fact that the empathy faded when her mind wandered.

Zeno leaned forward to say something to Len. She didn't hear what was said because her mind went into a slow-motion swirl, the sight of his slim back spinning the revolving door of her deep memory. She lay her head back on to the top of the seat and closed her eyes as a strange sequence of events began to unfold, as if a film seen as a child and forgotten ever since was now replaying. When it ended, the story of Zeno and Scarlett was no longer a mystery.

Most dreams are comparatively short. But within the dream dimension there is no way that waking time can be imposed on the dream reality, let alone measured. What made Scarlett's vision seem so subjectively long was that, as the dream progressed, so did the memory of a previous dream, and this movement of a dream broken within the dream opened other vistas of happenings long past and sealed with time's key.

Now recalled with such precision and clarity, she was unsure if she was remembering a distant fancy or a forgotten reality. And as it unfurled, so did the memory of others; events which were fixed, but locked into the dream landscape, were dredged up into her waking consciousness.

The fact that Scarlett entered the reverie just as the cab passed

Kensington Palace (by the clock, 2 a.m. Saturday) and was roused from it nine minutes later when the car arrived at its destination, belied the scale of the revelation. Even to Zeno. For it was from that moment that he, hitherto the guide of this nocturnal odyssey, was relieved of his leadership.

The only clue that the building was anything other than a residence was a discreet lettering on the door, informing the passers-by that this was a hotel. The fact that it was situated in Stanley Gardens – a short walk from where the party was taking place – didn't escape Zeno. Nor Scarlett, who was asleep in the cab when they arrived. But as Zeno said later, if an event was destined to happen in a particular spot, it would – even if you had scrimped on the postage.

'What's going on now, then?' asked Len. He was standing beside his vehicle looking at the moon.

'I'm going to nip in here and see if a mate of mine is on duty. The princess looks like she could do with a place to crash.'

'Seems a pity to disturb her, don't it?'

'Yeah. Don't want her waking up with a stiff neck, though – she'll have to start taking care of that throat.'

'Do you want me to come in and tell them the airline lost the luggage?'

'No, it's okay, Len. You keep an eye on her for me.'

'Pleasure, mate. Never seen a moon as big as that, have you?'

'I haven't been up this late for years.'

The foyer of the rock-and-roll hotel was deserted, save for a couple arguing on the stairs. On duty behind the desk was the night man, a West Indian with a penchant for Jimi Hendrix hairdos.

'Got a nice room for me and my chums, guv? SAS lost our luggage.'

The young man looked up from his *Melody Maker*. He grinned, showing immaculate teeth.

'Honkee,' he said. Somehow it was a friendly greeting.

'Hi, nigger – how's tricks?'

With the grin still starched to his face, he nodded towards the arguing twosome. 'Fairly normal.'

Zeno went and stood near the counter. Both listened. The man on the stairs with the key in his hand was a step below the reluctant woman, who might easily have been a transvestite. In between snatches of dialogue, he was trying to bring his quivering body into contact with hers. She was slowly retreating upstairs to avoid it.

'One for the road – okay, honey? Scout's honour.'

'I'm really tired, Harry.'

'One drink, okay? That's a promise. Then I'll drive you back to Romford.' Forcing her lips into a downward smile, the third sex said, 'Harree . . .'

'One drink?'

'You won't like it.'

Zeno whispered, 'You can say that again.'

'I can't stay all night, I haven't brought the insert . . . the thing that keeps it open,' she said. He had made it to the top stair.

'I'll keep it open,' he promised triumphantly, as they disappeared into heaven.

The night clerk said, 'Another ordinary night in a small hotel.'

'How're you doing, Wilf?'

'Still playing eight to the bar.'

'But you're in good shape?'

'Are a bull's balls beef?'

Zeno spread his hand on the counter.

'I know you're always full. We just need a place to be quiet, have a natter, maybe a nap. Doesn't have to be a room.'

'Don't know about quiet – we have a coach party in tonight. Block booking. Looks like a street outing to me – Sally Army stuff.' Wilf swivelled on his slim hips, scrutinised the board, and lifted a key from its hook.

'It'll have to be thirteen. The lavatory's broke.'

A middle-aged couple scampered across the room. The pursuer, a woman, was wearing a pair of joke teeth.

'You can use the loo on the landing,' said Wilf.

'Bless your heart – you're a prince. I'll get my chums.'

'The best of princes is he who visits the wise.'

'I bet not many princes know that,' said Zeno over his shoulder.

Len was sitting on the bottom step, whistling to himself, when Zeno reappeared.

'Everything all right?'

'Sure is a beautiful night, ain't it?' said Len.

'It sure is.'

'Get fixed up all right?'

Zeno nodded. 'Time for a cup of coffee – tea, maybe?'

'Naw, I'd better be pushin' off.'

'What's the damage, Len?'

'Forget it – it's on me.'

'Listen, it's very nice of you, Len. But don't be taken in by my threads – I've got dosh.'

Len laughed. 'Course you have, me old china. But I couldn't have bought tonight, could I?'

'How's that, Len?'

'Well, hanging out – with the customers. Just think about it. Every day, taking swells to grand places, having a bit of a chat on the way, and then off they go. And me left in the cab. Always making the tea, never drinking it – see?'

'Did I hear someone say "tea"?' said a little voice from the cab.

'I was just saying what a terrific time I've had, and how I'd better be getting . . .'

'. . . back to your trouble and strife,' said Scarlett.

'Miss, it was . . . splendid tonight. You singing like an angel, me being part of it all. I'll never forget it.'

'Thank you, Len. And thanks for being there for me when it mattered.' She kissed him. He climbed back into his cab and was blushing all over.

'Okay, me old chinas,' he called, pulling down his window and starting the engine. 'Don't forget, now – if you see me in this 'ere jamjar, give me a whistle. Special rates for chums.' And with a look towards Scarlett, 'Good night, star. Safe travelling.'

'Goodbye, Len,' said Scarlett, waving him on his way. She placed her arm around Zeno's waist and, noticing tears in his eyes, said, 'Well, me old china – what about a cuppa, then?'

Scarlett's first impression entering the hotel was that all the strangeness of the night was centred there. Not that she actually saw much – a gent in the passage was kneeling with his ear to a wineglass outside one room, but scuffled away as they arrived. Yet the murmurings, chuckles, and occasional cries strengthened the impression she had that, outside the walls of room thirteen, all the madness symbolised in the astrological configuration was concentrated around them.

Their supposedly unlucky room, albeit with its disfunctioning lavatory, was an elegant haven. A round bed occupied the centre of the room, and the adjoining bathroom – almost the same size – housed a Victorian bath, one end of which was cloaked by a wrap-around shower composed of circular brass ribs and copper joints. The showerhead itself was over a foot across.

Zeno had settled Scarlett, opened a window, and was exploring the bath-house when Wilf appeared, bearing gifts on a hotel salver.

'Didn't know whether to bring high high tea or a down-beat breakfast,' he said.

'Ah,' said Zeno. 'Salaam.'

'Asalaam alaikum,' replied Wilf, setting the tray within reach of Scarlett on the bed, and placing his fingertips to his heart, lips and forehead before offering it to her. On the tray were three plump tea-cosies. He lifted them one at a time, like an oriental jeweller displaying gems.

'Oh my!' exclaimed Scarlett at the array.

'Hot water. English breakfast and Formosan Oolong.'

'Oolong. My goodness,' gasped Zeno, joining them from the other room.

'The famous unbroken leaf with the peach flavour.'

'Not only a prince, but a scholar to boot.'

'The worst of scholars is one who visits princes,' said Wilf.

'Everything under control downstairs?' asked Scarlett.

'The lady in room five addressed me as "coon", and offered me a drink.'

'What did you say?'

' "On duty, madam." Fancy – thinking she could have the seed of Adam for a glass of cheap white.'

'Thanks, Wilf,' said Scarlett, examining the quilted tea-cosies.

'Friday night is carnival night – everybody gets a funny hat. I better get on before they shake the house down.'

When they were alone, Zeno kneeled beside the bed and reviewed the refreshment.

'Do you want to sleep or wake up?'

'Now, what do you think?'

She hadn't said much since they arrived. There was a transparency around her eyes, which he read as fatigue. He poured her a cup of breakfast. She plumped some pillows up behind her and leaned on them. Zeno made some Oolong for himself. Although she still felt absolutely comfortable with their moments of quiet, she thought he no longer appeared to be.

When he had made his tea and taken a sip, she watched him encounter the silence. It was a moment she knew well, usually filled by the fuss of lighting a cigarette. How strange, she thought – she had not felt the urge for hours. Zeno was sitting on his heels beside her. Maybe it was the posture, or maybe it was his own thought she picked up on, but she found herself concerned about his wife and child.

'Why don't you tell me about it, Zeno?' she said.

'Prudence?' he replied, as though expecting the question. 'Yeah – I did marry her, didn't I?'

198

Another silence. Scarlett, not wishing to influence his line of thought, did not prompt him. One of the things she noticed about herself now was that her mind was not pressing on all the time, trying to see around the corner of every moment.

'I was born with a longing,' he said finally. 'Well, I assume I was born with it. They say all little souls arrive with their own parcel of blessings to equip them for the trip. But I can't for the life of me figure what this did for me. You see, there was always something missing. I would see other kids happy, having a good time. I would have a laugh with them, but it wasn't spontaneous. There was always this melancholy. I was a bit sensitive when I was little – saw things others didn't, that sort of thing – and assumed it was part of it. You know, the price. I suppose I was a proper boy. Horny, too, but it was never that easy for me to get laid.'

Scarlett lifted an eyebrow. 'I'm sure the ladies hated you, Zeno.'

'I don't mean it wasn't there for me. It was that whenever I did, the isolation I felt increased. It wasn't that much of a problem until I got my break and saw how all the other guys handled it. They obviously felt no pain, and I began to wonder about myself.' He paused. 'Is this boring?'

'No. Did you ever think about trying guys?'

'Yeah, I thought about it. Always got along well with gays. Went to the pictures with a fella I knew swung. Thought I'd give it a try. But I didn't quite know how to start. I was thinking of what I'd do if I was with a girl, and then I realised it wouldn't work.'

'Why?'

'Well, it was leading to a kiss.'

'And you knew you couldn't?'

'Didn't want to. Which was a pity, because in lots of ways it would have suited me fine.'

'Casual sex, no emotional ties?'

'At the time, that's what I figured. Of course, homosexual relationships are as complex as any other – nobody escapes without pain, do they?'

'Why do you suppose that is?'

'Part of the trip. Compels you to train your ego, I guess.'

Outside, a shuffling started down the passage. It sounded like a line of people. A voice was singing something which sounded like 'Okee Cokee'. They listened for a bit until it went upstairs.

'Where was I? Oh, yeah. I always had a vague picture in my mind of the woman I was looking for. She would have red hair.' He smiled self-consciously, 'I was always a pushover for redheads. Don't know why. Then I met Prudence. By then I had worked it out this far: I was a man – not a gay man, yet I had been brought up primarily by my mother, who wanted a daughter. In comparison with other blokes, I was feminine.'

'And your wife?'

'Right. When I met her, I had accepted that I was sort of emotionally androgynous, but that I would be better of with a regular partner. One-night stands gave me attacks of conscience, you see. Then, two days before I met her, I had a dream about her.'

'That's curious.'

'Yeah. I met someone in the dream who looked like her. She looked enough . . .' He faltered and stopped speaking. There was an uneasy quiet. For in recalling the dream, a thought which had been edging into his head all night swelled, and he could no longer ignore it: that the girl of his dream was not the one he had married, but the one he was with now. And in this chill moment, a voice inside him told him he had sacrificed his chance of fulfilment with another because he had lacked the courage to wait.

'Talk to me, Zeno,' Scarlett was saying. She had seen the sudden stirring in his eyes, the pallor in his face, and had felt his panic. 'What is it, pal? You look like someone walked on your grave.'

Zeno forced himself to go on, almost as if nothing had occurred, but his voice was without its normal vibrancy. 'I . . . married her. She was so lovely – physically lovely. I guess I couldn't leave her alone for the first few years. I wouldn't acknowledge that it hadn't solved anything – that the same me was still there. But I was young, always ready for her. The passion enabled me not to think that maybe I had made a serious mistake. Later, whenever I thought about leaving . . . Women are intuitive, aren't they?'

He made an attempt at a grin. Scarlett knew he was talking to stop himself confronting something else.

'At any rate, she stopped taking the pill without telling me, and the next thing I knew she was pregnant. Sort of planned accident, see – and there was Zen. If you share your life with someone, things crop up – things you can't overlook, no matter how hard you try. I'm sure you know how it is.'

Scarlett thought of Julia, who perspired at night – how she had finally insisted on twin beds – but she brought her train of thought back to him.

'What problems, Zeno?'

'She always wore too much perfume.'

'Didn't you ask her to stop?'

'I did. But then I realised she wasn't well. I could smell that she wasn't well. So I changed our diet. It worked for me.'

'And Prudence?'

'This is what's so silly. I had the perfect regimen for her. And she stayed with it until Zen was born.'

'She was better?'

'Yes. She didn't get sick. She was less stressed, her headaches went, and she had this really healthy aroma about her.'

'Did it make you love her more?'

Zeno looked perplexed. 'No,' he said slowly. 'But she was better for it.'

'And it was better for you?'

'Yes. Well . . . yes. I felt closer to her. We had something in common. We were growing together.'

'And she broke the diet?'

'Yes. She didn't tell me, but I knew.'

'She smelled different?'

'Yes. I had not explained my motive to her. I figured it best if we were doing something together. So there was this dumb situation with her pretending she was sticking to the diet and . . .'

'. . . bingeing on the quiet.'

'Yeah, so I broke the regimen for a few days. We broke the regimen and . . .'

'And you went back to it?'

'Yeah.'

'With Zen?'

'Yeah, later on with Zen.'

'So Prudence must have felt left out?'

'Well, it was her choice. She knew what we were doing, saw that we were okay. Her colds got longer and longer. She knows it's all the sugar she eats.'

'But, wait a sec. Not everyone has the same amount of will-power. You don't seem to understand that.'

'I know.'

'And you don't talk to her much now? You don't fancy her? It sounds like you don't have much in common anymore.'

'You know I try. Every day I wake up, I say, "Today I'm going to be different. Spend time with her." And every day I wind up watching the telly, reading, even if it's stuff I've read before.'

'I think . . . I think I am going to run you a bath.' She bounced off the bed, strode into the bathroom, and investigated the hotel's choice of soaps and bath gels. Zeno was sitting on the bed fully dressed when she came back in. 'What do you think of this – it's Wallflower.' She held it under his nose.

'Trying to tell me something?'

She smiled. 'Smell it, you jerk,' she said.

'It's nice.'

'I know it's nice, but can I plonk it in your bath?'

'Sure.'

She returned to the bathroom and dropped the essence in the water. 'Still dressed, are we? Tell you what. As you're feeling so modest, I'll put on the smaller of these bathrobes so you don't feel alone. Okay? Deal?'

When she returned wearing the big fluffy robe, looking small and pink, Zeno was undressing. She watched him, and he seemed to shrug off his mood with his clothes. When he was naked, he strolled into the bathroom with the aplomb of a performer sharing a dressing room.

'That's a neat bod you have there, boy.'

'You think so? How do I compare with Nick?'

'Nick? You mean "old Nick"? Well . . .' she said, noticing Zeno was not exactly shrinking with embarrassment, '. . . I'd say he has more control, but less power.'

Zeno grinned and slipped into the foam. 'Worthy of a true companion of Zeno.'

'You can be quiet now and let me massage your neck.'

She did, Zeno thinking for a moment of his daughter and how many massages he had given without ever receiving one.

When she had placed her hands on his shoulders, she heard a noise similar to the sound of swarming bees. It took a moment before she realised that the sound had come from inside her own head. As she massaged the tense points on each side of his skull where it joined the neck, she had the strongest impression that she had done it before. And her focus changed.

This change of focus included the sensation that she was clasping a finely built woman, and that the hands, her hands, were doing it energised with manly strength. The moment wasn't fuzzy, but clean, precise; as natural as when, engrossed in a film, you become aware that you are seated in a darkened cinema.

'Now shower, put on the other bathrobe, and I'll do your feet.'

I can't believe this, thought Zeno. She's talking to me like I talk to my kid.

Downstairs in the lobby, Wilf was coping with the provocative woman. She was laid out on the front counter, skirt hitched up unceremoniously, yelling that it was time for her aromatherapy.

The high-pitched voice reverberated up the stairs and through the walls of number thirteen, where Scarlett was zoning Zeno's feet.

She had taken a loose hair from the collar of his jacket, threaded it through the signet ring, and was using the makeshift pendulum to 'douse' his feet. As the ring swung unaccountably back and forth over his right foot, Scarlett asked, touching the capsule of his big toe, 'Do you get pain in this joint?'

'Sometimes, when the weather is going to change – broke it running hurdles at school.'

'Athlete, huh?'

'I wouldn't go that far. Haven't competed for years.'

'Only with yourself nowadays.'

Zeno smiled into the pillow, 'You know an awful lot about me.'

'Does it disturb you?'

'No, I'm flattered.'

'What does disturb you?'

While he thought it over, she felt herself holding a freshly cut artichoke; its mauve tendrils shivered as she rubbed it into the slender foot.

'I always wanted someone to cherish. Someone of my own.'

'And?'

'I'm afraid it's come too late.'

She slapped the bottom of his foot. 'Okay, hush now. I'm going to fix this joint.'

'Where did you learn to do that?'

'Oh, I have an aptitude. I get taught things – people want me on their team.'

'I bet they do.'

As she worked his feet, he felt sorrow being rubbed from him. A constriction closed his throat and, as it passed, the tears that he had felt close to all night flowed on to the pillow.

When his body became still, Scarlett turned him over on to his back, loosened the tie of his robe, and laid herself on him, wiping his face with the palm of her hand and looking long into his cloudy eyes – which in that moment were vulnerable and, with their still dark lashes, feminine.

As she made love to him, it was to both a man and a woman, for the image beneath her kept changing, as did her notion of herself. Reassuringly caressing his hands whenever passion threatened to overwhelm him, she had a picture of two other hands, oiled and bound by a skein of silk. When orgasm finally released them into each other, she found herself gazing down into her own eyes, and knew she looked with his. She felt herself rising weightlessly on the essence of their energy – knew it to be the merging of two perfectly matched auras, knew she had experienced perfect love-making – the longing of many lifetimes to be at an end.

How long she floated out of her body she couldn't tell, but they were brought back to earth by a shaking of the adjoining wall. Someone said, 'You know about as much about foreplay as a cat knows about holidays.'

Neither of them moved. The wall shuddered again, and then a new voice, a woman's: 'I've had enough – fuck me, or leave me alone.'

This was followed by indistinguishable noises, then a more verbal, 'Oi, what you doing? Agh, you filthy bugger, you gobbed on my bum.' This was added to by a stream of words, of which only two – 'Quaker Oats' – were intelligible. And then more of the woman: 'Yes, you did. It's dripping down your chin . . . Oooh, what's that? Ooohh, oooh.'

A terrific scuffing and much thudding. The one picture on the wall of room thirteen groaned and threatened to fall. Zeno and Scarlett looked at each other, not sure whether to laugh or cry. Scarlett said, 'I think he must have decided to leave her alone.'

'Probably trying for the valley orgasm,' Zeno added.

In the corridor outside the room next door, the listener with the wineglass stethoscope had just positioned it on the door when it was whipped open, and four hands reached out and grabbed his arms and yanked him in. There was a pitiful cry, which Scarlett and Zeno overheard.

'You don't happen to wear a silk square, do you?' Scarlett asked.

'I do. Had it for years. Found it in Granny Takes A Trip.'

'What's it like?'

'It's Indian. I have it with me, I think.'

He fetched it from his jacket. How long ago was it that his daughter had slipped it into his pocket? He placed it over Scarlett's face. She could smell a mixture of rose and sandalwood incense. She examined it, hung it over the lampshade by the bed and, taking Zeno's left hand, placed the inside of her wrist against his and wound the warm scarf around them, using her free right hand to fashion a loose knot.

'What did you tell your wife when you met her?'

'I don't know. Some blarney, I guess.'

'What did you tell her that made her love you?'

'Don't know.'

'Come on – I thought you guys always knew the moment.'

'Well, I used to write to her when I was on the road.'

'Singing.'

'Trying.'

'Why did you stop singing?'

'Because I never wrote or recorded a classic. It only takes one, but it has to be a classic. That's why I'm not an icon, and that's why I stopped.'

'Okay. Now look me in the eyes and tell me what you told her. Not wrote to her – told her.'

'I know that love longs for beauty, I thought perhaps beauty thirsted for love.'

'You were right.'

'I just didn't wait for the right person, did I?'

'Don't say that. If we'd done it different, we might have not met at all.'

'True. Life is life, right?'

The lovers sat for a long time, facing each other, their hands bound. Zeno tried to reason with himself. Scarlett watched the darkness leave the sky, wondering if she had helped him the way he had helped her. She didn't think so.

'I shall be having to see a man about a dog soon,' said Scarlett.

'Good idea. You go first.'

They freed their hands. Scarlett tied her robe and cautiously peeped around the door.

'Be careful out there,' Zeno said as she slipped out. She walked down the passage and located the door without a number. She opened it to discover a tall man in a priest's garb with his tongue down a younger man's throat. They jumped apart when they saw her. The cleric screamed.

'Forgive me, father,' said Scarlett, slamming the door. She ran back to their room. Zeno was still lying on the bed.

'That was quick.'

'Haven't been.'

'Couldn't find it?'

'It's busy.'

'Somebody else caught short?'

'No. Bit of brotherly love.'

'What? Come on, I'll go with you.'

They relocated the toilet. It was empty. Zeno ushered Scarlett in.

'Do you want me to wait?'

'Would you?' She went in. A moment passed. Scarlett called, 'You still there?'

'Of course. Not stopping your flow, am I?'

'No. Why do you ask?'

'Funny how many people are uptight about the old bodily functions.'

From the floor above came a sudden cannonade of laughter. A little way down the passage a door opened and the couple from the reception – the woman still wearing the fake teeth – ran out of one room and into another. Zeno leaned against the wall and listened.

Man: 'No, not with the teeth.'

Woman: 'Wet blanket.'

Man: 'Teeth out and we'll talk.'

Woman: 'Talk? That's all I get from you. And I had all my teeth out special.'

Man: 'Exactly. Not with the teeth.'

The door opened and a pair of teeth were thrown out. The door slammed shut. The teeth bounced near Zeno, who picked them up. They seemed real enough. He placed them in the sand bucket, and they grinned up at him. A voice with an Irish accent echoed up the stairs, 'Now – do you think you can get your laughin' gear around that?'

Zeno called to Scarlett, 'I think we'd better be getting back – it's like Sodom and Begorrah out here.'

Scarlett came out, and they walked to their door.

'Okay,' said Zeno, 'you stay put. I'll go and see if there's any breakfast to be had.' He kissed her face and took off.

Scarlett stood in the middle of the room near the bed, looking at it. From the room next door came the same voices, but more subdued. The female voice said, 'You hurt me, you bugger – violated my temple.'

'Sorry.'

'No . . . it's all right – I bet you could be much rougher, if you wanted.'

Scarlett is drawn to the window. She pulls the drapes wide apart and stares at the skyline, noticing the first thread of daybreak. Her night is almost over. A blush of warmth starts at the base of her spine and rises up through her neck into her head. She closes her eyes and squeezes them tight – her 'big squeeze', as Miss Sage used to call it.

Into the dark comes a flash of light, rather as if she were facing into the sun with her lids shut and waving her hand in front of them. She starts to be aware of a voice. It is in her head, yet beyond the auditory nerve. It is her own voice, yet at the same time it isn't. It has a soft Dublin brogue. 'There are two shadows. The one known to everyone falls upon the ground . . .'

There is a sudden humming in her head, as before, but more profound – where sensation merges with hearing. From this low register, a new voice – masculine, musical: '. . . but the other is projected on to the sky.'

She opens her eyes. She is on edge, but not afraid. Beside her, also awaiting the dawn, is the reserved man. Finding her looking at him, he takes a step away, as if to allow her to appreciate his outfit. He is dressed as Ottavio from *Don Giovanni*. He extends a hand in front of his lips and blows across his palm, as if to send a gentle stream of air towards her. Scarlett becomes aware of a rich familiar perfume.

'Cosy room, isn't it?' The lilting voice. 'I'm John McCormack.'

Looking at the figure, her eyes really wide, she recalls first the man in the Soda Fountain, and then the person on the moving escalator. She has been seeing this . . . whatever-it-is all day.

'That's right,' the distinguished tenor says. 'But we haven't been introduced.' He sees her confusion. 'You'll get used to it in no time. Think of me as an old friend.'

'Are you a guide?' she asks aloud.

'Miss Sage said someone would come to help you, did she not?'

'I thought that was Zeno.'

'It was, and he helped you to me. He did the washing – and I am to do the ironing.'

She understands what he means, and her expression softens.

'There,' he says. 'See how easy that was.'

'Will Zeno be able to see you when he gets back?'

'No. But not to worry – he's not coming back right now. He's fixing some croissants as a surprise. Oops, sorry.'

Thanks a bunch, thinks Scarlett. 'But why? Why not him?' she says.

'Your longing reached the right pitch and was heard. Now you have to help him with his.'

'I can't think how. He seems to know it all – understands everything.'

'That's true. He does understand. To understand is relatively easy. Yet, to practise . . . is a great art.'

'But . . .'

'No, no – no "buts", fair Scarlett. He will listen to you, and I will help you to tell him. That's why I'm here.'

'Will we be able to stay together? I know it's difficult, but is there some way?'

'No.'

Scarlett goes to the bed and sits on it, her legs suddenly weak.

'You see, little one, sometimes pain is the only spur which will prompt a person from the easily understandable into the great art. Now, it would indeed be a luxury for you to be with him, but it is crucial for him to be deprived of you. You are going to have to trust me there. I expect to earn your trust, but for the moment you can take it on faith. We must not deprive him of his destiny. We must help him. And we shall, to be sure – to be sure, we shall.'

There is a knock at the door.

'You talk to me now in your head. Ask him to come in.'

'Come in,' she calls.

Zeno entered like a waiter, carrying a tray, with a napkin laid over his arm. He glanced around the room and then walked through McCormack (who smiled at Scarlett) and placed the tray with warm croissants and coffee on the bed.

'Breakfast,' he announced, rippling open a serviette.

'Croissants – my favourites,' advised McCormack.

'My favourites,' said Scarlett.

Zeno grinned and poured a sensible-sized cup of coffee, into which he scraped the foam of the milk. A second cup he filled with hot milk and stained with a dash of coffee. He presented her with the real coffee. 'Would you prefer your croissant buttered or for dipping?' Then he caught sight of the sky through the window, filled with the soft light of sunrise, and the brightness faded from his face. 'Our night is over,' he said.

'Not quite,' said the guide.

'It's getting light,' Zeno added resentfully.

'Light is only breath from another dimension,' said McCormack cheerily to Scarlett.

'Don't be down. It's another day – almost,' Scarlett said, taking her coffee and following him to the window.

The ghost joined them. They stood in a row – Zeno, Scarlett and McCormack. The latter whispered in her ear, 'Perceive the colours of his breath.' So that's what an aura is, she thought, seeing the cloud of indigoes and violets pulsating around Zeno. It's the fineness of his breath. How flawless it is – like a living rainbow.

'He's . . .' McCormack's voice was very close, almost a kiss, '. . . worth pushing a bit – don't you think?'

She didn't look around – she knew he was gone.

'Let's bring this little table to the window and watch the sunrise with our breakfast,' she said. While they drank their respective concoctions, Scarlett dipping her croissant, she started to tell him of her insight, all the while watching his eyes and the changing colours about him so she would know how he was taking it. Her voice took on the quality of a parent telling a child a story, a story no parent had ever told her.

'There was also a longing in *my* life, dear Zeno. It didn't take the shape of another person, as yours did, and it was only eased when there was music. Some deep wish was pinned to my heart, and my only choice was to follow the path that hurt least. In other words, the right direction was not doing the things that were painful. There was loneliness, of course, and occasionally there was a companion.

'In England, there was an exquisite old lady who taught voice. Before she died, she said there would be someone who would

211

come to ease the longing. That person is you, Zeno, and you have helped me more than you know. There is something we have to do together, it is part of the kismet that binds us. But first there is a story. It concerns us. It is our story.'

Scarlett looked out at the dawn, then poured another coffee for herself and added some to Zeno's milk. He didn't object. She felt the carpet reassuring beneath her bare toes, and began.

'As you said, we have been together before. And somewhere in that Romany soul of yours our last lifetime together is locked. With good reason it is too misty to recall. For three murders occurred the night our days as gypsies ended. Ours. And a great friend's. Our gift of song we owe to her. For truly her voice was an inspiration. In this drama, you, dearest Zeno, star as the older but married woman and yours truly as the enthralled younger man. Your husband, our elder, as coarse as you were fine, struck the night we were to elope.

'Our go-between was poisoned, and while dying she sang us her last melody. Using her final breath to warn us in song.' Scarlett reached out and covered Zeno's hand. 'If this is painful, it isn't meant to be – you know that.' She smiled.

'We refused to leave each other, preferring to die together. Yet even that was not to be. The young man was imprisoned in his caravan, and burned with all he owned, even his dog. To the sound of his cries, you were thrown headlong into a ravine. The night wind blew sparks into the camp and, by morning, most of our clan had perished. Some of our songs and the music we made must have been passed on but . . .'

Scarlett spread her hands. Zeno drained his cup and looked into the eyes of the storyteller and asked, 'How did you come upon this?'

'There was a new energy about this day. Last night, at Fleur's, there was fear. Yet it was the right place – it was hard not to run away, yet something was growing. When we met, touched, something blossomed. The fear – the fear of singing in public –

meant confronting the root cause of the desire to sing. And facing that fear was a preparation for addressing the greater fear, remembering the death by fire.'

She picked up his hand and held it to her cheek. 'And now it is orchestra and beginners, please, Zeno Studd.'

Zeno appeared calm, but when she defocused her eyes to glimpse his aura, she saw it was thinking yellow.

'His logic just took over,' said the now-familiar brogue.

'Whew!' exclaimed Scarlett.

'What?' asked Zeno.

'Coffee rush,' she said, standing up and moving to the bed.

'Now,' said McCormack, 'I'm going to tell him something – something he has wanted to know for a long time. You don't have to understand it, just repeat what I tell you. I'll start slowly.'

Four-four time, thought Scarlett.

'To be sure,' said McCormack, and he began.

'There is something I can tell you about your friend Zeno,' she said.

Zeno perked up. 'Didn't know you knew about the pre-Socratics.' She could see he felt safe now, on familiar ground. 'I'm all ears.'

'Very nice ears, they are, too.' And seeing she had his attention, it began.

'In the way that a movie projector creates an illusion of movement, the mind creates the illusion of past and future. A close examination of time will show that it is solely a concept in the mind itself – the mind being dependent on its creation for its movement. Space, likewise, is an extension of the mind's time concept.

'But, from the standpoint of reality, there is only "now". Since both space and time are illusions, it follows that any movement needing space and time is illusory as well. That is why the arrow in flight is at rest, movement being only in the mind.'

Zeno begun to slump in his chair.

'He's stopped listening,' the ghost pointed out agreeably.

'He must be tired,' offered Scarlett.

'Or indolent,' stated McCormack. 'Make him sit up.'

Scarlett walked behind Zeno, gave his shoulders a rub, and placing her knee through the staves of the chair, straightened his spine. At McCormack's instigation, she continued speaking into Zeno's left ear.

'This isn't intended to be cruel, but if it hurts, ask yourself what is hurting. And you'll discover it isn't the "I am", because that is not subject to pain. It is only the ego that squeals when it is scorched – which is what your mother meant when she said "you sometimes have to be cruel to be kind". Okay?'

Zeno nodded absentmindedly, his head giving the impression that it was experiencing difficulty remaining on his neck. He continued to gaze into the space midway between the bed and the wall. McCormack stepped obligingly into the area and continued.

'This is not at all hard for you to understand, as it is a topic you vapour on about mindlessly – namely "being there" and "all is one" – and what you need is a pin in your bottom from time to time, so to speak. In other words, all that is necessary is a little earnestness to "do it", rather than waffling on about it.'

Scarlett went on repeating the dialogue like an actress taking lines from the prompter. 'There is a bit of a discrepancy between what you say and what you do, isn't there, Zeno? This business of your wife, for instance.'

Zeno closed his mouth and was on the point of opening it again when the ghost carried on: 'Which reminds me. What he needs is a reliable clock.'

Scarlett held her hand up to Zeno while she consulted with McCormack to find out if he was speaking to her or to Zeno. McCormack waved her on, straightening a lace cuff, as though about to step on stage.

'Yes, a reliable alarm clock.'

'What?' queried Zeno.

'An alarm clock – what you need is an alarm clock.'

'If you say so,' said Zeno, confused.

'Let's say, for instance, you are being bored by your wife. That can be the factor that reminds you you're on "automatic".'

'Automatic?'

'Automatic in this instance . . .' said McCormack, getting carried away with making his point and waving his arms rather theatrically, '. . . meaning "preoccupied with the illusory individuality of life, rather than the oneness or nowness" – when you are not living up to your namesake's considerable example.'

A long pause followed, during which Zeno continued looking at Scarlett. Scarlett looked to McCormack, and McCormack concentrated on Zeno. When McCormack finally spoke, it was in a measured tone. 'After all, Zeno, you only need to be aware when you're unaware, don't you?'

There was a hush which made Zeno think of the moment when the lights went down in the cinema. McCormack lifted his arms, as if about to execute a high dive, and exited through the ceiling.

Wonder where he's gone, thought Scarlett.

'I wonder where he's gone,' said Zeno.

From above came the laugh again. Infected by it, they both started, until it became hard to tell who was laughing at who. Through the window came the new day's first rays of sun and Zeno – knowing the night was really over, and feeling a curious sensation in his chest he took to be happiness – broke into his renowned impersonation of 'Such A Night'. Not to be outdone, Scarlett joined in with Elvis's version.

With mutual applause they fell into each other's arms. Zeno had never wanted to kiss anyone so much, but he somehow felt he needed permission, and it seemed indelicate to ask.

THE DAWN

THEY WANDERED AROUND, saying goodbye to the room and its contents, Scarlett knowing she would never see it again, Zeno mentally arranging the next visit.

The dining room was filled with their erstwhile companions seated at breakfast, looking as cherubic as kids on a Sunday School outing. As he passed, Zeno said, 'Morning, all.'

Everybody smiled, the vicar toasted him with a glass of herbal tea.

' "Water from your own cistern", Padre?' God's servant was unsure, but finally smiled.

'Ah, yes. Proverbs. Ha-ha – very good, my son.' The cherub next to him grinned at Scarlett. 'Sleep well?' he asked.

'No rest for the wicked,' she replied with a sweet smile.

They strolled on through the tables into the reception area, where Wilf was at work polishing the brass.

'What's the damage, Wilf?'

'You owe me one, Zeno,' and Wilf said, to Scarlett, 'A pleasure to meet you, sweet thing.'

'Thanks, man,' said Zeno. Scarlett walked close to Wilf, removed a shaft of tinsel paper from his hair, and gave him a wink.

They stood on the top step, assessing the morning.

'What we need is wheels,' said Scarlett. Seconds later, they heard the unmistakable clip–clopping of shod horses and round the corner came the brewery wagon, pulled by two of its best shires. Scarlett nudged Zeno. A look was enough. They ran to the end of the block and, with surprising ease, lifted themselves unseen on to the back, behind the barrels.

'Just like old times,' said Scarlett. Zeno didn't respond. 'What is it, pal?' she asked.

'You know . . .'

They listened to the rhythmic sound of the hooves.

'I was thinking about what happens next,' he continued.

'Were you?'

'I was.'

'Did you get any of that – that we spoke about?'

'In the room, you mean?'

'Yes, in the room.'

'Yeah. Amazing about Zeno. Where did you get that? I mean, practically my whole adult life I studied that guy . . .'

'There was help.'

'Help?'

'A guide appeared when you went for the croissants.'

'Wow!' A thought stirred his eyes. It fired off a clip of blinks. 'Is it . . . Is he . . . Is he here now?'

Scarlett looked around like Oliver Hardy. 'No.'

'And he told you that?'

'Told me to tell you. Don't ask me what it means.'

'Oh, I understood it.'

'Did you?'

'Of course.'

'Did you? Did you really?'

Scarlett tried to defocus her eyes, but he only appeared fuzzy. He caught her looking at him and screwed up his face. Oh God! He's going to be hard to walk away from, she thought. She was remembering how sweet his breath had smelled when she had kissed him. They jumped off the cart as it turned into Sloane Street and walked to Hyde Park Corner. A naked man was handcuffed to the bus-stop, so they beat it through to the park and watched the guards exercising their horses before crossing into the solace of Green Park.

Early rays of sunshine were filtering shyly through the trees, and Scarlett caught a glimpse of a dervish lovingly whirling in a patched robe of many colours. She turned to share it with Zeno, but he was watching an old lady walking a pug, with a dummy in its mouth. The picture appeared to trouble Zeno. He's closing down, she thought, trying to make it easy for me.

'Don't forget: lots of raw food – good for rheumatism,' she said.

He looked up.

'Yeah, yeah, I know. There are a lot of things I'm going to start doing today.'

She thought he had resigned himself to the situation, but then he said, 'There's our tree.' And as they were both looking at it, he added, 'You know, I would give anything to see you again.'

'Please don't go all girlish. It's the end of an old romance – not the start of a new one.'

'I know.'

'I'll know you're out there. It will mean a lot to know that . . . you just are.'

'I am,' he said with his crooked grin. 'And what's more, this morning I know that I am.'

They had covered the length of the park and reached the exit nearest to the Underground entrance. It was the natural spot for goodbye.

'Now, you be nice to that pretty wife of yours,' she said, more to stop the tears coming to her eyes than anything else, 'or you may have to come back again as a toiling housewife.'

They stood for a moment looking at each other. Please walk away, Zeno. Please walk away, Scarlett said to herself.

'I'm walking away, then,' Zeno said finally. He was smiling, trying to be macho, but his feminine eyes were saying, 'It's burning holes in my heart to leave you.' In her heart, she was feeling, 'Only God knows how much I love him.'

Scarlett turned away, not wanting him to see how much it hurt. She heard his funny Cuban boots on the tarmac path. She moved to the gate and turned for a last look at his uneven walk. She heard her voice shouting: 'Zeno, I love you. Always have – always will.'

Zeno turned, raising his arms like a victorious boxer. An exaltation of larks flashed between them. Scarlett spun and ran into Piccadilly, the new sun shining full on to her face.

Zeno walked home, treading on reality one step at a time. A journey of a thousand miles starts under one's feet, he remembered as he planted one foot in front of the other. I will do something daring, something frightening to distract me – to stop me feeling sorry for myself. She told me she loved me. But I know that. She feels for me what I feel for her. She is the finer vessel. She must be doing this to help me. I will do something she would be proud of. The flying arrow is at rest. The arrow is me. We are not separate. It only appears so in the time–space concept. By the time he arrived at number seven Victoria Road, he had decided what to do.

It must be said that many of the plans hatched by Kenny Wisdom and Zeno Studd had no foundation in reality at all. Most of them were hash fantasies, induced by liberal quantities of Kashmiri khaki, Lebanese red, Peter's best Ibithincan black. All good smokes no doubt, but the ideas produced were like children born of barren women. All that Zeno knew for certain was that Kenny had climbed the tower and taken measurements. He and Kenny together had constructed the design of reliable, but lightweight, plywood, which Kenny had assured him could be carried by two – or Kenny alone, provided Zeno would lead the attack on the chimney and be prepared to take the backpack from Kenny when he reached the top.

It was Kenny's commitment to the project that kept Zeno from throwing the pieces away. Prudence was forever suggesting that he clean out the basement. In fact, some days, when he was lonely for some kindred spirit, he would go down into his workshop, unpack their effort, and erect and dismantle it over and over, sometimes making small adjustments, sometimes only staring in awe at Kenny's ingenuity.

On the morning after the night, he assembled it one last time before getting the pieces into travelling order for their ultimate destination.

The house was still as he left it and, cutting through the hole in the wall at Pooh Corner, he swallowed one of his herbal life-force Amazon pills to give him a lift. The wood strapped to his back was surprisingly light, and his old pair of Keds, which Kenny had recommended for the ascent, gave reassurance. No one would have guessed that this was a person with a freshly torn heart who hadn't slept for twenty-four hours. This was a man with a purpose.

Scarlett meandered towards Soho, seeking the nearness of other people and winding her tongue around her lips with unabashed determination, practising the exercise not only to strengthen her tongue, but her resolve as well.

She didn't stop until she reached Berwick Street. She leaned against the newsagent's and watched the flower stall being dressed. Wiping her eyes, she realised that she still wore Zeno's ring and started weeping again.

The florist, a handsome fellow with a ruddy face, noticed the pink eyes. 'Cheer up, lovely, it might never happen,' he said, giving her a cornflower for her buttonhole. And, with a cheery grin, 'Don't say Ron never gave you anything.'

'I won't. Thank you, Ron.'

'They do a good cuppa up there,' he said, pointing to a café a few shops along. 'Just like mother makes. Well, almost.'

She wandered over into the stallholder's retreat, bought a cup of tea and took it to the window seat, where she could stay in touch with the bustle. She touched the ring on her finger, examining the insignia cut into the blue stone, and wondering where Zeno had picked it up. What a fella – a smart, dumb, beguiling fellow. Her first man.

I'll think about that tomorrow, she said to herself, with the resolve of her namesake.

The climb up the scaffolding skirt was straightforward; a series of ladders placed between interlocking plank floors and tied off at climbable degrees. Zeno did not look down. He told himself every fresh platform was the first. It was pleasant; first two in the shade, third in the early sunlight, the final ladder dovetailed neatly on to the first of the iron rungs. Thinking how impressed Scarlett would be if she could only see him, he placed his left foot on to the first staple and, grasping the one above, began his final charge.

At the window table, Scarlett began to feel more herself. The tea – which would have disintegrated lesser mortals – was having an effect, and the earthy smell of vegetables, which drifted through the open door, comforted her. She was about to ask for a refill when it occurred to her that the feeling of well-being was too subtle to be a caffeine rush.

While pondering this vaso–dilation of her emotions, Scarlett had the distinct impression of being high up in a windy place, yet the comic book spread across the plastic table-top by the customer alongside her didn't even rustle. Scarlett finished her tea.

Zeno did fine until the sixth rung, which held firm while gripped by his hands, but came adrift when he placed his feet and full body weight on it. Then the surrounding cement crumbled, and it fell out.

In a thoughtless motion of pure reflex, one hand reached for the next rung while his foot jackknifed on to the rung where his hand had been. Both staples held firm while the dislodged piece of iron clattered through the scaffold ribs until it hit the ground a hundred feet below. Zeno heard its fall. He was clamped to the bricks as tightly as a gecko to a ceiling.

Proceeding with much more caution, and testing each rung thoroughly before setting his weight upon it, he discovered that the previous rung wasn't the only loose one. And he came to the conclusion that the scaffold was not in place solely for the biannual facelift, but to make secure the escalade to the top. It was now a climb worthy of a warrior, as Kenny once defined someone prepared to do battle with himself.

The sun which shone on the back of the early Saturday morning commuters was in her face as she made her way back to Green Park underground.

An amazing thing had happened. Both escalators were working. Two days in a row. She was definitely feeling more together, even giving a smile to the short-sighted do-gooder in the photobooth, gloating behind his 'change given if donation made to charity' collection box, as if the seeker of change was less worthy of a good turn than some abstract in need. It takes all sorts, she almost heard Zeno saying, as the proprietor of the booth returned a delayed-reaction rodential grin. Nobody had ever smiled at him before.

The up escalator was busy, filled with none-too-happy faces. She squinted her eyes, hoping to catch a flash of the collected aura, but her vision stayed three-dimensional. She did another set of tongue-strengtheners to keep her spirits up. Professional singers must practise diligently all the time, she told herself.

It was true. Intimations of a possible world opened to her; auditions, small parts – no problem starting at the bottom, it's all up from here. The sung words of 'I Hear You Calling Me' in a nut-brown tenor voice reached her, and she looked around for the singer. Earnest faces from the up escalator were looking at her, and she realised she was still flapping her tongue in and out. There he was. He appeared to be sitting cross-legged on the rubber hand rail of the escalator, moving towards her. She trilled along with his song. There was polite clapping from the commuters. The Papal Count smiled approval.

The top of the chimney was wider than he had imagined. He knew it didn't move, because he had watched it for so long. But it felt like it did. He removed his backpack, clinging to his memory of Kenny, but knowing he was in untested territory. He placed one leg into the chimney itself, and straddled the width of it as though astride a carthorse. Keeping his mind focused solely on his task, he managed to keep the nausea, always there, in abeyance.

When he realised that their handiwork was actually a good fit, he delayed positioning the final section, holding it to him and sitting in the space it left; a wind-breaker, almost cosy. He crouched, facing east into the path of the sun, looking into the windows of the house where his wife and daughter slept. And on the same line of vision, the tower of Big Ben, its face almost the colour of the cream sky behind it. And beyond this, the reassuring dome of St Paul's Cathedral.

He knew he couldn't risk the climb down, and had no way of knowing how long it would be before he was spotted, so he began exploring the ground of his fear. Concentrating first on his own front door (painted blue by Zen and himself a few months before), his eyes travelled the length of Eldon Road, slowly coming back to the base of the smoke-stack itself. There was a sickening heave in his groin, and he felt his testicles contract. He was going. He gripped his knees, fighting the blackout, but not allowing his mind to shy away from the sensation.

This is now, he told himself, fear is only in the future. The fact is, I am sitting on my chimney and the sun is shining on my face. I can feel its warmth. If I open my eyes, I will be able to see the house I own, bought fifteen years ago for £75,000. This is reality, all else is thought. My sometime enemy which I will make my friend.

The cramps in his gut began to subside, and became a pleasant tingling. He opened his eyes and looked down. A man in pyjamas was gazing up at him, as though he were an angel. He had bedroom slippers on. From Zeno's point of view, he looked like a striped animal with furry feet.

Scarlett changed trains at Mile End and found herself an empty carriage on the District Line. As the train pulled up the slope that would take her overground, she heard a beautifully projected high C, felt the presence of her guide, and saw him strap-hanging near the door. He looked astonishingly young, and dressed as Faust, his costume a deep purple velvet and mauve satin, trimmed with silver lace. As he turned to face her, he finished his note.

'Good morning, sir,' she said.

'You may call me John.'

'Thank you. Since we're being so informal, do you come when you feel like it, or are you summoned in some way?'

'I was wondering when you would get around to asking me that.'

'So, are you going to tell me?'

'Do you have a moment?'

'All the time in the world.'

'We are always here, always with you. For us it is a different dimension, for you a change of focus.' He glanced around the carriage.

'And Zeno?'

'Ah.'

'Why not him?'

'We spoke about him.'

Scarlett stuck out her lip.

McCormack took the hint. 'He has chosen another route. You see how he is: he is a mind person who is finding his heart by enquiry. When he is aware of himself, his mind is stilled. His way is hard – but no harder for him than yours is for you. He is seeking, and he knows what he seeks. That is rare.'

'And you're certain he'll be better alone?'

'But he's not alone. You are together. From the moment your breath was joined. Who is to divide you?'

'Oh my,' murmured Scarlett, recalling how Zeno had trembled in her arms.

'When he takes breath as his vehicle – instead of his body – he will soar to unimagined heights – to the source and goal of all things.'

'Miss Sage said something like that.'

'I know. Let's post him a wee something . . .'

Scarlett had felt her breath change rhythm. It slowed as she listened. Zeno's ring on her finger felt warm. She slipped it off and held it in her palm. She sensed the stone pulsating with his atmosphere, tuned herself to it, and began to breathe in harmony with him; picturing him, she breathed him to her, seeing his face with the eye of her heart.

An image came to her vision – a tall chimney. As separate frames of film on a zoom lens, it came closer and atop it all was Zeno surrounded by his handiwork. He was smiling, waving to the crowd below; writing on a scrap of paper, wrapping it around a coin, and dropping it to the spectators. She could hear the bell of the fire department. The crowd clapping and pointing. A worried woman arrived with a striking child. The red fire-engine reversed, extending its turntable ladder and cage. Zeno's face was in close-up; it grinned lopsidedly. Scarlett clasped herself, her heart thumping. She smiled back her best smile, and sent him McCormack's present.

Zen looked up at her mum's face, took her hand and waved with the other to her dad, who was being fireman-lifted on to the ladder and its extension. He waved back.

'So that's where he was,' Prudence said, biting her lip. 'Silly sod.'

'Mum, ssh – he couldn't get down.'

'He got up all right.'

'But he couldn't get back on his own.'

'He's such a kid.'

The two girls exchanged a knowing look. More bells were heard.

At Bromley-by-Bow, the young man got in, the regulation ghetto-blaster on his shoulder, earphones clamped to his ears. He spotted Scarlett, his only travelling companion, and sat opposite her, in the seat vacated by McCormack. He eyed her and turned up the volume. The carriage was immersed in electric overspill.

Scarlett tensed, and then Zeno's voice was in her ear, closer than a caress, 'Is not all one?'

She smiled – a thin smile – leaned forward, and grabbed the earphones, placing them over her ears. The young man pulled a second set from his dayglo windbreaker and plugged them in. He mimed smoking a cigarette, and Scarlett reached into her pocket, located the pack, and tossed it across to him. She looked down at the ring on her middle finger. An infectious chuckle filled the carriage.

Zen tugged at her dad's hand. He was enjoying the notoriety, but allowed himself to be pulled from the scene of the crime. An odd phrase popped into his mind, and it rolled around, changing colour like an aniseed gobstopper: 'What you're looking for is what is looking.'

Zen grabbed her mum with her free hand, and they walked towards the hospital exit. Tomorrow, Zen thought, everything will be back to normal. She whispered to herself the prayer he whispered when he believed he was alone. 'I will use my body and my mind wisely in the service of the self. Be true to myself, love myself absolutely. I will not pretend to be what I am not, I won't refuse to be what I am.

'Without self-realisation, no virtue is genuine. When I realise the depth and fullness of my love for myself, I will know beyond all doubting that the same life flows through all that is, and I will love all naturally and spontaneously. Alienation causes fear, and fear strengthens alienation. It is a vicious cycle – only self-realisation can break it. I will go for it resolutely.'

Gleefully preoccupied with Zeno's mantra, and swinging between their arms, Zen led the two people she loved back home.

Behind them, in silhouette, the back-lit smoke-stack transformed itself into Zeno's obelisk.

Vanella crept in. She removed the shoes she'd borrowed for the night at the bottom of the steps, and entered softly on bare feet.

'Somebody's been sleeping in my bed,' she said. No one had, but Captain Toby had used it to organise the bag of swag before his ill-timed getaway. She poked and sniffed her way around her quarters and, when she was satisfied that there had been no major violation of her territory, she set off to recon the rest of the house.

Madam must have turned the heating off in the pool, because the young man doing laps was blue with cold. In the drawing room was a policeman who looked like Burt Lancaster. He had taken his jacket off and was listening to a man with intense eyes who was discussing that the crucial thing to know when casting a movie was who wanted to screw who.

Peeping through the door of Madam's bedroom, she could see a man giving what-for to a lean woman with perfect legs. They didn't notice her, and she watched for some time, adding some new items to her study of the British.

In the gymnasium, she found Madam tied and manacled. Traces of gleet and saliva had dried on her thighs and pubis, but she didn't look spent. Vanella was padding out when her employer called. She padded back. 'Is Madam hurting?'

'Yes, Vanella.'

'Would Madam like to be relieved?'

'No, dear, but it's a little cold – just cover me up.' Vanella took a big flat cotton towel from the changing cubicle and spread it over her.

'Is Madam ready for coffee wake-up?' But Madam was already dropping into a contented sleep. How funny these civilised people are, she thought to herself. Much more interesting than the movies.

Mahajanga wouldn't seem the same.